Y0-CBD-325

The Windy Side of the Law

Books by Sara Woods

THE WINDY SIDE OF THE LAW

TRUSTED LIKE THE FOX

THE THIRD ENCOUNTER

BLOODY INSTRUCTIONS

SARA WOODS

The

Windy Side

of the Law

HARPER & ROW, PUBLISHERS, NEW YORK

FIRST EDITION

LIBRARY OF CONGRESS CATALOG CARD NUMBER: 65–27639

L-P

To avoid confusion it should be stated that the events narrated in this book occurred at an earlier date than those recorded in Trusted Like the Fox, while Antony Maitland was still at the junior bar.

Any work of fiction whose characters were of a uniform excellence would rightly be condemned—by that fact if by no other—as being incredibly dull. Therefore no excuse can be considered necessary for the villainy or folly of the people appearing in this book. It seems extremely unlikely that any one of them should resemble a real person, alive or dead. Any such resemblance is completely unintentional and without malice.

PROLOGUE

HE WAS CONSCIOUS of fear when he awoke, but he was not yet
deeply afraid. At first it seemed no more than the normal bewilderment of waking in a strange place, and it was only after
a few moments that instinct told him that by now he should
have remembered, and in remembering accepted the strangeness as something that had been planned, too commonplace to
worry about.

He had been lying on his side, but now he turned on his
back and stared up at the ceiling. It seemed a long way away,
surely the room was unusually high. But there was nothing
unusual in the conventional expanse of white, or in the old-
fashioned molding where once had obviously been a center
light.

He moved his head cautiously, half expecting a stab of pain.
Now, why should that have occurred to him? But there was
nothing wrong; indeed, now that he thought of it, he felt
perfectly fit. Except, perhaps, for a slight, not unpleasant feeling of lassitude. He'd know where he was, all right, once he'd
had a good look round. But it took a definite effort of will to
make the movement, to struggle into a sitting position and
survey the room.

A big room, as the height of the ceiling should have told
him. The curtains were still drawn, but imperfectly, and

enough light filtered through to show him a massive wardrobe, a dressing table bare of fittings, a writing table between the two long windows. There was a closed door in the wall opposite the bed, and a smaller one at the far side of the wardrobe that was open to show a tiled wall beyond. He had no recollection of ever having seen the place before.

He didn't know where he was . . .

. . . and hard on that realization the further thought came with the force of a blow. He didn't know who he was.

For a moment he was aware of an almost suffocating sense of panic. He must be ill . . . but this place wasn't a hospital. More like a hotel room. Yes, that was it, of course, he was at a hotel and he had only to stretch out a hand for the telephone to get in touch with . . . well, with whom? He spent a moment or two wrestling with that thought; he had no memory, no name, no past. If there were people in the world to whom he could appeal, he didn't know them. But . . . a doctor, perhaps. If he were ill, he'd better know it. He hadn't yet looked at the table by the bed, but unconsciously he took it for granted there'd be a phone there.

His right hand lay on the counterpane, and he looked at it now with the same sense of strangeness he had felt when first he examined his surroundings. A brown hand, well shaped, well kept; the pajama sleeve was blue, rather an expensive material, he thought. He twisted onto his elbow, still with the same feeling of languor, and was mentally rehearsing a guarded explanation to the hotel switchboard when he drew back his hand sharply and lay back against the pillows again to consider the matter further.

Funnily enough, it wasn't the difficulty of explaining his position that made him pause, though he foresaw that clearly enough; nor was it the thought, which had just occurred to him, that perhaps he was mad, and anyway the doctor would be bound to think so. The fear that took hold of him now was nothing to do with the panic fear he had felt a few moments before. It was cold, and compelling, and—because he did not know its cause—quite impossible to combat. He had to be careful: the thought might be instinctive, but he recognized its urgency. So before he did anything else he'd better see what he could find out for himself.

He threw back the bedclothes and swung his feet to the floor. The carpet was soft and thick, and he padded barefoot across to the dressing table. For a moment the mirror took his attention; a fair-haired man looked back at him, a man in his middle thirties, perhaps. Surely there must be something he would recognize; but, stare as he would, the face remained that of a stranger, neither familiar nor unfamiliar.

His eyes dropped away from the questioning stare of his reflection. There was a key on the dressing table, with a leather tag and the number "310" embossed on the leather. There was some small change, too: three half crowns, and a sixpence, and some pennies. There was a wrist watch . . . the time, he saw, was ten to eight. There was a small penknife and a crumpled linen handkerchief. His glance shifted a little, to a nearby chair with the jacket of a gray suit draped across the back. There should be a wallet in the pocket . . . some letters, perhaps . . . something that would tell him . . .

He stretched out a hand that was not quite steady to pick up the coat.

CHAPTER I

"I'M AWFULLY SORRY," said the man in the gray suit politely. "Ought I to know you? I don't seem to remember—"

His manner was so natural that the man who had greeted him started almost automatically to apologize and withdraw. But it was, after all, ridiculous . . . it might be some time since they had met, but there was no mistaking either look or manner: fair hair, straight and very thick, and cold blue eyes with a disarmingly mild expression; a deep tan, which was only to be expected; a hesitant, almost diffident way of speaking. "You're Peter Hammond," he stated, positively.

"Ye-es. Yes, I am." He seemed to make the admission cautiously, as if somehow the fact were discreditable. And his expression was puzzling: a look that was almost certainly relief, followed by a blankness that could only be designed to conceal some other, stronger emotion.

"Well, then!" said the man who had spoken first. "You can't possibly have forgotten me." He paused, and added, "Antony Maitland," in an encouraging tone; so that he felt, absurdly, for a moment, like a schoolmaster trying to bring out the dullest member of his class.

"So you're Maitland," the man in the gray suit exclaimed. And added, surprisingly, "I was coming to see you." For a moment he studied his companion with frank interest, and

4

then he began to look around him uneasily, as though he thought his words might have been overheard.

"Now, look here!" Maitland protested. "If you've forgotten me, that's all right. But *if* you have . . . what are you doing here?"

"I thought perhaps . . . I don't quite know." Hammond's eyes came back to meet his companion's, but he spoke uncertainly. Antony, with an increasing feeling of unreality, watched what was apparently a struggle for the right words, but the question that came only added to his bewilderment. "Who are you?" Hammond demanded, abruptly.

"Who . . . but . . ." Maitland broke off helplessly. There was nothing in Peter Hammond's appearance to suggest that he was off his head; but insane one of them must surely be, and he was beginning to have an uncomfortable feeling that it might—just possibly—be himself.

"I know you told me your name," Hammond was explaining doggedly. "But I mean, who are you . . . what is your occupation . . . how well do you know me? That kind of thing." Antony thought suddenly of a man groping his way through fog, and answered more mildly than his first instinct had dictated.

"I'm a barrister. I live"—he gestured—"three doors back. Jenny and I have a flat at the top of my uncle's house . . . Sir Nicholas Harding," he explained, seeing from the other man's expression that he did not recognize the name. "He's a lawyer too. Queen's Counsel. And we've known each other, on and off, most of our lives, though it's a year or two—" He broke off, and added, more puzzled than indignant, "Not as long as all that. You can't really have forgotten—"

Hammond had been frowning over the information, but he looked up now and said cautiously, "I'm afraid I . . . don't remember. I—"

"If you're feeling ill, Peter, you'd better come home with me. I'll call a doctor."

5

"Yes, I suppose . . . I'm perfectly all right, really." He paused, and then added with an air of desperation, "The thing is, I don't seem to be able to remember anything. Not who you are . . . who I am . . . anything!"

"In that case, you'd certainly better come with me," said Maitland, ignoring with real nobility the questions that were crowding into his mind.

"But you were going out." The protest was halfhearted, prompted perhaps by the distrust that Hammond still seemed to feel. Maitland ignored the words, and turned away as though he had no doubt the other man would accompany him.

"Only for a stroll," he said. "That doesn't matter." After a moment's hesitation, Peter Hammond followed him back along the pavement, and up the steps to the front door. As the key was fitted in the lock he asked suspiciously:

"Have I been here before?"

"Quite a few times, the most recent about three years ago." The situation was fantastic, of course, and Antony glanced again at his companion. "You'll remember when we get upstairs, I expect," he went on, deliberately matter-of-fact. "We haven't changed things much."

Jenny Maitland was in the upstairs living room, struggling—rather angrily—with an old-fashioned sewing machine, and what looked like about a hundred yards of flowered brocade. The new curtains ought to have been finished weeks ago, of course; and now, with the Trinity term closed and only a few loose ends to be cleared up in chambers before they went into the country, the task had assumed a disagreeable air of urgency. If only Uncle Nick hadn't had bronchitis, at such an unlikely time of year, too; but he had, and that was that, and a worse patient could hardly be imagined. When she heard her husband coming back, and bringing someone with him, she had to struggle momentarily with an impulse to heave the whole thing out of the window . . . sewing machine, material, and all. But not even Antony would have guessed it from her greeting.

"Why, Peter . . . how nice to see you after all this time."

Maitland, alert to every sign of the other man's mood, thought Hammond looked relieved at the words, but when she went on casually, "I didn't even know you were back in England," he began to look haunted again. If he'd really lost his memory . . . it did happen, of course, in spite of seeming so unlikely. He found his thoughts in confusion, and called them sternly back to order.

"It's early for tea, love, but do you think—?" He caught Jenny's eye as he spoke, and jerked his head slightly. She said, at once:

"Of course. Sit down, Peter. I won't be a moment, and then I want to hear all your news." Antony paused only to give the other man a reassuring grin, and then followed her out of the room.

Peter Hammond walked slowly across the room, and seated himself in the high-backed chair to the right of the hearth; perhaps it was by instinct that he placed himself with his back to the window. After a moment he leaned back, and stretched out his legs with a tired sigh. His glance might have seemed idle as it went round the room, but he was taking in each detail with the clarity that had attended every waking moment that day.

It was a big room, rather shabby, and not overly tidy . . . even if you disregarded Jenny's sewing which was heaped on the table at the other end. The furniture seemed to have been selected with a fine disregard for any matching qualities in the individual pieces; in fact, looking round, he could see only two things that were paired in any way: the chair he was sitting in, and its companion in the opposite corner. Altogether, he could well believe there had been few changes made over the years; a room that invited you to relax, to forget the vague fears and suspicions that darkened your mind, to take these two—Antony and Jenny—at face value. If he could trust them, they could tell him, he supposed, a great deal that he wished to know; fill in, at the least, the background details of his life. Out of his bewilderment he had fought his way to a precarious sort of calm, but he knew he must have help to hold on even to so small a gain; it seemed he had no choice but to listen to what Maitland had to say. Only he wished he could be sure. . . .

Antony, with an instinctive feeling that the visitor was likely to find reassurance in Jenny's presence, delayed his return until they could go back together; and Peter Hammond watched them as they came across the room to join him with an almost detached air. They both treated him in the offhand way of long acquaintance, but try as he would he could find no trace of the familiar. Maitland was tall, with a casual air that might or might not be assumed. He moved rather stiffly as he pulled forward a table for the tray his wife was carrying. Peter was not aware that he was looking at his companions with unusual clarity; in the ordinary way he might have thought vaguely that it was an odd way of doing things; now he realized that Maitland held his right arm a little awkwardly. That ought to give him a clue, but still he couldn't remember. . . .

He concentrated again on the other man's appearance. Dark hair, a thin, intelligent face . . . not the sort of chap you'd think you could forget; but then, neither was the girl. Peter's eyes rested thoughtfully on Jenny for a moment: on brown curls, not very tidy; gray eyes that had been bright with welcome when first he came in, but now very serious; an air of serenity—the word came oddly to his mind—a quiet way of moving, no fuss. A pleasant couple; he thought perhaps he could trust them . . . he didn't seem to have much choice.

Maitland had handed him a cup, and now presented him with milk jug and sugar basin, watching without comment as Hammond helped himself to each in turn without hesitation.

8

His own cup went onto the mantelpiece, he took up his stand with his back to the empty grate. "Well, now?" he said. And Peter, looking up at him, found his eyes alert and inquiring.

"It isn't easy to explain," he said.

"Have a stab at it," Antony invited. "To begin with, what *do* you remember?"

"Nothing beyond this morning." The simplicity of the question seemed to reassure him. "I woke up and . . . and I didn't know where I was. And then I realized I didn't know *who* I was, either. I got in a bit of a panic then." Neither of his listeners was at all deceived by the prosaic nature of the statement. Antony thought only, he's really afraid of something; fear was a thing he recognized when he saw it. But Jenny smiled with warm sympathy.

"I don't think that's surprising," she said. "It must have been a horrible feeling." Peter turned to her eagerly.

"It was horrible," he agreed. "I didn't know what to do, so after a while I got up and started to look around. It was a pretty comfortable room, but impersonal; there was some note paper in the writing-table drawer, with the heading 'Chiltern Hotel.' It didn't convey anything to me, but I wasn't surprised to find I was in London. Then I went through the pockets of the jacket that was thrown over the back of a chair: I found an envelope addressed to Peter Hammond, at an address in Ceylon, and a wallet without much cash in it, but quite a bit in traveler's checks. The next thing I came across was a passport . . . that's a bulky thing to have in your pocket and I began to think perhaps I hadn't been in England long. There was the name again, but I had to go to the mirror to check on the photograph . . . it sounds silly, doesn't it? So then I thought I knew my name, but it wasn't really very helpful."

"I can fill in a few details for you," Maitland offered. "But first, I take it you've seen a doctor. What did he say?"

"I . . . well, no, as a matter of fact, I haven't." He was aware of the other man's look, disconcertingly intelligent,

9

and added uncomfortably, "I told you, I feel quite well."

"I'd rather you told me the real reason."

"I don't think . . . oh, if you must know, I had a feeling something was wrong."

"I should have thought that was obvious."

"No, I mean something really important. Something in the background . . . something sinister." After the first reluctance, he now seemed eager to explain himself; but he paused a moment, and glanced at Jenny, before he added, more hesitantly: "I was . . . afraid," he said. "I didn't want anyone to know—"

"Why?" said Maitland. His tone was flat, incurious; and yet it demanded an answer.

"I don't know . . . how can I know?" said Peter Hammond. "I just didn't want to tell anyone. But then I saw I couldn't go on like that . . . I had to find out . . . so I thought I'd come to you."

"Why?" said Antony, again. He turned as he spoke, to pick up his cup from the mantel. "If you didn't remember that we had been friends—" he added, and let the sentence trail off invitingly.

"There was the notebook," said Peter. He looked up, and found, as he had expected, that the other man's eyes were fixed on his face. This trick of throwing out a question casually and following it up by a close scrutiny was beginning to annoy him, and he raised his voice a little as he went on. "It was a diary, actually, only there wasn't much written in it. My name again, and the Ceylon address, and some phone numbers and notes that seemed to be about appointments. But then there was a gap, with nothing written at all up to today."

"You remembered that . . . you knew what day it was?"

"No, but later on I had some breakfast sent in, and the morning paper. Then I knew. I knew I wanted the *Daily Telegraph*, too . . . but I didn't even recognize my own handwriting in the diary, I had to experiment to find out it really was mine."

"You were telling us what you had written," Maitland reminded him.

"Your name, and this address . . . right across the page that ends today. It didn't mean anything to me, but somehow it looked . . . urgent. I can't explain, really, only it seemed more forcefully written than the other things; at least, the name did." A new thought seemed to strike him. "You weren't expecting me, I suppose? It wasn't an appointment?"

"Nothing like that. As Jenny says, we didn't even know you were back in England."

"How long—?"

"About a year. A little longer, perhaps. I don't remember exactly." He let the silence lengthen between them for a moment, and then said casually: "Have you the diary on you, Peter?"

"Yes, I have." There was no mistaking the note of irritation now, but he pulled out a small book bound in pigskin, bent it open a little roughly, and leaned forward to thrust it into Maitland's hand. "There," he said.

Antony took the little book, and his face was expressionless as he examined it. Sunday to Wednesday on the left-hand page, Thursday to Saturday and an extra, blank space, on the other. And printed heavily across this right-hand sheet, in black ink and block letters, his own name; the address, below, was written more lightly, and in pencil. "Thank you," he said, and stretched out his hand; when Hammond made no move to take the diary he bent forward and put it down on the table at his guest's elbow, beside the untouched cup of tea.

"Not very informative . . . is it?" Peter's voice grated on the question, and Antony smiled at him disarmingly.

"Not at all informative," he agreed. "Don't be cross with me, Peter, I'm just as puzzled as you are."

"Well . . . all right." He picked up the diary at last, and held it between his hands as he continued. "I suppose you can tell me something about myself. You said we'd been friends."

"I can do that up to a point." His cup was empty, and he

handed it to Jenny before abandoning his position on the hearthrug and seating himself in the wing chair opposite the one Peter was occupying. "Can't you remember anything?" he demanded.

"Only since this morning. I seem to *know* things, though. Impersonal things, I mean."

"I know. The way to Buckingham Palace, and which newspaper you read, and the station to travel from if you want to go to Basingstoke," said Antony, helpfully.

"That sort of thing. So I don't see why I can't remember the rest."

"Perhaps you will when I tell you—" He broke off, and said in rather an awed tone, "It's quite a tall order, isn't it?"

"All the same—" said Peter; but he sounded resigned, rather than eager. Antony grinned at him.

"I needn't go further back than where you were born, I suppose. That was at Tilham, in Sussex. Your father was headmaster of the Grammar School. That's when we all first knew each other."

"All?"

"Jenny's family lived about three miles outside the town. We saw a good deal of each other at one time; Jenny and her brother, Graham; Bill Cleveland; Gerry Martin; you and me." He was watching Hammond as he produced the names in turn; but there was no sign of recognition, only of deeper strain.

"I'm sorry. I don't remember."

"I left Tilham when my father died, when I was thirteen. But I used to go back to stay with Doctor Martin, and later— incidentally—to see Jenny. So we were more or less in touch until the war started. You'd just gone up to Cambridge then, but I remember hearing a year or two later that you were in the Army . . . Engineers, I think; or was it R.E.M.E.?"

"I don't know," snapped Peter.

"Sorry. Just a manner of speaking, I wasn't trying to catch you out. I heard of you from time to time, pretty vaguely; and I heard that your mother had died—"

"In 1942," Jenny supplied, as her husband paused. "And just before you were demobilized your father died too and Pamela . . . you didn't tell him about Pamela, Antony."

"No, I forgot. She was a bit older, you know, and I didn't know her so well—"

"Who," asked Peter, "is Pamela?"

"Your sister." His pause was a brief one, he didn't really expect any comment. "As Jenny was just going to say, after your father died she came up to London to live, and was married a year or two later. By which time you had come out of the Army and gone back to Cambridge; from whence you emerged, after an appropriate interval, to take a job with Cardew and King. That took you abroad a good deal, but you used to show up here from time to time, staying with Pamela and her husband, so we still saw something of you."

"Pamela?" said Hammond. His tone was questioning, but the question seemed to be self-directed. He shook his head after a moment. "Tell me about her," he requested. Antony looked rather helplessly at his wife.

"I can't give you a very good description, I'm afraid," said Jenny. "She was tall and fair—very like you, really, Peter—and always beautifully turned out. Only, you see, we thought she was grown-up when we first knew you . . . when we were children . . . though I expect she was quite young; so, even though we used to see her sometimes when you came to town, we never got to know her well. I liked her very much, though. She was a kind person, rather quiet—"

"Was?" said Peter. Tone and face were alike without expression.

"She died a year ago, just before you went to Ceylon. You must realize," Antony went on apologetically, "that we're spanning a good many years, very briefly." For the first time since they had met that day, Peter smiled back at him with something like real amusement.

"Yes, I appreciate the fact that my life wasn't really one rapid succession of funerals," he said. "I'm a bit curious, though. She can't have been very old. What was wrong with her?"

"Cancer," said Antony, briefly. He was watching the other man carefully, but still there was no shadow of emotion; there came instead—as might have been expected—a spate of questions.

"Well, have I any other relations? And what about my work? Am I still with that firm you mentioned?"

"As to relations, none that I know of. You changed jobs about six years ago—we had a night out to celebrate—and went to work for your brother-in-law's firm."

"Yes, but—" Peter broke off. "There are so many questions, I don't know which to ask first," he added, with a gesture that nicely blended exasperation and helplessness.

"Well, you're a civil engineer, if that point is puzzling you. Pamela married Bernard Shenstone, who is managing director of Kinlocks. They are pretty big, and important, and have fingers in more pies than I could possibly name. You joined them, as I said, after working on projects abroad which sounded impressive to my uninstructed ear, and took charge of the Birmingham office; which, funnily enough, meant that we saw less of you than when you were living abroad. The last time we met was at Pamela's funeral, and you told me Shenstone had asked you to go on this trip to Ceylon . . . trouble shooting, you called it. Something to do with a dam . . . I think."

"I see." He seemed to be turning the information over doubtfully in his mind, and after a moment he looked up and added seriously. "It all sounds ordinary enough, doesn't it? Nothing that could account for the way I was feeling."

"You said you were afraid," said Antony. "Don't you think that was natural enough?"

"I suppose so." But he still sounded dissatisfied.

"So the best thing we can do," said Antony, "is get you to a doctor. You can think about seeing Shenstone when you know what he has to say."

"Yes," said Peter, still unenthusiastic. "I don't know any doctors," he added, as if this put the whole suggestion out of court.

"Then you can see ours, for the time being," said Antony, taking no notice of this rather weak evasion. "That's the best thing, isn't it?" he appealed to Jenny.

"He's really very nice," she said, addressing Peter directly, in an encouraging tone, "and if he doesn't know about—about amnesia, he can certainly send you to someone who does."

"Well—" said Peter; obviously he was still hesitant. "I suppose I must," he added, and smiled faintly, first at Jenny and then at her husband.

"Right!" Antony was on his feet. "Shall I ask him to come here, or shall we go back to the hotel?"

"The hotel would be best, wouldn't it? I don't want to put . . . either of you . . . to any more bother."

"As to that . . . well, just as you like. But I'm coming with you," said Antony, firmly.

After a little argument they went back to the Chiltern Hotel by taxi, leaving Jenny to phone Dr. Prescott. Peter Hammond still seemed uneasy, and as they drove through the busy streets his eyes went from side to side in a troubled way. Maitland had plenty to think about, and felt, besides, that he had done enough talking for one day. He didn't know much about this loss of memory business, but obiously it was a hell of a thing for the patient. Peter seemed normal enough, in all but this one particular; but the thing was to see what the doctor had to say about it.

The Chiltern was an old-fashioned hotel with a reputation for solid comfort. Antony waited while Peter went across to the desk for his key; obviously his subconscious—or whatever it was that guided his actions in these matters—was in good working order, whatever tricks his conscious mind might be playing.

The clerk recognized him before he mentioned either name or room number. He said, "Yes, Mr. Hammond," rather more loudly than seemed necessary, fumbled in his search for the key, and then added, by way of afterthought, as Peter was turning away, "There were two gentlemen, sir."

Peter swung round to look at him. "To see me?" he asked. But Antony was looking across the wide hall, where two men had got up purposefully when the clerk spoke his friend's name. A thickset man in blue serge, with stolid brown eyes and a five o'clock shadow; and a younger man, with an alert, lively manner, slim, good-looking, just a little too well dressed.

Peter, too, had noticed the men, and started across the hall to meet them. Antony followed him, and frowned as he went; his thoughts were confused, but he had an inward smile for the most insistent of them, rueful and wholly self-derisory. Now what was he getting into? For that matter, what had Peter got himself mixed up in? Memory or no memory, this seemed drastically out of character . . . because if these two chaps didn't represent officialdom of some kind, he'd never take a bet with himself again. And, obviously, the receptionist had got their measure too. Still, the most likely thing was a Customs inquiry . . . a matter of routine that had nothing to do with his friend at all; in the circumstances, even that was wildly inconvenient, and it didn't explain why Peter had been afraid.

The party converged a few paces from the lift, whose doors were held open invitingly by an elderly attendant. It was the younger of the newcomers who spoke; he had rather a pleasant voice, with an accent Antony couldn't quite place. "Mr. Hammond?" he said, but did not wait for the answer to the question his tone implied. "We'd be glad of a word with you, if you can spare the time." He didn't really mean that, Antony thought; for all his surface affability he was obviously quite determined.

Oddly enough, the request did not seem to add to Peter's uneasiness. His quick look round was intended only, it seemed, to locate the hotel lounge. When he had done so he gestured.

"I'm expecting a visitor presently, but we could talk for a few minutes if you like."

"Perhaps it would be better if we went up to your room." He glanced at Maitland as he spoke, and his meaning was unmistakable. "It's . . . rather a private matter." And as Peter still hesitated he added, in a low voice, "My name is Shelley . . . Inspector Shelley. I'd rather go into my business with you in a less public place."

"We'll go upstairs, then. We'll all go upstairs," said Hammond. The look he gave his friend was a compound of bewilderment and entreaty. Antony followed as they crowded into the lift, and searched his mind as he went for any scraps of information concerning the Customs & Excise Act that might be lodged there. Peter said, "Three ten," the attendant clattered the gate cheerfully, and they began to move upward. Shelley gave Maitland a sour look, but made no open protest. His colleague's face was expressionless; obviously a man, thought Antony with sudden amusement, who could take the rough with the smooth.

As Hammond had told him, Room 310 was comfortable, though Shelley's look seemed to disparage the rather old-fashioned furnishings. Even with the four of them there was plenty of space. "Now!" said Peter; and turned to face the two strangers.

Shelley was feeling in his pocket for what Antony presumed to be some form of identification; all his movements were sharp and decisive, and he produced without fumbling what looked like a detective's warrant card. "I'm afraid it's rather a serious matter, Mr. Hammond. We're from New Scotland Yard, Sergeant Watkins and I." He paused, and seemed to be considering whether Peter's look of stupefaction might possibly be genuine. Antony, still in the background, was startled into a new alertness; more serious then than he had thought, and yet . . . "I'm hoping for your co-operation, sir," said Shelley, blandly untruthful. "We've a question or two to ask you, and then perhaps you'd be kind enough to let us have a look round here."

The request seemed to have had a numbing effect on Peter. Antony moved forward and asked softly: "Have you a search warrant, Inspector?"

Shelley turned to face him, and eyed him appraisingly; a look that said, as clearly as words, that here perhaps there might be someone to be reckoned with. Antony spoke again before he had time to reply. "A foolish question. If you had a warrant you wouldn't be wasting time asking, would you?"

"I should not." The words were snapped, and judging from his wary expression he would have spoken still more curtly had he been quite sure of the other man's status.

Antony smiled at him. "Then—as you're asking for Mr. Hammond's help, Inspector—it's surely not too much for us to ask what you expect to find here."

Just for a moment Shelley hesitated, and it was his more stolid colleague who broke his long silence and said, without inflection, "Acting on information received—" Incredibly, there was a gleam of amusement in his eye, though otherwise his expression remained solemn. Shelley interrupted him, hastily and with an air of frankness.

"I should have explained, perhaps, that we are from the Narcotics Branch." He turned a little, to include Peter more directly in what he was saying, and he seemed to be choosing his words carefully. "Our information is that a quantity of heroin came into the country in your baggage, Mr. Hammond. So I'd like the opportunity of seeing whether there's any truth in the statement, or not."

"Yes, I see." Peter spoke dully, but the glance that flickered to meet his friend's startled look for the first time conveyed to Antony some of the sense of horror that must have attended his waking that morning. "What shall I do?" he asked.

Antony, who had shifted the field of his mental researches to one more familiar to him than Customs offenses, was looking quizzically at Inspector Shelley. "You'd claim to be 'reasonably suspicious,' I take it?" he inquired; and took a certain malicious pleasure in the policeman's start of surprise. Again it was Sergeant Watkins who replied before his superior officer could do so.

"You've hit the nail on the head, sir. And that being so, I'm sure you'll advise your client—" Maitland shook his head at him.

"My presence, Sergeant, is purely fortuitous. However, I'm sure Mr. Hamomnd will be only too glad to co-operate." Watkins gave him a friendly smile, but Shelley came back into the conversation, saying forcefully:

"Under the Dangerous Drugs Act—"

"Part Three," murmured the sergeant.

"—we have, as you surmise, the right to arrest without warrant in certain circumstances."

"But, Inspector—" (Antony's protest had a plaintive note, his look was blandly innocent) "—all this is surely unnecessary."

"So long as you understand the position," Shelley nodded.

"So long as Mr. Hammond understands it, surely. In other words, Peter," he added, turning again to the cause of all the bother, "you haven't much choice in the matter. It's a case of co-operate . . . or else!"

Peter seemed to have been following the exchange easily enough. He ignored Shelley's inarticulate protest at this all-too-simple exposition, and waved a hand in unenthusiastic invitation. "Do what you like," he said. "You won't find anything." But again his eyes betrayed his uncertainty.

CHAPTER II

"IF YOU THINK," said Sir Nicholas Harding trenchantly, "that
I propose to involve myself in the affairs of a man who professes to have lost his memory—"

"Who *has* lost his memory, sir," said Antony. He paused,
and added, "I think," conscientiously, if not altogether wisely.

His uncle said "Ha!" in an accusing tone, and sat back as
though that settled the matter. Antony eyed him with exasperation.

It had been nearly eight o'clock when he finally got back to
the house in Kempenfeldt Square. Sir Nicholas, he knew, was
celebrating his emancipation from the sickroom and imminent
departure for Switzerland by dining with them that evening;
he reflected ruefully as he went up the stairs that he'd better
have his explanations in good order, but try as he would he
seemed to be able to put together no very coherent account of
what had happened. Jenny, of course, would already have told
Uncle Nick where he had gone, but that was no longer the
whole story . . . not by any means.

Jenny, indeed, had been attempting to beguile Sir Nicholas
with an account of their unexpected visitor, and when Antony
came in he had no difficulty in correctly interpreting her look
of relief and his uncle's rather dazed air.

The room was surprisingly cool, considering how hot the

day had been, and a little breeze ruffled the curtains. He paused a moment in the doorway—somehow he had never ceased to savor the moment of home-coming; but he thought now, with amusement, that the word that came to his mind— tranquility—was a very poor description of any place that contained his uncle. He crossed the room, and smiled at Jenny in passing, but his eyes were on Sir Nicholas as he spoke.

"I see I've no need to apologize," he remarked. "Jenny's been telling you—"

"That alone should be cause for contrition. I'm in no fit state to be subjected to such an ordeal." But he showed signs of being mollified as he watched Antony refill his glass.

Jenny wisely ignored the implied criticism of her powers of narrative. She had been curled up in the corner of the sofa, but now she unwound herself and stretched contentedly. "Why did it take so long?" she asked. "I thought you'd be back ages ago."

"Well, so did I." Antony was pouring his own sherry, and did not meet her eye. "One or two things came up," he added, evasively, and realized as he spoke that it was foolish to parry the question. He had done so instinctively, but of course they had to know . . .

"Well, what did Doctor Prescott say?" Jenny demanded. "That's the important thing, after all." She was on her feet now, poised for departure kitchenward; Antony seated himself, and looked up at her over the rim of his glass.

"He didn't commit himself. Not one of his things, apparently. He's sending Doctor Macintyre to have a look at Peter."

"But will he get his memory back? And how long will it take? And why did it happen?"

There was a simple answer to all those questions. "I don't know," said Antony. He found his uncle's eyes fixed speculatively on his face, and added soberly: "You're quite right, of course, sir. There's more to it than that."

Jenny looked from one of them to the other, and when she

saw her husband's expression her animation left her and she sat down again on the arm of the sofa. Sir Nicholas said gently: "I am sure you would not wish to try my patience," and Antony grinned suddenly.

"The thing is," he confided, "Peter's been arrested. There were two chaps at the hotel—"

"For heaven's sake," exploded his uncle, "try to give us a straightforward account."

"It isn't straightforward, Uncle Nick. Not a bit."

"Well, to begin with, you say he has been arrested. On what charge?"

"Smuggling," said Antony, succinctly. His glance went briefly to his wife's face. "Worse than it sounds, I'm afraid," he added deliberately. "Not just perfume, or watches—"

"You may spare us a list of the things he did not bring illicitly into the country," snarled Sir Nicholas. "What exactly has he involved himself in?"

"Dope," said Antony. "Heroin, to be specific. But—"

"I have always admired," said Sir Nicholas thoughtfully, "the unerring instinct with which you choose your friends."

Jenny said, "I don't believe it. He couldn't have changed so much." But she was still watching Antony, and there was an uncertain note to her indignation.

Antony picked up his glass, and seemed to be giving it all his attention. "They found a packet of the stuff in his suitcase," he said slowly. "Done up in plastic and shoved inside a pair of walking shoes. Inspector Shelley said it was heroin— I don't expect he'd be mistaken about a thing like that, in his line of business. They'd been tipped off, I gather; anonymously, I should suppose, but no doubt we shall learn that in due course." He had been choosing his words carefully, and now he looked up and met his uncle's eyes.

"What exactly are you proposing?" inquired Sir Nicholas dangerously.

Antony gave an expansive gesture, found himself in danger of spilling his sherry, and paused to drink a little before he replied. "Someone's got to defend him," he said, stating the obvious. "Of course, if you're not feeling well enough . . . but the trial can't come on till the Michaelmas term now."

"I am perfectly well," snapped Sir Nicholas. "But the whole affair will be dealt with summarily . . . won't it?"

"Well—" said Antony.

"Tell me the worst," sighed his uncle; but he did not sound resigned.

"They mean to prosecute on indictment, and don't seem to expect any difficulty in getting permission to do so."

"Do you really imagine that makes the matter more attractive?"

"Not really."

"In any event, if you think I have the slightest intention of involving myself with a client who professes to have lost his memory . . . I should have thought even you would realize that it's no sort of a tale to give the jury, besides being about as unpopular a defense as you could well devise."

"Yes, but I don't think it is a tale," said Antony.

"It is altogether too convenient, too specious," his uncle told him. "Do you expect the court to share your credulity?"

"Unfortunately, no. But you might persuade them, sir."

"I don't intend to try."

"Well, but look here, Uncle Nick . . . suppose he really has forgotten. You say it's too much of a coincidence, but suppose it isn't a . . . natural thing . . . suppose it was artificially induced."

"If you're implying this young man is an addict, as well as a purveyor of the drug . . . I don't think that's an extenuating circumstance. And I don't believe heroin would have that effect."

"No, but there may be something else that would. Doctor Prescott didn't know, but he did say Peter showed signs of having had some sort of a sedative. If someone was making use of him—"

"You're twisting the facts to suit your theories, Antony."

23

He watched as the younger man got up and began to move restlessly across the room. "This fellow Hammond," Sir Nicholas asked, abruptly. "Are you so very fond of him?"

Antony paused halfway to the window, and turned slowly to face his uncle again. "Fond?" he said, and seemed to be considering the aptness of the word. "I've always liked him. But the thing is, sir, I don't think—"

"You don't think he'd do a thing like that," said Sir Nicholas, snatching the words from him savagely. "How many times have you listened to that, and cursed your luck at having a fool for a witness?" He paused, but Antony did not speak. "Well?" he demanded. "On what do you base your opinion?"

"On character, sir."

"A dangerous business, Antony."

"Yes, I know."

"He may have changed; at least, he may have developed aspects to his character of which you know nothing."

"I realize that. But if he *is* telling the truth—"

"Don't tell me," said Sir Nicholas, tight-lipped (for his nephew's passive acceptance of his strictures was having the worst effect on his temper), "another lame dog!"

"Is that so strange, sir?"

"No, not strange, merely pigheaded, and no more than I should expect."

"Well, then," said Antony, still meekly.

"I cannot imagine," said Sir Nicholas, as though goaded beyond bearing, "why you should wish to embroil me in the affair."

"Because I shall have my work cut out, without having to worry about the presentation of the case in court. Don't you see, Uncle Nick—"

"I am glad at least that you realize there may be some difficulty in defending a man who claims to have no memory of his movements during the period in which the crime occurred.

Who does not even know," Sir Nicholas added, with deliberate malice, "whether he is innocent or guilty."

"Well, I know it's awkward," Antony confessed. "But I can't leave it where it is, sir, you must see that."

"To my sorrow, I can well believe it." He paused, looking his nephew up and down, and then added tartly: "Just what are you proposing to do?"

"Find out what happened," Antony replied without hesitation. "All the things Peter can't tell me." His uncle eyed him stonily.

"Meddling again," he commented. And added, ungraciously, "You'd better tell me the rest of the story, I suppose."

Antony came back to his chair. "Are we keeping you, Jenny? This will wait."

"I want to hear," she told him. She got up from her perch and came round to take her usual place on the sofa, settling herself with a deliberate assumption of ease, and folding her hands on her lap.

Antony looked at her for a moment before he spoke again. "It won't take long," he promised. "I told you when we got to the hotel there were two chaps waiting . . . Inspector Shelley and Sergeant Watkins, of the Narcotics Branch. That was a bit of a facer, I can tell you. They hadn't a search warrant, and they were there because someone had told them Peter had brought heroin into the country—he arrived at Southampton yesterday on the *Atlantis*, by the way—and I imagine it wasn't an isolated incident, or they wouldn't have been quite so excited about it."

"At this stage," remarked Sir Nicholas, "I could very well do without your speculations."

"Yes, but . . . well, anyway, Peter said 'go ahead'—he hadn't really any choice, as I told you—but he was beginning to look pretty jittery, a fact which wasn't wasted on either of them, I assure you. But I was watching him while they searched, and he may have guessed they were going to find something, but I'll swear he didn't know where it was."

"However, they did find it."

"Yes, I told you about that. And just when Shelley was look-ing triumphant and demanding an instant explanation, Doctor Prescott turned up. Well, I could have done without him at precisely that moment."

"So I imagine." Sir Nicholas's smile was malevolent. "You were prepared to suppress your friend, Hammond, to institute yourself his spokesman—"

"Exactly, sir. Well, what would you have done? But instead of that, the doctor came in prattling gaily of loss of memory. And then the fat was in the fire," Antony admitted. "It wasn't without its funny side, I suppose, because Shelley was already bristling with suspicion, and that just made things worse. But I didn't see anything comic about it at the time. Shelley did consent—er—under pressure to let Doctor Pres-cott examine Peter before they took him down to the station and charged him. All I could do then was get Geoffrey Horton down there in a hurry; and he's arranging for Doctor Mac-intyre to see Peter, and all the rest of it."

"So much for propriety," murmured Sir Nicholas. (Geoffrey Horton was a solicitor.) "What is the position now?"

"I don't see any chance of getting Peter out before the Magistrates' Court on Monday. They may oppose bail at that stage, but I doubt it. I tried to get on to Shenstone—his brother-in-law, sir—but he's out of town for the weekend. I'll see him when he gets back. Of course, the police have Peter's luggage now, so we'll have to rely on Geoffrey for any further information from that source." He paused, and seemed to be wondering how best to word his next remark. "At least, it will be a new experience, acting for a client who can't tell us any-thing," he said. And Jenny was reminded, suddenly and ir-reverently, of a carrot dangled enticingly before a donkey's nose; but she wasn't feeling like smiling just then.

Sir Nicholas showed no enthusiasm at the prospect; perhaps

he was allergic to carrots. He said sharply, "I have given no undertaking—"

"No, sir, of course not." Antony's tone was undeniably soothing, and his uncle eyed him suspiciously. "But there's no harm—is there?—in making a few preliminary inquiries."

"I don't see how I can stop you," said Sir Nicholas, disagreeably. But Jenny realized that his interest was caught, and his help as firmly pledged as if he had made the most solemn commitment. She found the thought depressing, because her imagination had taken her already beyond the familiar, comfortable room, and the routine discussion of a new brief, into all the strange and perhaps dangerous byways down which her husband's unorthodox ways might lead him.

"If Peter has been framed—" she said, and knew as she spoke that there lay the basis for all her fears; but she broke off as both men turned to look at her.

"If he has, love . . . what then?"

"I don't know." She looked at him helplessly. You might call it a passion for truth, for justice; you might call it—when you were angry—just plain vulgar curiosity; you might call it weakness, that he could never refuse an appeal. Whatever it was, it was part and parcel of Antony's nature, and there was nothing she could do—or wanted to do—to alter it. His eyes were fixed on her with a sort of amused comprehension; she got up with a purposeful air and said, defiantly if obscurely: "There's nothing else to be done."

"There isn't, is there?" he agreed. "Not for either of us." He glanced at his uncle and added, provocatively: "It might be a good idea if you fed us, Jenny. A good meal has a notoriously mellowing effect."

But they argued all through dinner, and it was late that evening before they finally abandoned their discussion.

: :   : :

That was on Saturday. On Sunday afternoon Geoffrey Horton came to tea. He was a few years younger than Maitland, had red hair, a normally cheerful disposition, and a carefully nurtured criminal practice. Sir Nicholas had been known to complain of the amiability which led him to comply with Antony's sometimes erratic requests; but he had a great regard for him nonetheless.

Geoffrey came in now with a rather exaggerated air of caution, and was obviously relieved when he saw Sir Nicholas was not present. "For I don't mind telling you, Jenny," he said, "I wasn't at all sure how he'd take this business."

"Just as you'd expect," said Antony, closing the door and following him across the room. "But you can relax for the present; he's out today, and he's leaving for Switzerland tomorrow."

"Already?" said Geoffrey, sinking with a sigh of relief into one of the wing chairs. "I thought he'd . . . well, I was sure he'd want to reorganize, or disorganize, everything in chambers before he went."

Jenny pushed an ashtray toward him, and settled herself more comfortably with one leg tucked under her. "I blackmailed him," she said, composedly. "I threatened to go away myself, and leave him to Mrs. Stokes. He really has been ill, you know, Geoffrey; but he hates fuss, and she won't leave him alone."

"You haven't been particularly aloof yourself," said Antony, taking his favorite place with his back to the empty grate. "But I admit, you get your effects with more subtlety." Jenny pulled a face at him.

"I thought it was the best thing," she said, with dignity.

"The original managing woman." Antony was unimpressed. "So, as long as we've a nice, neatly-documented case ready for him by the end of the long vacation, we've nothing more to worry about."

"Oh, haven't we, though? If you ask me," said Geoffrey with feeling, "what sort of a defense I should *not* choose to put forward in this or any other action, I'd say 'loss of memory.'"

"Well, I dare say. It wasn't exactly a choice, however." He

met his friend's look with a challenging one of his own. "Or don't you think so?" he asked.

"Well . . . you must admit, it's damned unlikely," Geoffrey grumbled. He looked at Jenny, as though for support, and found her eyes fixed on him accusingly. "Never mind," he said, in a hurry. "Skip it."

"Then perhaps," suggested Antony, a little too politely, "we could leave our opinions to one side, and come to matters of fact."

"Such as they are," said Geoffrey. "They won't comfort you. The police are being pretty cagey about details, but I'm sure this is part of a racket that has been going on for some time; which is why they were only too eager to pounce as they did."

"Well, Peter hasn't been drug-running regularly," Jenny objected. "If it was a racket, one journey now and then wouldn't be much use, would it?"

"No, but . . . well, the facts are there," Horton pointed out. "I mean, the stuff was in his suitcase, and he can't explain how it came into his possession." His sense of grievance overcame him, and he added rather querulously, "It's all very well for him to sit back, and say blandly that he doesn't remember anything. It leaves us in a hell of a position."

"It leaves us with all the world before us," said Antony, blithely. Yesterday he had been depressed and uncertain, but his doubts had cleared today. He saw that the other man was really annoyed, and added coaxingly, "Tell me what you know, there's a good chap."

"I know what you've told me," snapped Geoffrey. "And very little besides." A silence spread itself between them which Antony did nothing to break; and after a few moments Horton added ruefully: "He came in on the *Atlantis*, she docked at Southampton on Friday. There's no report from the Customs people yet, but there can't have been anything suspicious."

"I knew that bit," said Antony. "There were some menus and things on his dressing table."

"I saw the contents of his wallet at the police station; and also what was in his brief case. You had a look at his passport, he tells me, and he showed you the diary. There were some traveler's checks in the wallet, and a few pounds in cash, and a picture of a girl. He says—of course!—that he doesn't know who she is."

"No letters?" asked Antony, ignoring this attractive byroad.

"No personal correspondence. Except insofar as some of the stuff in the brief case affected his future. I've heard of Shenstone," he added, perhaps not irrelevantly. "What's he like?"

"Tycoon," said Antony. "I've met him, but I don't know him well enough to give you a more definite opinion than that."

"He's smooth," said Jenny. She pondered. "He always seems to say the right thing, but I never really felt comfortable with him."

"What about him, anyway?" asked Antony.

"Just that they'd been having some discussion about what Hammond would be doing when he came home," Horton explained. "It got a little heated in places—the correspondence, I mean. The job he held had been filled, and he didn't seem to like the sound of the alternative that was offered. To tell you the truth, Antony, it made me wonder whether he might not have taken something on . . . in desperation, you know; perhaps not really knowing what it was he was being asked to bring through."

"If you think he brought in that bloody great package deliberately, without having the faintest suspicion of its contents . . . well, I don't think he's such a fool as that," Maitland protested. "And if you're trying to be tactful," he added, with a spurt of indignation, "you needn't bother."

"Well, you must admit, it's . . . not unlikely," said Geoffrey.

"You've talked to Peter," said Antony abruptly. "What did you make of him?"

"Not relevant, and you know it. He's a pleasant enough

chap, so many of my clients are. But I haven't the benefit of your previous knowledge of him to enable me to form an opinion." Horton so obviously meant just the opposite of what he said that Antony's hackles rose again.

"I'm not prejudiced," he protested. "It's a considered opinion . . . quite dispassionate . . . based on my knowledge of his character." Geoffrey gave an incredulous snort, and Jenny said quickly:

"Well, I *am* prejudiced, and I don't care who knows it. If it were something else I might believe it . . . but not dope."

"Let's leave it there," said Geoffrey, pacifically. He had no real objection to sparring with Antony, in fact he rather welcomed the opportunity; but if Jenny was going to join the defense team, he was off. "All this doesn't affect the immediate issue, after all," he said.

"Irrelevant, incompetent, and immaterial, as our American friends would say," agreed Antony solemnly. But he was quite well aware of the reason for his friend's sudden capitulation, and burst out laughing as he caught his eye. After a moment, Geoffrey laughed too; and Jenny, despairing of seeing the joke, went out with her feathers only a little ruffled to put the kettle on.

CHAPTER III

THAT THERE were difficulties inherent in the situation, Antony Maitland would have been the first to admit; but certain minor inconveniences were not immediately apparent. He had a pretty fair idea, for instance, of the strength of the case that could be made out against Peter Hammond, and was able to listen with equanimity to Inspector Shelley's careful presentation of the evidence in the Magistrates' Court. And if he suspected, by the time the hearing was over, that the police had their own reasons for not opposing bail, that didn't worry him unduly. But it was not until, halfway through the afternoon, he took a taxi cityward, that his thoughts began squirreling round Hammond's predicament, the embarrassments of the next half-hour, and his own growing—if illogical—sense of responsibility for his friend's welfare. As he paid off the taxi it was the awkwardness he foresaw in explaining the matter to Peter's brother-in-law that mainly occupied his mind.

Kinlocks' head office was in a tall new building of quite startling mediocrity which had recently risen on one of the bomb sites. From a study of the board in the entrance hall, he gathered that the firm occupied the whole of the two top floors, and having been lured into the lift-cage by a uniformed siren, the ascent was accomplished without delay. Once there, however, it took ten minutes of earnest endeavor to break through the various lines of defense with which the managing director had surrounded himself; but at last he was able to embark on the last stage of his journey, following a fair-haired girl down a long corridor that presumably led to Shenstone's room.

Down the left-hand wall of the corridor a procession of framed photographs marched beside them. A bridge across a deep ravine; a bewildering complex of buildings which reminded him of nothing so much as the interior of an anthill designed by a particularly devious-minded ant; a sweep of concrete . . . the retaining wall of a dam? The other wall presented a series of windows, each giving the passer-by a slightly different view of the activity beyond; Antony was aware of men hunched untidily over drawing boards; men who stared raptly into space, apparently awaiting some direct inspiration from on high; men who argued over drawings with various degrees of heat. He wondered vaguely whether his own chambers in the Inner Temple would present to a stranger so alien an impression; but the question was no sooner formulated than dismissed.

The fair girl, whose manner and dress proclaimed a maturity her face and figure denied, had passed the last of the windows and come to a stop before an imposing mahogany door; a door that looked out of place, somehow, in that modern building. Before she knocked she glanced anxiously over her shoulder, as though fearing her companion might have fallen by the wayside. When quite satisfied that he was still in attendance, and showing no immediate signs of riotous or unseemly behavior, she tapped lightly and opened the door. Her manner was as grave and decorous as an acolyte dedicated to the service of a hasty-tempered deity, and in spite of his forebodings, Antony was grinning to himself as he went in.

His first thought was that the room was almost startlingly impersonal. His second, that his own recollection—and Jenny's—had been at fault in categorizing Shenstone as "smooth." The man who rose to greet him was well over six foot, immaculately groomed, but retaining even so a somewhat rugged appearance. The sort of man, you might imagine, who would find himself more at home in the great outdoors.

If this were so, he had certainly done his best to provide himself with breathing space. Antony crossed a vast blue sea of carpet to reach the desk, and when he reached it its surface still stretched between them . . . void and empty, he thought, with one of his brief, amused extravagances. An apt enough phrase, anyway. Shenstone might be a busy man, but his office gave little indication of his activity.

"Ah, Mr. Maitland. Have we met, I don't seem to remember—?" After all, his voice belied his appearance. It was satin-smooth, and—paradoxically—it rasped Antony's nerves like a rusty file.

"We have met. It was years ago." His tone, more curt than he had intended, dismissed the meeting as unimportant.

"Then, I wonder . . . but won't you sit down?" A gesture stressed the invitation; Shenstone seated himself when he saw his visitor had obeyed him, and pushed a streamlined gold cigarette box hospitably across the desk. "Whatever your business is, you seem to have impressed my secretary with its urgency," he added; and smiled as he spoke.

"It is urgent, I'm afraid. It concerns Peter Hammond."

"Peter—?" The smile lingered on Shenstone's lips, but his eyes were suddenly wary. "What about Peter?" he asked; and now his tone had a sharpness. "I was expecting him here this morning. I hope . . . not an accident?"

"No," said Antony; and afterward wondered what had possessed him to make his disclosure so abruptly. "But he is in trouble . . . with the police."

Shenstone looked incredulous, and when he spoke the honey had quite left his voice. "I hope you mean to explain that," he said, harshly. But then his bewilderment seemed to lighten. "Oh . . . Customs!" he said. "Is that all?"

"All?" snapped Antony, suddenly and inexcusably annoyed.

"He could get ten years." He paused for this to sink in, and again noted the other man's startled look with something unkindly approaching pleasure. "I'm talking about a charge under the Dangerous Drugs Act," he added deliberately. "It's a serious business."

"This is intolerable!" He got up as he spoke, and began to pace restlessly up and down behind the desk. Antony sat watching him quietly, and wondered as he did so which aspect of the situation had engaged his anger. After a few moments Shenstone paused, put one hand in his pocket and withdrew it rather quickly, and directed a piercing look at his companion. "May I ask what is your connection with this affair, Mr.—Mr. Maitland? Are you here in an official capacity?"

"Nothing like that. I'm a friend of Peter's."

"Then I need not scruple to tell you—" But he obviously thought better of what he had been about to say, for he broke off there and gave his remarks another direction. "I suppose he's in custody?" he asked.

"No, he was released on bail this morning."

"Then why isn't he here himself? I suppose you're trying to tell me he wants my help, but doesn't care to face me." His tone was bitter, and Antony was aware of an increasing feeling of uneasiness. This man, after all, knew Peter Hammond intimately, and if he thought . . .

"There are complications," he said. "I'd better explain."

Shenstone listened, tight-lipped, while the story was told, and when it was finished he made no immediate comment. After a while he came back to the big chair behind the desk, seated himself deliberately, and looked at Antony with something like amusement. All his irritation seemed to have left him, and when he spoke his voice was again as bland as butter. "My memory is improving, Mr. Maitland. I seem to remember . . . you are a barrister, are you not?"

"I am." His own angry reaction to Shenstone's manner was indefensible, he knew, and he was determined to keep his temper.

35

"And you're telling me that Peter, with no memory and a serious criminal charge hanging over him, conveniently found your name written down in his diary, and made straight for the one person of his acquaintance more capable than any other of helping him in his predicament?"

Antony considered. "That seems a fair enough statement," he said at last. "Of course, it would have been more to the point if I'd been a solicitor, but one can't have everything," he added.

"No, indeed. As it stands, the coincidence is quite sufficiently unbelievable." He made the statement deliberately, watching his companion.

"I happen to believe it," said Antony, mildly.

"Do you, Mr. Maitland? I hope you will forgive my frankness, but the only doubt in my mind is whether the story was concocted before, or after, Peter came to you." Antony grinned at him.

"I'd have thought up a much better tale than that," he said cheerfully. "If you think loss of memory makes a good defense, you're mistaken."

"Well, I must take your word for it." Shenstone was eyeing him doubtfully, obviously a little taken aback by this good-humored acceptance of his insinuations. "But you say Peter asked you to come here—?"

"To be exact, I offered to do so. It seemed only fair to tell you, before you saw the evening papers."

"Obliging of you," said Shenstone, dryly. "As for Peter . . . you say the police released him, Mr. Maitland. Where is he now?"

"I tried to persuade him that he'd be better off in hospital. But he's gone back to the hotel."

"I suppose he's seen a doctor, however, if only to lend color—"

"Two, to be exact." Again Antony ignored the evidence of the other's disbelief. "They agree there's nothing physically wrong with him. As for the mental condition, they've no idea what caused it, or how long it will persist."

"I see. Well, I suppose, if he maintains this story of amnesia, Peter hasn't told you anything of his engagement." Antony shook his head. "A girl called Robbins, I haven't met her. But it seems she should be told."

"Yes, of course." (More explanations, he thought despondently.) "It'll be rather a shock for her, I imagine. Was he coming home to be married?"

"He'd finished the job he went out to do. I know nothing of his personal affairs . . . well, very little," he amended. "You say he went back to the hotel. Where is he staying?"

"At the Chiltern."

Shenstone seemed to be considering this, and to judge by his expression his thoughts gave him no pleasure. "He'd better come and stay with me," he said at last.

"I don't know—"

"Can you suggest anything better?" Antony shook his head, and the other man added, bitterly, "I will be quite plain with you, I don't like the situation. But I should prefer to avoid a scandal, and in the circumstances the best thing seems to be to accept Peter's story, at least so far as the world is concerned." He paused, and suddenly looked at his companion with genuine, if rueful, amusement. "That's the best I can do, Mr. Maitland. I don't think it's a bad offer, on the whole."

"It's . . . extremely generous." He liked Shenstone much better blunt than honeyed, but this didn't seem the time to say so. "Shall I tell him—?"

"Let's see." Shenstone glanced down at his wrist watch. "I'm engaged this evening, so perhaps it will be easier all round if we make it tomorrow."

"It's Lyall Square, isn't it? Number Eleven?" Antony got to his feet as he spoke, and added slowly, "It would make it easier if you could believe him." Shenstone laughed shortly.

"Perhaps," he agreed. "But you mustn't ask the impossible, Mr. Maitland. After all, even if I accept the amnesia, there's still this business of the drugs."

"Legally, he's innocent until he's proved guilty."

"Certainly. But we're not talking of the law now, we're talking of our personal beliefs." He had risen as his visitor did, and they faced each other again across the desk, their eyes almost level. There was something searching in Shenstone's look, and when he spoke again his voice sounded to Antony for the first time to have a note of genuine concern. "Has it occurred to you, Mr. Maitland?" he asked; "Peter is my brother-in-law, a member of my firm; I probably know him a good deal better than you do."

"Yes . . . it had occurred to me." His tone was level, but he was thinking, if Shenstone can accept so easily the fact of Peter's guilt . . .

He left the building a few minutes later with kinder feelings toward the managing director of Kinlocks than a quarter of an hour ago he would have believed possible. But he still felt depressed.

: :   : :

Jenny had driven Sir Nicholas to Dover that morning, and they had time to lunch together before he had to go aboard. The dining room was crowded, but the hotel was an old-fashioned one for all its present popularity, and it was surprising how much flavor of the "shilling ordinary" still clung about it; an illusion which did not persist once the menu had been studied.

As is usual with people who see a great deal of each other, they had plenty to talk about; but toward the end of the meal Jenny fell silent. She had no intention of speaking her thoughts, which, indeed, were unformulated: a vague uneasiness, an equally vague wish that Sir Nicholas would postpone his trip, in spite of the fact that she could see a dozen difficulties which would arise if he decided to do so. But Sir Nicholas, meeting a rather wistful look across the coffee cups, shook his head at her and said, smiling:

"It wouldn't help, you know." His reflections had reached much the same point as hers, though by rather a different route.

"I don't know what you mean," said Jenny, on the defensive.

"Don't you, my dear? I thought perhaps you were worried. About this latest freak of Antony's," he amplified.

"Well," said Jenny, drawing out the word doubtfully. "Yes, I am, Uncle Nick."

"I don't think there's any danger involved . . . except perhaps the danger of disillusionment," he said. "At which stage you can pick up the pieces, and I'd be no use at all." He saw her uncertain look, and added with a show of irritation: "Be sensible, Jenny. You can't really believe—"

"You don't think Peter's telling the truth?"

"He may have lost his memory, though I wouldn't be inclined to place too much reliance on the statement. But he's certainly involved in some sort of criminal activity," said Sir Nicholas, bluntly.

"Antony's very sure—"

"I am well aware of it. But as he'd say himself, 'who lives may learn.'"

"Yes, but—" She picked up her coffee spoon, and began to trace a complicated pattern on the tablecloth.

"But—what, my dear?"

"He's often right about people, Uncle Nick. And you don't know Peter . . . we do."

"I hesitate to remind you, Jenny, of the occasions when Antony has *not* been right," said Sir Nicholas, austerely. "Do you remember Henry Traynor? A fine mess that was . . . and not the only time." Jenny laughed suddenly, and put the spoon back neatly in her saucer.

"Your memory's too good," she said. "If you're going to start digging up the past—"

"It was your idea," he pointed out, reasonably. "And I've just cause for complaint . . . he always involves me in his escapades, sooner or later."

"Well . . . yes, but—" She caught his eye, and added, defiantly, "I don't know what I want. If Peter is involved in drug-running, Antony'll find out and not get mixed up in it. But I don't really want to believe that Peter would do a thing like that."

: :   : :

Antony went straight back to chambers after his talk with Bernard Shenstone, and spent a harassing half-hour with Sir Nicholas's clerk. Jenny was visiting friends on the way home, so he went round to the Chiltern as soon as he could get away from old Mr. Mallory, and took Peter out to dinner. Hammond seemed impervious to the rather odd looks they got as they left the hotel, but he was obviously worried and nervous, and Antony thought that the sooner they could get him away to a lodging slightly less in the public eye, the better it would be.

He elaborated this opinion over the dinner table, when Peter looked doubtful about accepting Shenstone's invitation. He had reported their talk without comment, but now he said firmly: "You can't avoid meeting people forever. And if you won't go to hospital—"

This had at least the effect of rousing Hammond, if only to a display of revulsion. "No!" he said. He was showing a disposition—which his friend regarded as unhealthy—to crumble his roll and ignore what was on the plate in front of him. Antony tried another tack.

"Doctor Macintyre thought—"

"He seemed to believe me when I told him I couldn't remember anything," said Peter, gloomily. "But probably you know more about that than I do."

"He said he'd want to see you again," said Antony.

"Well, that's all right, it doesn't have to be in hospital." The brief show of energy had been succeeded by a return of listlessness, but there seemed to be some firmness behind the words. "I don't altogether understand the position," he added. "You've talked as if the doctor would be a witness, but I don't see what my . . . my state of mind has to do with smuggling."

"In theory," Antony told him, "there's no reason why you should be called to give evidence when it comes to the trial. In practice, it would be better to explain your silence. Even an unconvincing explanation," he added, unkindly.

Peter looked up at that. "Then he didn't believe me?" he asked.

"That's not what I said. As a matter of fact—" He paused, and cast his mind back to his interview with Macintyre, hearing again the doctor's laconic tones. "He said he was pretty sure in his own mind that your condition was as you described it to him. But he also said we could get a whole squad of experts, and between them they wouldn't be able to swear to more than an opinion. Which isn't enough."

"No," said Peter, sadly. He had been pursuing a piece of potato around his plate in a desultory way, but now he put down his fork and said bitterly: "He told me to relax . . . not to worry. What the hell does he think I am?"

"A human being," said Antony, "who'd be all the better for taking his advice." The other man looked at him angrily for a moment, but he did not seem able to sustain any emotion for long.

"He also said it's a 'not uncommon form of amnesia.' But why should it have happened now? And how long—?"

Antony ignored the second part of his query. "I asked him that," he said. "Whether amnesia could be induced in any way." He laid down his knife and fork, and looked reproachfully at the congealing food on his companion's plate. "Are you going to eat that, Peter; or shall we have some coffee?"

"I'm not hungry. What did he say?" asked Peter. But again the brief show of animation died as he listened to the reply.

"He said he didn't know of any drug that would do that. He said the commonest causes of amnesia were a blow on the head—but he couldn't find any trace of injury—or the 're-treat from reality' the psychologists are always talking about."

"Not particularly comforting," said Peter, dismally.

"So I told him what Doctor Prescott has said, and he

agreed you'd probably had some kind of sedative; but he thought most likely it would be no more than some antisea-sickness pills, probably the kind that have a basis of scopola-mine. It was too late when he saw you to do any tests, but he thought it might have been that."

"Well, I don't even know if I get seasick." Peter paused a moment while the waiter, a volatile Italian with an air of dis-illusionment, removed his almost untouched plate; but ob-viously his thoughts had gone running on in the same direction. "When you talk about getting away from reality," he went on, as soon as they were alone, "it could be that . . . couldn't it? I mean, for all I know I may be up to my neck in this racket."

Antony had allowed his attention to wander, but some-thing in the other man's tone disturbed him, demanded his full attention. He leaned his elbows on the table, and said earnestly: "Drug-running isn't a pretty business, when you think about the people who take the stuff . . . who become addicts; which is just a nice, tidy word for something less than human. How do you feel about the idea that you may be responsible—?"

"It revolts me!"

"There you are, then. That's exactly what I thought. And unless you've changed—"

"I see what you mean." Hammond seemed to be thinking this out, and after a moment he added, "Thank you," politely. Antony grinned at him.

"I know it's maddening," he agreed. "But I'm not pretend-ing to any very profound knowledge of your character, after all."

"You know more about me than I do about myself," said Peter. Adding, with a burst of candor, "I find that intoler-able."

Privately, Antony agreed with him, but there seemed no point in discussing a situation that neither of them could do anything to remedy. Now that he was away from Shenstone's company his own doubts had receded, but they remained uneasily below the surface of his thoughts. His next remark, however, was probably intended to divert his companion by providing a counter irritant.

"I found out one thing which may be a bit of a shock to you." He was fishing in his pocket as he spoke, and produced at length a battered envelope. "Shenstone tells me you're engaged to be married," he added.

Peter took the news without visible emotion, but after a while he said carefully, "Who—?"

"A girl called Nan Robbins." Antony glanced down at his envelope, though he didn't really need to refresh his memory. "She lives near Midhurst."

"I wonder," said Peter, "if she was expecting to meet me in town. I'd have thought—" He stopped, and shook his head as though the movement might clear his bewilderment. "If it's true," he went on, "it's awkward . . . isn't it?"

"Very."

"I suppose we'll have to tell her. I mean . . . the papers—"

"Obviously, we must tell her." Antony's tone was tart, but when Peter made no immediate comment he added, in a resigned way, "I suppose that means you want me to see her."

"You're being very kind," said Hammond, formally. But there was no real feeling behind his words; he seemed that evening to have gone beyond emotion. He took out his wallet then, and produced the photograph Geoffrey Horton had mentioned. "Do you suppose this is her?" he asked. "A pretty girl, wouldn't you say?"

"Extremely." Maitland's tone had no more enthusiasm than politeness demanded. Not conventionally pretty, he thought, but an attractive smile . . . provocative . . . tantalizing? He was trying each word in turn, and none seemed precisely to fit.

43

"I thought perhaps it was my sister," Peter was saying.

"Pamela? Nothing like her."

"It's queer, though, isn't it?" He was frowning at the photograph. "If I knew her before I went away—" He looked up then and met his friend's eyes; and Antony was shocked by the realization that the lack of emotion was a very thin veneer indeed, that below the surface indifference were fear, and uncertainty, and a very deep loneliness.

Because there was nothing he could say that would be of comfort, he was relieved to see the waiter approaching with their coffee. He made use of the interruption to turn their talk to less personal matters.

:   :   :   :

When he got back to the Chiltern Hotel that night, Peter Hammond crossed to the desk to collect his key. "I'll be checking out tomorrow," he told the clerk. "Will you ask them to have my account ready by midday?"

The clerk murmured a polite acquiescence, but something in his expression—a curiosity not quite hidden—sparked Peter to a show of anger. "There's no real need to advise the police," he said. "I'll be giving them my new address."

"Yes, of course, Mr. Hammond." The man's eyes dropped with an odd effect of coyness. Peter turned on his heel, and went toward the lift.

Up in his room, with the world shut out for the moment, he took off his jacket and flung himself down on the bed. He was extraordinarily tired, but this couldn't be physical, he realized, looking back over the day's activities. He began, rather hopelessly, to try to sort out his impressions. The police had been polite enough, but with a kind of irony behind their civility; or so he had imagined. The Magistrates' Court . . . it was like watching a bad play, he thought, where the chief actor didn't know his part. But what had he felt? Not the appropriate emotions of shame and fear . . . not just then. Incredulity, perhaps, that this should be happening to him. But later, when he had time to think, he realized that this was illogical . . . for who was he, anyway . . . what sort of a man . . . ?

What had he done?

The words seemed to echo in his brain, as though he had shouted them. He was lying on his back, and now he shifted his position a little, as though the movement might provide an escape from his thoughts. Gradually the feeling of panic subsided. He thought, my name is Peter Hammond, and I was born in this room three days ago. He thought, in that other life I had relatives, and friends, and acquaintances I can't remember; I did a job that I can't remember, though it must have been important to me, because a man's work is his life; I made promises which I can't remember . . .

If I have forgotten all these things because I am afraid, because I will not face reality, I have been guilty of betrayal. Logically, then, I must admit that I may also have betrayed . . . myself. If the police are right . . . I don't want to believe they are right . . . but, if they are, I am a criminal. And, if not, where did the stuff come from? Maitland seems to think . . . but he wouldn't tell me what the other chap— Shenstone, my brother-in-law—what he thought, whether he believed me. I've said I'll go there tomorrow; I don't really want to go. I don't mind them watching me here, and talking . . . well, not much. But I dare say they'll ask me to leave when they get round to it, and I've got to stay somewhere until the fog clears . . . until I remember . . .

He lay for a long time, straining against the barrier that had somehow grown up between sleeping and waking, two nights ago. The room was very quiet; in spite of the hotel's central position his window looked on to a courtyard, and there was only a murmur of traffic to be heard, too faint to be disturbing. From time to time there were sounds from the corridor; once a woman laughed, clearly and joyously, and he heard the rumble of her companion's voice; once there was

45

a rattle of crockery, though the trolley that held it ran silently on the carpeted floor. He wondered if it was for the same couple, a late supper after a show; and then thought of the strangeness of knowing that was a thing that was done, when he couldn't remember ever having done it.

At last he sat up and swung his feet to the floor; and glanced at his wrist watch as he unfastened the strap. It was later than he had thought, he'd get himself to bed and try to read for a while. He had found two books in his brief case earlier in the day, a paperback *Don Camillo*, and a new-looking novel which he supposed, rather doubtfully, must be to his taste.

He was pulling off his tie as he went toward the bathroom door.

He never knew what it was that set him on his guard. The door was a little ajar, and the room dark beyond it; there was no stir of sound or movement; nothing strange or unexpected. But he stopped short on the threshold, and his hand went out unwillingly to push the door farther open. It moved for six inches, and stopped. He pushed harder, something softly insistent held it against him. His left hand went out to the light switch, he moved forward until he could see past the half-open door, and found himself looking down at the body of a man, tumbled face downward on the floor in front of the washbasin.

He stood quite still for a moment of frozen disbelief . . . for just long enough for his eyes to force acceptance of a fact his brain rejected. Then he bent down and tugged gently at the man's shoulder, until the face was visible.

It wasn't easy to recognize him, though the uniform should have given him a clue. It isn't easy to recognize anyone who has died by strangulation. But after a moment the face of the hotel valet came into his mind; and he forced himself to look closer, to trace—with difficulty—the resemblance between the little, quiet-moving man he had seen earlier in the day, and the thing on the floor . . . face suffused and swollen, tongue protruding between blackened lips, bloodshot eyes staring and seeming still to hold the frantic terror of his last moments.

But the little man lay quiet now, with the cord of Peter's dressing gown tight about his throat.

CHAPTER IV

THE PHONE CALL came when Antony had been in bed about half an hour, and dragged him unwillingly from the first quiet depths of sleep. He sat up and switched on the lamp on the table beside him, and listened for a moment to the bell shrilling imperatively from the living room before he threw back the clothes and swung his legs to the floor.

Jenny lay almost undisturbed by the noise, though she made a sort of groaning sound when the light went on, and burrowed deeper into her pillow. Antony padded reluctantly across the room, and hoped as he went that perhaps the caller would despair before he reached the phone, so that he could go back to sleep again. But the bell rang on.

When he took up the receiver he was not feeling particularly amiable, and his "Hallo" held more of growl than greeting. But he went very still as he listened. "Could you come? It's urgent . . . really urgent. Could you come at once?" Peter had solved the tricky problem of how to address an old but unremembered friend by never using his name. He was speaking quickly, too quickly to be easily intelligible; but for all that something insistent in his tone checked Antony's angry retort before it was uttered. Instead he said, sharply:

"Where? To the hotel?" And added, as Peter's agreement reached his ears, "Why do you want me?"

48

Several minutes later he replaced the receiver, but did not immediately move away from the desk. Instead, he sat gazing blankly at the wall in front of him, and might have remained there for some considerable time had not Jenny's voice from the doorway roused him from his fit of abstraction.

"Is anything wrong, Antony?"

He turned then, and smiled at her. "Nothing for you to worry about, love. Just an S.O.S. from Peter. Some fun and games at his hotel." But it was no use thinking he could get away with this casual explanation, as he might have known; Jenny was fairly bristling with suspicion, and he added—though still in an offhand way—"Well, the valet who looked after his floor has been killed. He seemed to think he'd like me to hold his hand."

Jenny came farther into the room. Her feet were bare and she hadn't stopped to put on her dressing gown, and she shivered a little as a gust of wind billowed the curtains. Antony said: "Darling, you look like one of those cold, pink shapes Mrs. Stokes used to be so fond of giving Uncle Nick. You'd better get back into bed."

"Not until you tell me . . . I suppose you mean the man was murdered . . . but what has that to do with Peter?"

"Well, he found him," said Antony, apologetically. He met Jenny's stony look (the look of one quite prepared to stand her ground indefinitely, even in a flimsy nightdress, with a chilly wind blowing around her ankles), and added with a directness that only just missed brutality, "The chap had been strangled, and left in Peter's bathroom." He crossed the room then, and began to urge her back toward the bedroom, and said, more gently, "I'll have to go, love. I'm sorry."

"Are the police there?"

"As a matter of fact . . . no." This was altogether too pertinent a question, and he added defensively: "I tried to persuade him, but he seemed a bit jittery and said he wouldn't do anything till I got there."

Jenny got into bed again, and sat there hugging her knees

49

and looking at him reproachfully. "They'll think it's funny," she prophesied. "Couldn't you call them from here?"

Antony picked up his dressing gown, and draped it round her shoulders. "Not really fair," he said. "I don't know what he might say, if they got there first. Besides, I don't *know* it's true, not for sure. It might all be imagination."

"I suppose so." Jenny's agreement was reluctant. "But I don't like it," she added, firmly. "I'm sure Uncle Nick—"

"Uncle Nick isn't here," said Antony, who had gone across to the highboy and was rummaging for a clean pair of socks. "Thank heavens," he added, devoutly, as he found what he wanted and shut the drawer. Jenny made a queer, snorting sound, which might have been a suppressed giggle. But when he turned to look at her again her gaze was still solemn and accusing.

But the argument didn't really delay him, and he felt he had made good time when he got to the Chiltern at last. His tap on the door of Room 310 was answered quickly with a suspicious question; a moment later he was stepping past Peter Hammond into the room, and hearing without surprise—and with only a faint feeling of injury—the complaint that he hadn't been quicker.

"You've been an age. What kept you?"

"Picking daisies," said Antony, shortly. His eyes were on the door on his right that still stood ajar and gave a glimpse of a tiled wall beyond. "In there?" he asked, jerking his head.

Peter nodded. He went back a pace as Maitland moved toward the bathroom, and watched passively the brief pantomime of his inspection. Antony pushed the door gently, as he himself had done, but his hands were in his pockets, and he shoved with his knee; then he was round the door, looking down at the thing on the floor, and still with that detached air. After a moment he backed out again, and turned an expressionless face to his friend.

"Not pretty," he said. "In fact . . . was he lying like that when you found him?"

"I couldn't see his face. But I didn't really move him, only to turn him a little."

"I see." He was crossing the room as he spoke, and having pulled round the rather spindly chair that stood by the writing table, he sat down with an air deliberately contrived to convey a leisurely approach. "You'd better tell me," he invited. "Did you come straight back here when you left me?"

"Yes, I did. And I didn't go out again. I know what you're thinking, of course," said Peter, with something like desperation in his voice. "Why didn't I find him sooner?"

"Well, why didn't you?" The casual air persisted.

"I was . . . thinking." Hammond sounded angry now; angry and defiant. Antony let his eyes wander for a moment; the room was tidy, he thought, almost too tidy; but the bed was convincingly rumpled. Then he looked up at his companion and gave his sudden smile.

"Very understandable," he remarked. "And that poor chap is the valet?"

"I saw him earlier in the day, when I came back to the hotel."

"I wonder . . . well, never mind that now. Don't you think it's about time we confided in the police?"

"I suppose we must."

"We can hardly ignore the whole unpleasant business," Antony pointed out.

"No, but—"

"You didn't kill him, did you?"

"No!" The denial came explosively; but there was no assurance in his voice as he went on. "It's just that . . . don't you see? . . . I'm not sure what it means."

"Too much of a coincidence not to have some sort of connection with your affairs," Antony agreed.

"Then the charge . . . that dope business . . . doesn't this make you think it may be true?" He was speaking carefully, as though every word mattered, and his tone had a desperate earnestness. "I've tried to persuade myself it couldn't be; you seemed to believe in me, I thought perhaps you'd know . . . if I could have done a thing like that. But now . . . how can I expect you to trust me, when I can't even trust myself?"

Antony leaned back; the little chair creaked alarmingly. He said: "There could be more than one interpretation of what has happened." And again his voice was quite without expression.

"Then you don't think—?"

"Well, this smuggling racket isn't something new; at least, not if the attitude of the police is anything to go on. But . . . oh, for heaven's sake, Peter, we haven't time to talk about it now." He got up as he spoke, and went across to sit on the bed and pick up the telephone. "I suppose I'll have to go through the switchboard," he said; and the thought seemed to depress him.

"If you'd just tell me—"

"Have you never wondered," said Antony, with an air of patience that was only slightly exaggerated, "who tipped off the police about the dope in your suitcase? It doesn't affect the question of your guilt or innocence—and don't think I don't sympathize with your desire to know about that—but it does make it extremely urgent to get in first this time." He had picked up the receiver as he spoke; but now, before there was any sign of life from the hotel switchboard, there came a knocking on the door, not very loud, but sharp and insistent.

"Damn," he said softly, and then, "Open up, Peter. Someone wants to see you." He was in the act of replacing the receiver as the door swung open and three men surged past Hammond into the room. Or, more accurately, two of them passed him; the other paused to shut the door firmly and take up his stance with his back to it; all with a casual air that wouldn't have deceived a child.

He recognized at once Sergeant Watkins, stolid as ever; and the broad-shouldered, shockheaded individual who was acting as doorkeeper could only (in that company) be a plain-clothes constable. But it was the man who had come in first who caught and held his attention: a thin-faced man with a square jaw and a tight-lipped look of displeasure. He had met Inspector Conway before. Antony sat for a moment, his hand still on the telephone, and then got up slowly. But for all his inward reluctance, his greeting sounded spontaneous enough. "Well!" he said, and smiled with an affectation of pleasure that might easily have passed for genuine. "You come most carefully upon your hour, Inspector." He looked past the detective, and found Sergeant Watkins's mild brown eyes fixed on him ruminatively. "More information received?" he asked gently.

The thin-faced man showed no signs of pleasure, feigned or otherwise. He said: "Mr. Maitland!" rather as though he had found a cockroach in his salad, and went on with very little pretense of cordiality, "What are you doing here?"

"Visiting," said Antony. "By invitation," he added, with just enough emphasis to make the words a reproach.

"I have business with Mr. Hammond," said Conway, austerely, declining to be drawn.

"So I suppose." He turned a little, to catch his friend's eye. "Your acquaintance among the police force is growing, Peter. This is Detective-Inspector Conway, of Central. Not the Narcotics Branch, this time . . . his specialty is murder. Just the man we want, in fact."

"Oh," said Peter, blankly. Antony sympathized with his feelings, in the circumstances there didn't seem to be much else the poor chap could say. Again he looked past Conway's shoulder until he met Sergeant Watkins's eye.

"As a matter of fact, we're holding a wake," he confided.

"Are you indeed, sir?" said Watkins, politely. He was looking round him as he spoke, and Antony came forward until he stood at Peter's elbow.

"I was just going to dial 999," he said, "but I suppose someone else was before me."

53

"We did receive a message," said Conway, cautiously.

"Well, then!" He gestured as he spoke. "You'll find him in the bathroom," he added.

Inspector Conway gave him a hard, suspicious look, glanced briefly at Peter, and then turned and marched stiffly toward the half-open door. Sergeant Watkins smiled, sleepily and apologetically, as though this activity in some way constituted a breach of etiquette. He made no attempt to follow his colleague, but stood rubbing his finger reflectively along the line of his jaw with a faint, rasping sound.

Conway's inspection lasted little longer than Antony's had done. His air of severity was even more marked as he came back into the bedroom, ignored the sergeant's look of inquiry, and dispatched the constable to find another telephone. Watkins must have found the instructions he gave sufficiently illuminating, for he made no attempt to interrupt with questions of his own. When he had finished, Conway turned to Peter. "Well, Mr. Hammond?" he said.

Antony took one quick glance at his friend's face, and intervened before he could say anything in reply. "We've nothing to tell you, Inspector. We don't know anything."

Conway turned his head, and gave him an unfriendly look. "Are you here in a professional capacity, Mr. Maitland?" he asked.

"I'm quite prepared to give Mr. Hammond a little friendly advice."

The detective compressed his lips over what he evidently took for an understatement, a euphemism for what might more correctly have been described as "damned interference." "In the circumstances, Mr. Maitland, I'm sure you will advise him that it would be . . . unwise to withhold an explanation."

"When you've told me the circumstances—" Conway exclaimed impatiently, and Antony gave him a sympathetic nod. "I know. Here we are with a body in the bathroom, and you want to know all about it. But don't you think we've a right to know . . . what you're doing here, for instance. After all, we've made you welcome, and given you every facility—"

"Whereas you might, of course," said Sergeant Watkins, his eyes on the ceiling, "have barricaded the door."

Antony grinned at him. "Your point," he conceded. "All the same, it's not really so difficult to tell me what I want to know. Just begin at the beginning, and as long as you stick to the truth you'll find it quite easy," he added, encouragingly. His words were directed to Conway, but again it was the sergeant who answered.

"Someone phoned us. Nothing was said about murder."

"Oh, wasn't it?" said Antony, unbelievingly. "Then what's *he* doing here?" he asked, his eyes moving reproachfully from one to the other of the two policemen.

"There were . . . implications," said Watkins. For all his bovine look, his brown eyes were full of amusement. "And you won't deny, Mr. Maitland, it seems our interpretation of them was justified."

"And so," said Inspector Conway, frigidly, "we come back to my original request. If I may be permitted—"

"But, of course!" Conway was quite rigid with anger now; whether at Antony's obstructive tactics, or because he felt his subordinate was talking too much, was not readily apparent. "Mr. Hammond will be only too glad to help you," Antony went on, "especially as I gather you don't feel it necessary to caution him." He turned his head as he spoke, and met Peter's eyes; and realized with dismay that all this skirmishing had missed its purpose. Hammond still seemed dazed, and had made no apparent effort to rally his forces to meet the police attack. "But there isn't much he can tell you."

"I think you must allow me to judge—"

"Why, certainly, Inspector."

"Then I must ask you, Mr. Hammond, what you know of this affair."

"Nothing, really. Only that I found him." His tone was flat, unemotional, and Antony thought, with sudden extravagance, that he had gone beyond fear now . . . far beyond fear to the ultimate depths of despair.

"Do you know the man?" Conway was asking.

"I saw him earlier today."

"You'd notice his uniform," said Antony. "He seems to have been the valet on this floor."

"Thank you." Conway made no attempt to hide the fact that he felt no gratitude for the information. "You say you saw the man earlier today, Mr. Hammond. Not before that?"

"You must know I've been in . . . in custody over the weekend, Inspector. I may have seen him on Saturday, but if so I don't remember."

"You arrived at the hotel on Friday evening, I understand."

"So I am told. I don't remember that either," said Peter, steadily.

"At best," said Antony, "hardly an extensive acquaintance." The smile with which Conway greeted this intervention was suspiciously like a snarl.

"Well, at least, Mr. Hammond, you have admitted to seeing the—er—victim—"

"I don't care for that way of putting it," said Antony. This time the detective ignored him altogether.

"He came in when I got back here after lunch," said Peter, for the moment unexpectedly garrulous. "Wanted to know if he could do anything for me, and gave me a knowing sort of look when he said they hadn't known if I was returning. I thought he was just inquisitive, and got rid of him as quickly as I could."

"And when did you see him again?"

"Tonight. He was dead when I found him."

"You came in, I am told, a little before ten o'clock."

"I don't know exactly. I think that's near enough."

"And it is now twenty to one. *That* needs some explaining, don't you think, Mr. Hammond?"

"I didn't go to bed straight away. I didn't go near the bathroom. I was thinking," said Peter, and turned his head to look at Antony. His expression was hard to read.

"That hardly covers the delay, Mr. Hammond."

"The inspector wants to know, Peter, the exact time you found him. And what I'm doing here." He looked from Conway to Watkins and added amiably, "An odd time of night for a social call. I'll admit that, if you like."

"Well, I didn't notice the time," said Peter. "But I think it was quite a long while after I came in. I phoned Mr. Maitland," he added. "It was almost immediately after I made the discovery, so perhaps he can tell you. I thought . . . things seemed to be happening that I couldn't understand . . . I thought perhaps—" He let the sentence trail, almost as though he had forgotten how he had meant it to end. Conway said sharply:

"What did you think? That he could explain these things that puzzled you? Or that—"

"If you're going to say 'that he could help you cover them up' . . . I shouldn't," Antony advised him. "I might get annoyed, Inspector."

"We should get on a good deal quicker without all these interruptions, Mr. Maitland," said Conway, severely.

"You have my sympathy, but I can't at the moment think of anything that would induce me to leave," said Antony, frankly.

"We can use Mr. Maitland's help, sir," said Watkins. It was the first remark he had contributed that evening that didn't seem to have been specifically designed to annoy; but Antony's look showed no appreciation. A formidable man, he thought, uneasily, finding himself maneuvered into a position he had no desire to occupy. Conway might resent his colleague's intervention, but he had no hesitation in following the suggestion.

"Well then, Mr. Maitland. What time did you receive Mr. Hammond's call?"

"I didn't notice exactly. Eleven-thirty, pretty near."

"And you came straight here?"

"I had to dress, Inspector, and find a taxi. That took a little time."

"But, even so, it didn't occur to you that perhaps the police might feel some interest in the matter."

"I think you must realize—" Antony began; and at the same time Peter said, with a good deal more energy than he had previously displayed, "That was my fault, Inspector. Mr. Maitland told me what I should do, but I didn't take his advice."

"That needn't have stopped him from getting in touch with us," Conway pointed out.

"I don't think that would have been very sensible," said Peter, coolly. "You must have been told I've lost my memory. How could he know I wasn't suffering from hallucinations, too?"

Antony was a little taken aback at this sudden reversal of roles; he met Watkins's amused look with a grin that was a little rueful, but it was Conway, after all, who was running the show. "That brings us back to the point I wished to make, Inspector. Don't you think it was natural in the circumstances that Mr. Hammond should want some . . . well, some moral support?"

"I might think so," retorted Conway, "if I believed for a moment that he was really suffering from amnesia."

"There you are, anyway. There's your explanation. If you don't like it—"

"I don't." Conway was emphatic. But whatever else he might have been about to add (and Antony could not feel that his remarks would have been made in a spirit of brotherly love), he was interrupted by the return of the constable, who sidled in apologetically.

"The squad's here, sir. And I told the manager, he says you can use his office."

Before they left the room to the ministrations of finger-print men and photographers, Sergeant Watkins strolled over

58

to the bathroom to take his first look at the dead man. He stood in the doorway for rather a long time, until Antony could hardly contain his curiosity; but when he moved away again he had no comment to make, and only shook his head when Conway looked at him inquiringly.

They found when they went downstairs that the manager was not quite so philosophical over what he obviously regarded as desecration as the constable's message might have led them to believe. Antony was impatient during the interlude which ensued, while the poor man was calmed down and such information as he had to give extracted; but afterward, as the night wore on, he came to think that there were —after all—worse things in life than boredom. And answering Conway's questions was one of them.

::   ::

He got home a little after five o'clock, to find Jenny precariously perched on a chair by the window, just finishing the hanging of the new curtains. This time she was warmly engulfed in his winter dressing gown—a venerable garment to which they were both inexplicably attached—and she descended with more haste than dignity when she heard him, and nearly fell over because she trod on the hem. Antony put out a hand to steady her, and said sharply: "There are more accidents in the home . . . have you no sense?" But his expression did not match his tone, there was a vagueness about him that might, or might not have been merely the result of exhaustion. Jenny picked up her skirts, and started purposefully across the room.

"I thought you couldn't be much longer," she told him. "I'll just make some tea."

Antony followed her into the kitchen, sat down on the rather penitential chair at the end of the table, and pushed the fingers of his left hand through his hair until it stood up in wild disorder. "What a mess!" he said. "What a damned, unadulterated mess." And added, with an obvious sense of injury, "Why do these things always happen to me?"

59

Jenny had the cold tap turned on full. She smiled at him over her shoulder, but did not attempt to answer. When she had plugged in the kettle and filled the teapot with hot water, she came to stand near the table. "Was it true?" she asked.

"What? Oh, the murder. Yes, quite true."

"You said . . . one of the hotel people."

"A chap called Wilson, he'd been with them nearly ten years." He stopped to consider this statement, and decided, with reluctance, that it could not be left to stand alone. "I'm not quite sure how they're organized," he went on, "but I gather he had a sort of supervisory position, and only went on duty when someone was away, or if they were extra busy. He was last seen tonight by the chambermaid, 'after half-past nine' she says. And if Peter's telling the truth Wilson was already dead in the bathroom when he got in at about ten o'clock. I told you he'd been strangled, but we don't know who did it, and we don't know why. If Peter's telling the truth."

"Have they arrested him?"

"No, they haven't. I don't quite know why. The hotel rather grudgingly fixed him up with another room." He had been avoiding her eyes, but now he clasped his hands on the table in front of him and looked up at her with a sort of weary candor. "You were quite right, love; the police got there before I had a chance to call them."

Jenny made no direct reply to this. She went to the cupboard and brought two cups, and spent more time than was necessary rummaging for teaspoons. When she could think of nothing else to fiddle with she came back to her former position by the table. Antony gave her a rather halfhearted grin. "Admirable woman," he said. "I know you're full of questions."

"You're tired," said Jenny, as though that covered everything.

"Yes, but . . . I think I'd better tell you. The situation is a trifle . . . complicated," said Antony. "To begin with, the informant—whoever it was—had phoned the Narcotics Branch. I gather his remarks were pretty cryptic, but suggestive . . . enough to arouse suspicion; so Sergeant Watkins was sent along to investigate, and Inspector Conway accompanied him with a sort of watching brief in case there really had been foul play. You remember Conway, don't you? A sour-faced chap with a sarcastic tongue and the temper of a fiend."

"I remember you talking about him," said Jenny, precisely. Antony laughed, and sounded, oddly, as if he were genuinely amused.

"It wasn't exactly a joyous reunion," he confessed. "I mean, I've known situations which pleased me better. But I never can resist . . . oh, well!"

On the stove the kettle began to splutter, and Jenny went back to make the tea. She said, not looking round from her task: "You say they didn't arrest Peter, but don't they suspect—?"

"They're as suspicious as hell," said Antony. "And not only of Peter. And I don't know that I blame them," he added, reflectively. "As for why they didn't arrest Peter, I think they're still hoping he'll lead them somewhere. Then, they can't explain the information that was laid, you know. The whole thing looks fishy, but it's by no means watertight. Not yet."

Jenny was pouring tea, and her whole attention seemed to be taken up by this simple task. "Won't it make things difficult, if Inspector Conway is angry with you?" she asked.

"Well, I wouldn't say tonight was exactly a picnic," Antony admitted. "Questions, questions, questions . . . I thought we'd never get to the end of them. However, I've a suspicion Sergeant Watkins may be helpful. He's a queer chap, I haven't the remotest idea what makes him tick; but he's not really in sympathy with Conway, I'm pretty sure of that."

"I don't see how that will help you," Jenny objected.

"No, but I was going to say, he's certainly got a sense of

humor, and though we had one or two brushes I don't think he's exactly unfriendly. I'm not being constructive, am I?" he added, dejectedly.

"Not really," said Jenny. She thought a moment, and then went on: "This murder . . . it must have something to do with the other things that have happened, mustn't it?"

"I think so. I think the dead man must have been part of the setup, whatever it is. Though I can't for the life of me think how he fits in." He picked up his cup, but found the tea too hot for comfort and put it down again with something of a clatter. "The trouble is," he said, "it's given Peter the jitters. He says he didn't do the murder, and I believe him . . . I think. But he doesn't trust himself over anything that happened before he lost his memory. I'm not quite sure why, but he seems more or less to have given up the struggle."

"Oh, dear," said Jenny. "Do you think—?"

"No, I don't. No, really, Jenny love, you know Peter. He's still the same person. And the funny thing is . . . you know how prickly he's been, but tonight he seemed to be slipping back into something like our old association."

"You mean, he remembered?"

"No, I mean . . . I don't quite know what I mean. He was pretty apathetic, you know—well, that wasn't like the old days—but whenever he thought Conway was backing me into a corner he fired up immediately in my defense. In its way, it was amusing." Jenny was looking puzzled, and he was frowning with concentration as he went on; perhaps he was trying to make his explanation convincing to himself, as well as to her. "I've never lost touch with Peter, but I've never been so constantly in his company as when we were very young, before I went away to school. And he was just like that then, he'd fire up in an instant if somebody had me on the defensive. I expect tonight's doings set up some sort of connection in his mind." Another thought seemed to strike him. "Do you think that's a hopeful sign?" he asked.

"I don't know," said Jenny, slowly. But her thoughts were

not on the question. "I can't help being worried, Antony. Uncle Nick says—"

"Yes, I thought we should get to that." The brief spurt of energy left him, his tone was flat and weary. "He'd murder me if he was here, so let's just be thankful he isn't. Though I suppose he'll see the papers," he added, gloomily; and drank some of his tea in a dispirited way.

"He won't see the shocking ones," Jenny said to comfort him.

"No, but—" He grinned up at her, and again—surprisingly —his eyes were bright with amusement. "Have you thought, love? Everyone discounts the embellishments of a story in the popular press, but this particular tale . . . the more soberly it's told, the worse it'll sound. Don't you think?" When she did not reply he added, with a sort of gloomy relish: " 'Acting on information, the police went to a room in a West End hotel, where they found a man remanded earlier in the day on a charge under the Dangerous Drugs Act, a member of the legal profession, and the strangled body of one of the staff.' That sentence seems to have got out of hand somewhere, but you see what I mean? Uncle Nick will have a fit."

"It isn't funny," said Jenny. The reproof in her tone did nothing to hide her anxiety. Antony abandoned his tea without further ado, and got up and went round the table to comfort her.

CHAPTER V

HE WAS ON THE telephone soon after nine o'clock that morning, with his final cup of breakfast coffee on the desk beside
him. He was talking to Roddy Gaskell, the head of the company that owned the passenger liner *Atlantis*. Roddy was a
connection of a sort (he had married Jenny's cousin), and
believed himself to owe Antony some gratitude into the bar-
gain; but the enthusiasm with which he tackled the problem
which was propounded to him owed more to his own character than to either of these things. He never could do anything by halves.

"The cabin steward?" he asked now. "You don't know his
name, of course . . . well, I can find that out all right. I'll
have them send him up to see you . . . would tomorrow do?
I shouldn't think he'd object to a jaunt, and it'll save your
time."

Antony expressed his gratification, but he sounded a trifle
wary. Talking to Roddy was rather like swimming against a
tidal wave, you never quite knew where you were going to be
washed ashore; and this morning he felt positively battered by
the exercise. "I also want to know who Peter Hammond
mixed with on board," he added, pushing out the suggestion
cautiously, as though afraid of being overwhelmed in the ensuing flood of helpfulness.

64

"Ask me something difficult," requested Roddy. "Tell you what, I'll have a word with the captain. He's a discreet sort of chap." The idea of Roddy commending anyone for discretion was almost too much for Antony, who privately considered the other man didn't know the meaning of the word. He choked over a mouthful of coffee. "Did you say something?" Roddy asked. "Oh . . . well . . . I'll find out for you if *any-thing* queer went on during the voyage; and who shared Hammond's table, and played games with him, and all that sort of rot. *Atlantis* will be in for about a fortnight this time, so you can always go down to Southampton later on, if it seems a good idea."

Several minutes later Antony turned from the telephone, to find Jenny's eyes fixed on him with amused sympathy. She was showing no signs at all of their disturbed night; in fact, she was almost disconcertingly wide-eyed and alert. "I wish you were coming with me," he said.

"I thought you'd be in chambers all day," said Jenny, "or I wouldn't have promised to drive Joan to Oxford. And it's too late to back out now."

"Yes, I know. But you won't be late?"

Jenny shook her head. "Do you want me to phone Mr. Mallory before I go, Antony? What shall I tell him?"

"Anything you like. Called out of town on urgent business, I suppose. There's another thing, Jenny . . . when were we going to the farm?"

"On Friday." She did not attempt to elaborate the statement.

"Well, I wonder . . . I mean, I don't suppose . . . oh, damn it all, love, I can't just go away and leave things like this." Jenny laughed, and took pity on him.

"Don't worry . . . I phoned Bill when I got in last night." She flushed faintly as she met his eyes, but her own were steady enough.

"Burning your boats?" he asked gently. "Why do you always let me have my own way?"

65

"*Let* you!" said Jenny. But his guess was only too near the mark. So now she added crossly. "That's one way of putting it." But then, with unexpected honesty: "If it was just something you wanted to do, I might make a fuss. But for something you feel you *ought* to do . . . that's different." She glared at him for a moment, as though daring him to argue, and then got up and began to clear the table with an air of fierce concentration that did not invite any further comment.

: :   : :

As an intensive search of the local telephone directory had failed to yield any information under Nan Robbins's name, Antony had decided that the only thing to do was to go and look for her. At worst, someone at her home or among the neighbors could probably tell him where she was to be found.

Inquiry at the station at Midhurst revealed her address as being some four miles distant; a nearby garage provided him with an elderly car and still more venerable driver, who took him at a sober pace to a cottage on the outskirts of a village, and showed a proper disregard for time by expressing an obviously genuine willingness to wait all day, if need be. Antony, viewing with some anxiety the extremely dangerous and unsuitable corner on which the old man had chosen to stop, advised him to wait in comfort at the pub they had passed a few minutes ago, where he could probably get some lunch. It wasn't until this scheme had been examined carefully from all angles that the driver gave it his blessing, executed a horrifying U-turn and departed. At which moment Antony began to wonder uneasily what sort of a drive back to Midhurst they would eventually have. But it was too late to worry about that now.

The cottage was attractive, with a thatched roof, walls of an ancient and mellow brick, and leaded windows peering shortsightedly through a screen of wisteria. Inevitably, the gate creaked as he pushed it open; the narrow, flagged path

66

passed between flower beds which were alive with color to a green front door.

He had nearly reached the house, and was considering his gambit, when the door opened and a girl backed out dragging a heavy-looking suitcase. She had pulled the door shut before she looked round and saw him, when she let go of the case, straightened her back, and said, "Oh," blankly. Adding, not very encouragingly, "Do you want me?"

"If you're Miss Robbins . . . yes, I do." But remembering the photograph in Peter's wallet he was pretty sure she was.

"I'm Nan Robbins." There was still a question in her tone, and she added with sharp suspicion, "What do you want?" (So she's seen the papers, he thought. But it could only have been the smuggling business, the murder won't have been reported yet.)

"I'd like to talk to you, if I may. It's about Peter Hammond."

Funnily enough, though he had wondered about his reception it hadn't occurred to him that if she knew what had happened she would probably take him for a reporter. He realized his error as soon as he saw her reaction—tightened lips; a quite fiery look; a quick, decisive shake of the head. "I'm a friend of Peter's," he said. "Not from a newspaper, if that's what you're thinking. Did he ever speak of Antony Maitland?"

She did not answer immediately, but her look lost some of its hostility and became merely appraising. After a moment, "Have you seen him?" she asked. "How is he?"

"Fit enough, in one way," said Antony carefully. "I take it you've seen a newspaper?"

"Yes, this morning." All of a sudden she was speaking in a rush, the words tumbling out as if they had been bottled up inside her, just waiting their chance of escape. "I was expecting him on Saturday, you know; he phoned on Friday, from Southampton, just to say he'd arrived, and he'd be in touch next day. I waited and waited, and then I rang up the hotel in the evening. The man who answered didn't seem to know if he was there or not, so I thought perhaps his business had dragged on, and he hadn't had time to call. But on Sunday when I rang they were quite definite, he wasn't in the hotel. So then I thought I'd just have to wait till he phoned me, and try not to worry."

"What did your paper say?"

"That—you must know all this, Mr. Maitland, if you've seen him—that he's accused of bringing drugs into the country." Her voice rose almost to a squeak; conveying, rather touchingly, her sense of outrage at the suggestion. "And it said he'd lost his memory."

"I'm afraid that's true, Miss Robbins."

"So he doesn't remember . . . me?" She gave a sigh as she spoke and Antony, in spite of his sympathy, smiled at her involuntarily. Her chin went up as she met his look, and she added with resolution: "Well, he couldn't, could he? But then, how did you know—?"

"Shenstone told me about you."

"I see. What do the doctors say?"

"They won't commit themselves, but it's usually only a temporary condition." He knew as he spoke that he was being less than honest, and felt humbled by the sudden friendliness of her smile.

"I was just going up to town to see him," she said. "Do you want to talk to me first?"

"It would be best, I think." Probably she sensed his seriousness, for she opened her handbag without another word, and started to scrabble through the contents in search of her latchkey. A moment later she was leading the way into the cottage; Antony picked up the abandoned suitcase and ducked under the lintel.

The room had not yet had time to feel deserted. There were fresh flowers on the chest under the window, and tall delphiniums in an earthenware jug masking the empty grate.

The furniture ought to have been antique, and wasn't; but it had obviously been chosen with care and Antony thought the overall picture—the low, beamed ceiling, dark oak, bright chintz—as attractive and cheerful as the girl herself. And that was, perhaps, an odd choice of words. Nan wasn't looking especially cheerful now.

His first thought when he saw her had been that the black-and-white of the print in Peter's wallet was singularly inappropriate. She was a small, brown girl—brown hair, thick and rather simply dressed with only the hint of a wave; brown eyes, very direct and serious; a clear, brown complexion. For all her present solemnity, a vital and invigorating person. He found himself wondering whether, if she smiled at him now, her eyes would light up as they had done when the photograph was taken. But there wasn't much chance of finding out while he was on his present errand, and had to tell her . . .

He had half expected tears, and afterward he thought perhaps he had only escaped because she was so incredulous. "I don't believe it," she said when he had finished. "It can't be happening to us." He knew how she felt, and accepted the statement without comment; and after a pause she added, with a businesslike air that was obviously quite unreal, "I think I ought to know what you're thinking, Mr. Maitland; you haven't told me that."

"I believe what he's told me," said Antony. "Well, more than that, as a matter of fact; because he hasn't said anything about the smuggling except that he doesn't know if he did it."

"And you're trying to help him?" He nodded. "I can't help feeling," said Nan, with difficulty, "that it's uncommonly good of you."

Antony—who had hoped she would take his own part in the affair for granted—said quickly and unfairly, "I'm acting in conjunction with his solicitor, of course. If you think some other arrangement would get better results—"

"No. No, of course not."

"Well, then," said Antony. And gave her a friendly smile. "Can you help me at all, do you think?"

"I don't see how."

"The two things must be connected in some way. We've got to find out about the smuggling before we can hope to know anything about the murder."

"That's all very well, but how can we?" said Nan, despondently.

"Have you had any letters from Peter recently? Did he say anything that might give us an idea—?"

"If you mean, did he tell me he was planning to bring me some—what was the stuff?—heroin for a wedding present . . . he didn't," said Nan, suddenly flaring up.

"That wasn't quite what I had in mind. He might have said something in one of his letters that seemed unusual. Or when he phoned you on Friday from Southampton."

She took her time to think that over, but said at last, regretfully, "The phone call was just what I told you, and he isn't much of a letter writer. All this year he's been away he's written about plans . . . our plans; and about how Mother was; but he never *told* me anything much."

"Was that true to form?"

"I don't know. We only met six months before he went, but when he was in Birmingham and I was here he used to phone mostly, or send a telegram. We'd have been married—of course—before he went to Ceylon," she added, with an inconsequence that Antony took as proof of a cherished theory—that no woman could ever stick to the point. "But Mother was ill, I didn't feel I could leave her."

"I hope—"

"She's better now. In fact, she's gone to Madeira with Aunt Betty. But," she added, returning disconcertingly to the point from which she had wandered, "all I got from the ports of call was a postcard or two."

"No mention of the people he met?"

"Oh, no. He'd have told me about them when I saw him, I expect. But he wouldn't write."

"Never mind. Do you still want to come up to town, Miss Robbins?"

"Yes, of course. But . . . it's a little daunting, isn't it? I mean, being forgotten." She smiled when she saw his look of dismay, though her eyes were still solemn. "Don't worry, there isn't an answer to that. I don't expect it will do any good, my coming. But I don't see what else I can do."

"I've a car in the village," said Antony, declining to follow this line of speculation. "I sent the driver down to the pub for some lunch."

"Can I come with you, then? I was going to catch the bus, but it will have gone now."

"You'll come with me, of course," said Antony, suddenly decisive. "We'll have lunch in Midhurst—I'm hungry, and you'll be the better for food, even if the thought of it revolts you; then we'll take the next train to town, and I'll take you to see Peter. Right?"

"Right," said Nan. "And to tell you the truth," she added, "I'm quite shockingly hungry." From which simple statement her companion drew a good deal of encouragement.

: :   : :

Antony's more gloomy forebodings had not been realized; the driver had apparently partaken of refreshment sparingly, and the return to Midhurst was accomplished as sedately as the outward drive had been. Nan was a talkative and friendly companion, but once she had finished cross-examining him about the doctor's report—which she did very thoroughly at the first opportunity—she seemed disinclined to speak of Peter. She had spent Christmas, eighteen months ago, with her married sister in Edgbaston, and that was where they had met. After that, Peter had taken to spending rather frequent weekends in Midhurst, and they were engaged by Easter. He was very worried, all the time, about his sister, who died just before he went to Ceylon. The trip had cropped up rather suddenly, she thought. No, she hadn't met Mr. Shenstone. At which point Antony, feeling he had asked enough direct questions, decided it was time to let her have her head, conversationally. Left to herself she talked more freely, and less to the point.

It was past six o'clock when the train got in, and they stopped to leave Nan's suitcase at a hotel in Victoria, which Antony silently condemned as a dump. She was quiet when they were back in the taxi again, on their way to Lyall Square, and he had time to wonder what had been happening in his absence. Shenstone might have thought better of his invitation, or Peter might again have been arrested, this time on an even more serious charge.

The parlormaid reminded him, somehow, of the girl who had conducted him down the long corridor at Kinlocks: a pretty girl with a good figure, severely neat in her uniform. But the likeness—if there was one—lay in her manner; there was the same air of decorum, the same effect of conferring a favor . . . and wondering all the time if the recipient was really worthy. It was almost surprising that she did not deny her employer, or at least shut the door in their faces while she went to inquire.

Following her across the hall and up the wide staircase, Antony became conscious that the sports jacket he had put on that morning was no longer appropriate to the occasion. For that matter, neither was Nan's rather faded summer frock, with a camel coat flung on casually over it. The house was a show place, beautifully appointed. Enough to get on a man's nerves, he thought, treading gingerly past a niche on the half-landing where a hideous vase was displayed with a care that could only mean it was valuable. So far as he could tell, Nan was unaffected by the atmosphere; but she was, of course, ahead of him on the stairs, and he couldn't see her face.

The drawing room had the same air of spaciousness he had noted in Shenstone's office, being big enough to carry a great deal of ornament without feeling cluttered. It was a long room with a highly polished parquet floor and a liberal sprinkling of oriental rugs. There didn't look to be a single comfortable chair in it.

For a moment as the door opened Antony had a view over Nan's head and past the maid's shoulder of the two men, before they had time to come to their feet. Bernard Shenstone was leaning back in a chair which must be sturdy for all its grace, but still looked too small for him. Peter, on the other hand, was making no more than a fair attempt to seem at his ease, and the constraint between the two men was almost tangible.

But the glimpse was momentary only, the tableau dissolved into action and Shenstone was crossing the room toward them. As he spoke an introduction, Antony had time to admire the big man's ease of manner, his apparent lack of embarrassment.

Peter had made no attempt to join them; Antony even had the impression that he was incapable of movement. "You found her?" he asked, and his air of unconcern was almost painfully overdone. But then he looked back at the girl again, and his expression was both eager and doubtful. Nan went across to him, and gave him both her hands. She said, "Peter," but she spoke quietly, undemandingly; and when he looked down at her with a question in his eyes she added with much more force, "Don't worry, darling. Don't worry about anything." She turned her head then, and smiled at Bernard Shenstone. "You're being very kind," she said, "I don't know what we'd have done."

For the first time in their brief acquaintance, Antony thought his host seemed abashed by this remark. They exchanged glances, each aware of a certain, wry amusement in the situation. And then Shenstone said, as suavely as ever,

73

"My dear Miss Robbins, it can only be a pleasure to serve you," and Antony was conscious again of the irritation he had felt at their previous meeting.

But he had to give Shenstone credit for his handling of a difficult situation, offering hospitality from a quite fantasically well-stocked cabinet of Chinese lacquer, and making a small ceremony of getting them comfortably seated. Or as comfortably, thought Antony irritably, as one could be in that damned, impersonal room. There was nothing cozy about it, nothing that invited relaxation; rather he was conscious of a stern expectation that he should be on his best behavior. Looking at Nan—a faded copy, only, of the lively girl he had met earlier in the day—Antony became aware of an almost intolerable sympathy. To give her a chance to talk to Peter he turned to Shenstone with the first question that came into his head. (But what was there to be said between those two, after all?)

"You've heard," he asked, "what happened last night?" He realized, as he spoke, that the other man's control, both of himself and the situation, was even more admirable than he had supposed. Under the bland exterior Shenstone was seething with anger; but the revelation was momentary only, his voice betrayed no resentment.

"If you mean that murder has been added to our other problems . . . yes, Peter told me," he said.

Antony mastered an insane desire to apologize. "At least," he remarked, "you didn't reconsider your invitation."

Shenstone smiled, but his eyes were still cold and unfriendly. "I think, Mr. Maitland, you have forgotten my reasons for extending it. They still remain valid, you know . . . perhaps they have even a greater validity. But I don't pretend to like the situation."

"I don't suppose you do."

"But that doesn't worry you? How right you are to concern yourself only with essentials." He picked up his glass, and seemed to be studying it for a moment; then he looked up again and his eyes met Antony's challengingly. "Is your own opinion unchanged?" he demanded.

"Quite unchanged," said Antony. And found himself adding, "I see no reason to amend it," as though the statement needed some qualification.

"Of course not," said Shenstone, obscurely. He drank, and put the tumbler down again, and added smoothly: "I have been much occupied today with the police."

"It could hardly have been otherwise."

"No? I'm afraid I have very little experience—" And again the smooth tone flicked Antony, illogically, to anger.

"You will welcome the chance, no doubt, of enlarging your outlook," he said. And did not know that his manner wickedly parodied Shenstone's blandness. Then, with an abrupt change of tone, he added, "They wanted the background, I suppose. But did they tell you anything?"

"They did not. And, as you say, they wanted all the details," said Shenstone heavily, "that Peter professes himself unable to supply." He was watching Antony as he spoke, and smiled benignly when he saw his lips tighten. "Exactly!" he said, as though his companion had spoken. "But you must allow me the freedom of my own ideas, Mr. Maitland."

The trouble was, of course, his attitude was all too reasonable. Antony let a silence lengthen between them, and heard for the first time the murmur of Nan's voice from the other side of the room, and wondered what sort of an understanding she had established with Peter. Because he didn't want to listen he began to look more closely at the grotesque carving which shared the table at his elbow with a bowl of colored glass it would have seemed sacrilege to use as an ashtray. "You have some very beautiful things," he remarked insincerely; thinking as he spoke how twisted and ugly the figure was, though its smoothness might well be pleasant to the touch.

Shenstone's reply was equally convenional, and equally ignored the tension that was building up between them. "That is . . . Lamashtu," he said, "she's quite one of my favorites." The bland voice took on an almost lyrical quality. "Lamashtu, the she-devil, known for her anger, her fierceness. She has the head of a lion, as you see, and is reputed to howl like a bitch."

"Good lord," said Antony, startled.

"She has, besides, other less pleasant attributes. In particular, she delights in causing miscarriages, both human and animal."

"A jolly sort of companion for the long winter evenings," said Antony, idiotically.

"You don't admire her? But look at the delicacy of the work, Mr. Maitland. Jade is a particular passion of mine."

"Jade?"

"White jade . . nephrite. You will find several more modern pieces in jadeite, from the Chi'en-lung period, in the cabinet behind you. But the earlier work . . . look at Shoulao in the window there, no more than three inches high, but most exquisitely carved." His eyes came back to Antony's face again. "He may comfort you if you find Lamashtu's habits distressing. A more amiable character, the god of longevity. But I'm boring you, Mr. Maitland."

"Not at all. I'm not very knowledgeable, I'm afraid. And I really ought to be going." He picked up his glass to finish his sherry.

"I was hoping you'd dine with us."

"I'm sorry—"

"Well, Miss Robbins will stay." He raised his voice a little, and Nan turned her head when she heard her name. "I was saying, my dear, I hoped you'd stay—"

The girl's eyes had a blank look; Antony thought uneasily that she looked as though she couldn't take much more. Peter's expression was wooden, and gave no clue to his feelings. And before Shenstone could complete his invitation the door opened and the parlormaid said clearly, "Miss Burdon, sir," and a dream—or perhaps a vision?—walked past her into the room.

76

That, at least, was what Antony later told Jenny. Just then the effect was quite stunning enough to preclude the possibility of any very rational thought. There was a noticeable pause while the three men stared at her, before any of them was collected enough to get to his feet.

She was tall—not too tall—and slender, with smooth ash-blond hair piled high on her head. Her gray linen dress was uncreased, and beautifully cut. She looked cool, and elegant . . . too well-groomed, perhaps? A trifle cold? But for all her perfection of feature—which was undeniable—her eyes had a sparkle that gave the lie to any suspicion of frigidity. She paused in the doorway for just long enough to register a kind of faint surprise at finding so many people in the room; then, ignoring the others for the moment, she swept across to Peter's side and placed a hand on his arm. "My poor darling," she said. "How dreadful for you."

Peter said, "Forgive me, I don't—" and broke off and looked round him in a hunted way. Nan was staring at the newcomer as though she were indeed a vision; and Shenstone was angry again, so angry that he made no attempt to hide the emotion. Antony abandoned with regret his impulse to retire into the background.

"The circumstances are a little unusual, Miss—Miss Burdon?"

She moved a little so that she could face him, but her hand remained resting lightly on Peter's arm. "I know something of the circumstances," she said. "I've read the papers, so I know Mr. Hammond can't remember me. Which is rather a blow." She paused, and favored Peter with an intimate, dazzling smile, and then turned back to his friend again. "Please forgive me," she said. "Are you Peter's brother-in-law?"

"This is Mr. Shenstone." Antony looked inquiringly at his host, who showed, however, no disposition to take control of the situation. "And Miss Robbins," he said, "My name's Maitland."

She was smiling again, completely at her ease. "I'm Elaine

Burdon," she said, and patted Peter's arm. "We met on the boat," she added. "And I'm very sorry, Mr. Shenstone, but when I got back to town today and read the papers I just had to see him."

Bernard Shenstone seemed to have recovered his self-possession, and with it his customary blandness. "It is indeed a pleasure—" he began; but Nan interrupted him, saying bluntly:

"How did you know where to find him?"

"I knew he was staying at the Chiltern. They gave me this address."

"But I telephoned," cried Nan, "I telephoned twice, and they pretended they didn't know." Elaine allowed her the briefest of glances.

"Did they?" she said, with no trace of interest in her voice. And added, with the sort of insolence a woman uses only against another of her sex, "I just told them how much it meant to me to know."

"Oh!" said Nan.

"Perhaps we should explain," said Shenstone, "that Miss Robbins is engaged to be married to Mr. Hammond."

Elaine's eyes turned to Peter. "That's really too bad of you, darling," she said, gently reproachful. And then, to Nan: "I'm really very sorry. Do you mean he didn't write to you?"

Antony heard Shenstone mutter, "I expect he forgot." Nan tilted her chin, and said aggressively, "What about?"

"Why . . . about us," said Elaine, as though that explained everything. She looked at Shenstone, and then at Antony, and added earnestly: "It wasn't just a shipboard romance, you know . . . not at all like that . . . we were quite, quite serious."

Nan stood very still for a moment, looking at Peter, then she turned and held out her hand to her host. "It was kind of you to ask me to stay for dinner, Mr. Shenstone. I'm afraid this evening—" As she went toward the door, Antony had the impression it needed a definite effort not to run out of the room, to maintain a dignified pace. He made his own farewells rather quickly, and caught up with her on the stairs. The parlormaid was in the hall below, waiting to open the heavy front door.

Outside he took her by the elbow, and began to walk down the street. "If you explode here," he told her, "I'll . . . I'll wash my hands of the whole affair."

"That . . . that . . . *creature*," said Nan. She was almost running now to keep pace with his longer stride, but she managed to look up at him and added stormily, "Of course, if you think it's funny—"

"I don't," he assured her, grimly. "But she routed us properly, didn't she? And we've left her in possession of the field." They reached the corner, and he steered her round it, without any immediate thought for direction. He slackened his pace then, and released her arm. "What are you going to do?" he asked. Nan came to a sudden halt, and turned to face him.

"If you mean about . . . her," she said, "I just don't believe it." She scowled up at him. "I know exactly what you'll say," she added. "I hardly know Peter . . . I must have been mistaken in him . . . people change their minds, and it's better to know before you get married—"

"I shouldn't say anything of the sort," Antony pointed out. "I've known him forever."

She pounced on that statement, unconsciously underlining her own uncertainty. "Then you don't think—?"

"I don't think he's the sort of chap to change his mind on the eve of his wedding," he said. "And that makes me wonder—" But even as he spoke he was aware that the doubts were crowding back. "Look here, when were you going to be married?" he asked.

"Next Saturday." Her look dared him to sympathize. He made no immediate comment, but began to walk down the street again, and after a while said in a matter-of-fact way:

"So you're going to stay and see it through. Do you really want to go back to that frightful hotel?"

79

"I must," said Nan. Her voice was carefully expressionless. "It isn't expensive," she explained. "But anyway, I'll have to find a job."

"Not just now," he protested.

"Yes, you see . . . I haven't much money left. When Aunt Betty said she'd take Mother to Madeira it seemed like a godsend; I mean, it will be good for her, of course, but it meant we could have a quiet wedding . . . no fuss, and not much expense. Mother only just has enough to manage, so when I knew Peter was coming home I had quite an orgy of spending—that's really why I didn't meet him—and I've only about three pounds left. That would have been enough for groceries till the weekend, but now I owe you already for my train fare—" She stopped, and then said, "It's none of your business," crossly. "I don't know why you made me tell you." Antony took her arm again.

"What we want," he told her, "is to find Jenny. I expect she'll be home by now."

"Who—?"

"My wife. I dare say she'll know what to do. And I tell you quite frankly, Nan Robbins," he added, looking about him for a taxi, "I'm flummoxed!"

CHAPTER VI

IN THE HOPE of appeasing old Mr. Mallory by the appearance, at least, of diligence, Antony had arranged to see the steward from the *Atlantis* in chambers next day. He was to regret this move later, when the clerk came in with a calculating look in his eye, and an innocent query as to whom it would be proper for him to consult on the subject of fees. But for the time being he was glad of his choice, comforted by the feeling of normality the familiar surroundings gave him. The events of the last few days, reviewed over the breakfast table, had an air of unreality that he found almost terrifying.

Jenny had been home when he arrived there with Nan the evening before, and had accepted tranquilly their rather disjointed chorus of explanation. "If the hotel's uncomfortable, you must find somewhere better. As for a job, it shouldn't be difficult to get a temporary one, at this time of year." She paused, and seemed for the first time to be wondering if this optimism was altogether justified. "At least . . . what can you do?"

"I can type," said Nan. She sounded depressed and uncertain, and the vitality which Antony had thought characteristic seemed to have left her. "I did learn shorthand, but I haven't used it for years."

"Then that's settled, half the typists in London must be on

holiday just now." It wasn't like Jenny to sound so positive; perhaps she meant it as an antidote to Nan's depression. "But first—don't you think?—we'd better fetch your luggage."

"Everything's packed," said Nan. "Everything that's fit to wear. I know I look a mess," she added.

"As a matter of fact, you don't. But it isn't how you look," said Jenny oracularly, "it's how you feel. So I think I'd better drive you down to fetch your things tomorrow."

She had gone off to pick Nan up at the hotel at quite an early hour that morning, with a blithe confidence that Antony would have found somebody, before nightfall, who needed an addition to his staff for the holiday period. As a matter of fact, it hadn't been difficult, so now he was able to give his attention to the steward with that, at least, off his mind.

The man's name was Alfred Loring, and he brought to the Inner Temple an odd blend of hilarity and subservience; together with a bulky envelope from the captain of the *Atlantis*, which presumably had been sent at Roddy Gaskell's instigation. Antony put this on one side for later consideration, provided a carefully-rehearsed minimum of explanation, and embarked cautiously on his questions.

"You were looking after Mr. Hammond on the recent voyage, I take it?"

"In a manner of *speaking*, sir; I'm one of the deck stewards."

Now what the hell was Roddy thinking of, to disregard his request like that? But obviously the cautious approach had been unnecessary, almost ludicrously so. Loring leaned back, and prepared to enjoy himself. "Not to worry, sir; the old man—the captain, that is—told me all *about* what you was wanting. And the *first* thing he told me to tell you was the names of the people who sat at table with Mr. Hammond; and *when* he told me who they was, that's funny,' I said, 'they're the very ones he saw most of, right through the voyage.'"

"Is that so surprising?"

"Well, sir . . . yes, and no. They mixed with the other passengers, of course. But still, they did seem to—to sort of drift back together again." He saw Antony put out a hand to take up the envelope, and added quickly: "That's right, sir, you'll find all about them in there. There was Miss Burdon, and Mr. Miller, and Mr. and Mrs. Brayshaw, and Miss Winthrop. A regular old acid-drop, she was," he added reflectively.

It was obviously no use to try to maintain an attitude of professional reserve. Antony smiled at him encouragingly. "So those five people could tell me, you think, how Mr. Hammond seemed—perhaps what plans he had made—before he lost his memory?"

"Better than anyone else, sir. Why, they was thick as thieves, the lot of them; and Miss Winthrop, which wasn't altogether to be expected, her being a different style, as you might say, from the other ladies. Miss Burdon . . . well, I'd say there wasn't a man on the boat as didn't make a pass at her, one time or another," said the steward happily. (Perhaps, after all, it had been the captain's decision to send him, and for reasons that were becoming obvious; whatever his other qualities, he was neither self-conscious nor tongue-tied.) "A regular smasher," Loring went on, "and Mrs. Brayshaw, she was a looker too, but not so much class. Like to have clawed her eyes out, once or twice, when she found her husband with Miss B. on the boat deck. But there, that kind of thing happens on shipboard, as you know, sir."

"Yes, indeed," said Antony, vaguely; though he was not unappreciative of the implications of this remark. "Was Mr. Hammond especially friendly with Miss Burdon?" he added. "You see, it might help him to remember—"

"Now that's a funny thing, sir, I wouldn't have said so. Not especially." Antony was getting used, now, to the queer trick of emphasis. "I'd have said she preferred Mr. Miller. But Adams (he's the cabin steward, sir), he thought different.

Well, sir, we're not *paid* to gossip, but from what he says there was goings on, and . . . and so forth." The sentence trailed off, so that Antony was left wondering whether Loring had been overcome by an unexpected delicacy, or whether—as seemed more likely—the cabin steward, having made so much of his disclosure, had belatedly considered the virtue of discretion.

Whichever it was, Loring seemed to have no more to tell him, though he talked on happily enough until Antony began to have a desperate feeling that he might become a permanent fixture. There wasn't even much more detail to be had about the five people who had been Peter's most constant companions. A dull lot, reflected Antony angrily, when at length he was alone again; a line not worth pursuing . . . if it wasn't the only hope he had! And he'd have to see the cabin steward, sooner or later. Damn Roddy's incompetence.

When Mr. Mallory made his stately entrance a few minutes later, the contents of the envelope were strewn untidily across the desk; but apparently Maitland had already digested them. He was drawing with vicious strokes across the corner of a sheet of double demy, and seemed completely absorbed in what he was doing; but after a moment he looked up and smiled at the clerk, who was standing perfectly still but contriving somehow to register extreme anguish of mind.

"I'm sorry," he said, and pushed the stiff sheets across the desk. "Part of that bundle of deeds from Bellerby," he added. "You'd better ask Willett to erase the sketch . . . it might shock him." Mr. Mallory picked up the document and averted his eyes after one quick look. "Irrelevant . . . precisely," said Antony, with sympathy. And set himself to listen, with unaccustomed patience, to the clerk's cautiously-worded condemnation of time-wasting practices. But the old man was no more than getting into his stride when the phone on the desk rang.

"Sergeant Watkins, Mr. Maitland," it announced apologetically.

"Well, put him through, then."

"No, sir, he's here. Could you find time—?"

"Yes, of course." This rather incoherent approach, he realized, was not for his benefit at all, but because Hill was well aware that Mr. Mallory would not relish the interruption. He looked up at him now with a grin, and said sepulchrally, "The police are here!"

The old man, of course, was not to be drawn. He compressed his lips slightly, and withdrew without any more overt comment, meeting the detective in the doorway and acknowledging his existence with a slight bow . . . royalty being gracious to a not-undeserving commoner. Watkins looked around him appreciatively as he crossed the room, and when he came to the desk he stood looking down at Antony and ignored his conventional greeting. "Turning the tables, Mr. Maitland?" he asked.

Antony had indeed been conscious of satisfaction that he was meeting the policeman on his own ground, instead of being taken at a disadvantage as he had been at Peter's hotel; and he did not think it necessary to mention that he was using his uncle's room. He grinned his appreciation of the aptness of the comment, pushed a box of cigarettes across the desk, and leaned back in his chair. "Sit down, Sergeant. What can I do for you?"

The brown eyes met his guilelessly. "A few questions, Mr. Maitland."

"I'm working on the Hammond brief, even if he isn't precisely my client," said Antony.

Watkins heaved a sigh. "You talked to Inspector Conway the other night," he pointed out. And noted shrewdly the slight frown with which his companion greeted the reminder.

"Had I a choice?" said Antony, abruptly. "But you're concerned only with the Dangerous Drugs charge . . . about which I can tell you nothing, of my own knowledge."

"You could tell me again how Mr. Hammond came to consult you," said Watkins, humbly.

"I could, of course." But he did not offer to amplify the statement. Watkins sighed again, and said with an air of candor:

"Well, you see, Mr. Maitland, it's like this." But he didn't proceed to an explanation. Instead he paused, drew meditatively on his cigarette, exhaled slowly and added, without any change of tone, "Do you believe he's lost his memory?"

"I do."

"Oh . . . well . . . it makes no difference really. The heroin came into the country in Mr. Hammond's luggage . . . you'll admit that, I dare say."

Antony shook his head. "Tell me something, Sergeant. This isn't an isolated case, is it? You'd hardly have reacted so violently to your 'information received' if it was the first hint of smuggling that had come your way."

"The traffic has been going on for some time, and I don't need to tell you it's a serious business. Lately we've redoubled our precautions, but still the stuff has been coming in." The answer came without hesitation, and Antony realized, to his discomfort, that the purpose of this visit might well be to impart information, rather than to receive it. The question was, what was the detective's angle?

"How do you know?" he asked, cautiously.

"Unfortunately, it's only too obvious; if people are getting hold of drugs . . . I don't really need to explain that to you, Mr. Maitland. Besides, it's not only being brought in for home consumption: there's an outward movement too, or so they believe in the States."

"That's queer. Why not direct?" This time he spoke without thinking, caught by the interest of the problem and forgetting his brief uneasiness.

"If I knew the answer to that," said Watkins, "I'd be a wiser man . . . and a happier one. But the direct route is more obvious, there may have been advantages in the element of surprise."

86

"Does it mean that the traffic is being organized in this country?"

"I think it does."

"And do you suspect Wilson of being part of the setup?"

"The thought had occurred to me."

"Well, at least, you can hardly imagine that Peter Hammond is deeply involved. He isn't a regular traveler these days—"

"As to that, Mr. Maitland, I'm keeping an open mind."

"As witnessed," said Antony, dryly, "by his arrest."

"You're not saying we acted without evidence?" The sergeant's tone was gently mocking. "But I'm open to conviction, Mr. Maitland . . . and I have an open mind about the —the ultimate responsibility. Which is what I'm chiefly concerned with." The mild brown eyes were intent now, and Antony was reminded of the assessment he had made of his visitor's character. Well-disposed . . . perhaps; but quite surely a potential danger.

"It's odd," he said, ignoring the note of inquiry in Watkins's voice. "Don't you think it's odd that you were tipped off twice? First about the heroin, and then about the murder."

"Not particularly. It's surprising the things that come our way, as you probably very well know."

"Well, who—?"

"We don't get a name tag with every tip we get. And I don't imagine you're so guileless as to believe that a man is innocent because he's informed against."

"The motive," said Antony, "was obviously to involve him."

"But perhaps not unjustly. Do you think?" The sergeant's inquiring look ought to have amused him, but Antony was conscious only of irritation. He got to his feet restlessly and moved across to stand with his back to the empty grate.

"What do you want?" he said.

"I told you: to find the man who's behind . . . all this."

"Not Peter?"

"If you really want my opinion, I think he killed that chap, Wilson, or that he knows who did. But that isn't my concern. I want the man behind this smuggling racket, the one who's responsible for the whole thing; and what I think is that your friend could lead us to him."

"I see." His tone was even enough, but he didn't like the way the conversation was heading. "If he recovers his memory," he insisted, automatically. "Meanwhile, I'm trying to find out—"

"What, Mr. Maitland?" The detective spoke quietly now, as though he were afraid to disturb some train of thought. Antony, whose sentence had trailed into silence as an idea struck him, came to himself with a start.

"If the heroin was in his luggage, someone put it there . . . most likely someone on the ship," he said. For the first time, Watkins showed some signs of annoyance.

"I hoped you'd be frank with me, but I really don't need instruction in the obvious." He showed no signs of being appeased when Antony laughed, for the first time that day with genuine amusement.

"I'm sorry," he said. "Really . . . I'm sorry! But I've a simple mind, and when I think aloud—"

"I'd say, Mr. Maitland, you're about as 'simple' as a corkscrew," said Watkins grumpily.

"All right then, suppose you tell me—" Antony suggested. The detective eyed him warily.

"What, for instance?"

"Well, to begin with, what time did Peter Hammond arrive at the Chiltern on Friday evening?"

"He went there straight from the boat train, and arrived about eight o'clock. Came down to dinner almost immediately. If he had any visitors in his room, nobody knows about them," said Watkins glibly.

"Thank you, Sergeant. And how long has this drug traffic been going on?"

"We've known of it for over four years." He paused to produce a squashed-looking packet of cigarettes, and to pat his pockets until he located a matchbox. When he went on his voice was mild again, and friendly. "It's a sore subject, as you might say."

"So I imagine."

"It wasn't too bad to deal with at first," said Watkins. "I'll say they were ingenious, but—well, we have a trick or two ourselves. Inspector Shelley now—I could see you didn't take to him the other day—but he's as bright as they come. I don't mind telling you, we thought we'd got it beaten. Two years ago, that was. Not a sign of the stuff for six whole months, but then we found it was still getting through. That was a blow, I can tell you, we'd put up a screen you wouldn't have thought a fly could pass."

"And so?"

"The screen's still there." Watkins sounded aggrieved. "And the chaps at Customs are on their toes, but we don't get much joy out of it. Now it seems the casual traveler is being used, the people we don't have to worry about as a rule for anything more than a pair of stockings or a bottle of perfume; and, you see, it has been pretty soft for them, because the more time is spent on *likely* suspects, the less there is for the unlikely ones. And have you any idea what that'll stir up when we start acting on it . . . when everyone's luggage has to be checked as thoroughly as we're already checking the regulars."

"It won't be exactly a popular move," Antony agreed. "But these occasional travelers—Peter Hammond, and the others you seem to be postulating—there's obviously some contact on the ship, but do you think they know—?"

"You're suggesting Mr. Hammond was made use of without his consent. I might be more ready to believe that," said Watkins, "if Wilson were still alive."

"But you're checking up—"

"Of course we are. But the real difficulty—if what you're

suggesting is true—is, how would the distributors get the dope back from the 'innocent' conveyors?"

"I can think of ways," said Antony.

"Ah, but can you prove anything?" Antony shrugged, and did not reply. After a pause, Watkins went on, "Not that we reckon much to this idea of yours, that the stuff was planted on Hammond. There's not a scrap of evidence from the ship, and the people with most opportunity—because they were most friendly with him—sound a pretty respectable bunch to me. But you've met one of them already—what did you think of Miss Elaine Burdon, I wonder?"

"The circumstances of our meeting," said Antony, carefully, hoping he did not look as startled as he felt, "did not really allow me to form an opinion." It was Watkins's turn to laugh now, which he did so heartily and incautiously that he spluttered over his cigarette, and ended up coughing and wiping the tears from his eyes.

"Perhaps *she's* the reason your friend, Mr. Hammond, found it convenient to lose his memory," he suggested, when he could speak again. And Antony—who did not like the suggestion at all—grinned at him and shook his head.

"I'm more interested in Wilson," he said, after a pause. "But, of course, you're not concerned with that."

"No," said the sergeant, doubtfully. "Only insofar as the murder touches our affairs. But I've learned quite a lot about him . . . eh?"

"Tell me," Antony invited. He thought afterward it was strange he should take it for granted that Watkins would comply with this request, but at the time it simply didn't occur to him.

"He was a married man, couple of youngsters, lived in Fulham. Employed at the Chiltern Hotel for the past ten years or so—you heard that bit on Monday night, I think. He was looking after the third floor when he was killed, because one of the regular chaps was ill."

90

"The valet who should have been looking after Peter's room?"

"No . . . actually, one of the men on the top floor. Wilson sent the third-floor valet up as a replacement—he says he thought it was just because the top floor would be busy, and Wilson wanted the easier job. Convey anything to you, Mr. Maitland?"

"Not a thing, Sergeant." (But it was suggestive, wasn't it?) "Where was Wilson when Peter arrived at the hotel?" he asked, with a vague air that did not quite disguise his interest.

"Now that's a funny thing," said Watkins, nodding his head as though in approval of this line of questioning. "On Friday and Saturday he was off duty. His wife says he was ill, but I think it was a hangover."

"Bad enough to keep him from work two days?"

"I wouldn't be surprised. He might have renewed his binge on Friday night. Mrs. Wilson says she phoned the hotel for him on Friday, but he must have been feeling pretty bad on Saturday morning, because there was a man phoned, asking for him, and all he would do was pull the bedclothes over his head and groan."

"About Wilson himself, then. What was he like?"

"Harmless little man, at least that's what everyone agrees to; and apart from the occasional overindulgence, a good husband, a bit too careful with his cash, but not really mean. It paid off, anyway, he'd upwards of six thousand pounds in one of The Trustee Savings Banks."

"Well, now!"

"Not bad," said Watkins, judiciously. "His wife says, 'he was the saving sort,' and 'the tips were good,' but somehow I don't think—"

"Neither do I, Sergeant. Neither do I."

"Going back to the night in question, the chambermaid saw him on and off up to half-past nine, when she had to go to help an old lady get ready for the night. She had quite another reason for the fact he'd sent the regular valet off the floor . . . said he was 'a good friend' of hers. She kept a pretty good tag on what he was doing, which was nothing out of the ordinary. He wasn't around when she got back from her old lady, but it was some time before she thought anything of that. She didn't know he'd gone to Mr. Hammond's room, and she hadn't seen anyone else going there, but she seems to have been out of the way during the crucial time."

"No suspicious characters hanging about . . . no, I didn't think so," said Antony despondently.

"He had one friend he met sometimes after work, whose name his wife doesn't know, and whose description she can't identify," said Watkins. "You wouldn't know anything about that, would you, Mr. Maitland?"

The query came casually, but it demanded a reply. "How should I?" said Antony. But he was frowning again as he spoke.

"Name of Dooley," said the sergeant. "That meant something to Records, if it didn't to us. Ex-con man—small-time stuff—going straight for two, three years now. So far as anyone knows."

"And how did you happen to hear of him, Sergeant? The chambermaid again?"

"That's right. Helpful's the word, but all we got from her was a description. However, it just happened," said Watkins blandly, "that one of our chaps saw him hanging round the hotel during the weekend; and when we showed her a picture she identified it all right." He got up as he spoke, and looked across at his companion, his brown eyes amused and friendly. "I think that's about all I can tell you, Mr. Maitland."

"Am I supposed to thank you for the information? I can't help feeling there's a catch in it somewhere."

"Shall we say I was hoping the force of my example would encourage you to be equally frank?"

"You can say so, if you like," said Antony bluntly. "I shan't believe you."

"There is still the question I asked when I came in," Watkins reminded him.

"The question—? Oh, *why* Peter came to me? But you know that already."

"I know what you told us."

"It happens to be the truth."

"Well . . . perhaps. But even if we allow that Mr. Hammond is suffering from amnesia, the question remains—why was your name written in his diary?"

"I c-could give you a suggestion about it, but it'd be g-guesswork, and on the whole I think I'll keep it to myself," said Antony. He was holding on to his temper with difficulty, but there was still a question he wanted to ask. "I don't quite understand, at one point I thought you really wanted my help. But now you seem to be accusing me of s-something."

"I'm making no accusation, Mr. Maitland. I just thought it was time someone pointed out a few home truths." The very placidity of his tone was an added irritant.

"F-for instance—?"

"For instance, that if Inspector Conway—say—asks you some questions that seem to go beyond the night of the murder, you might be well advised to answer them. You might even say," Watkins went on soberly, "that he'd have good reason."

"C-Conway!" said Antony, bitterly. "I s-still d-don't see—" But it should have occurred to him—of course, he should have thought of it—that to an outsider there was one obvious and simple explanation for the beeline Peter Hammond had made for Kempenfeldt Square.

"Take my word for it," Watkins assured him. "And there's another thing—"

"Well?" But even as he snapped the query he realized, dimly, that Watkins's attitude—amused, gently malicious— was not altogether hostile. "Did Conway send you here?" he asked, abruptly.

"He did not. I don't think," said the sergeant, gently regretful, "he altogether approves my methods. I believe," he went on, with a bland disregard for the truth, "in a straight-forward approach. Now, I don't say Conway's wrong in his suspicions, mind you, I don't say that at all. But I felt suffi-cient doubt in my own mind to feel you should be warned."

"Warned? Of what? Of what Conway thinks?"

"No, Mr. Maitland, that was by the way, and perhaps I shouldn't have told you. But if he's wrong, if you're just mixed up in the affair by chance, I'd keep out of it now, if I were you."

Antony was again conscious of a strong feeling of unreality. This couldn't be happening . . . that he should be sitting here in chambers, while a stolid-seeming member of the police force solemnly offered him these quite outrageous sug-gestions. With an effort, he wrenched the conversation back somewhere within the limits of sanity.

"Peter Hammond's solicitors are briefing my uncle," he said. "In his absence I'm bound to put in a little work on the Dangerous Drugs charge."

The brown eyes twinkled. "A survey of the documents in the case needn't necessarily take you outside chambers, Mr. Maitland. Is that all you have in mind?"

"Well . . . no." He hesitated, and Watkins took up the explanation in a serious tone.

"You're going to tell me that friendship has its obligations," he said. "But it can be dangerous work . . . asking ques-tions. You've seen already these people don't pull their punches."

Antony laughed. For the moment his anger seemed to have left him, and he sounded genuinely amused. "You've got me really confused now," he complained. "The alternatives of deep-dyed villainy and lamblike and helpless innocence are rather too violently opposed."

Watkins heaved another of his large sighs. "You're going to tell me you can look after yourself," he said sadly. "Well,

94

maybe that's so, but don't say I didn't warn you." He began to look about him. "I had a hat," he said.

Antony came forward, and walked with him toward the door. "Disingenuous," he remarked. The sergeant turned on him an innocently questioning look. "You've given me a very good reason for continuing to ask questions," he pointed out.

"To vindicate your honor?" The tone, despite its apparent solemnity, betrayed the detective's amusement.

"How well you understand me," said Antony, blandly. "Don't tell me it hadn't occurred to you." But when the door had closed behind his visitor he stood very still for a moment looking at it blankly. And his thoughts did not give him any pleasure at all.

CHAPTER VII

AFTER A WHILE he shook himself out of his abstraction, and went back to the desk. He had already decided on his course of action, and took up the telephone without delay. He couldn't get hold of Roddy Gaskell, but a few moments later he was talking to Geoffrey Horton.

"I've got a statement you'd better have, from the captain of the *Atlantis*," he told him, without preamble. "I'll just note down the addresses I want, and bring it round after lunch." The solicitor's voice crackled urgently in his ear, and he went on impatiently: "Yes, of course I mean to see them. I've a good excuse, haven't I? To help Peter to remember . . . just that, and nothing more."

"A likely story," said Geoffrey sourly.

"Well, anyway, I've got to see you. I don't quite like the way things are going."

"If you mean you're seeing reason at last about Hammond's involvement, I can only say, I'm all for it."

"I don't mean anything of the kind. I—no, I can't tell you now. I'll see you this afternoon. And, Geoffrey—"

"Well?"

"Can you ask Cobbolds' if they can trace a chap called Dooley. Rush job. He was a small-time thief, who later evolved a rather unconvincing line in confidence tricks. I

defended him once, way back, not long after I was called."
A nice little coincidence, he thought, as he cradled the telephone; and should I have confided in the good sergeant . . . or not? He picked up the receiver again, and presently heard Dr. Macintyre's laconic tones.

"Now what do you want?" But he didn't wait for a reply. "I've nothing to add to what I told you, nothing at all."

"Hammond told me he'd been to see you yesterday," said Antony. "I hoped—"

"There's no change in his condition—at least, as he reports it to me."

"No, Doctor. Then you still can give no more than an opinion—"

"If you mean, can I swear to the truth of his story, I've told you, no one could." He paused, and then asked with a slight sharpening of tone, "Where's your uncle?"

"In Lausanne by now. Unless he stayed in Paris for a day or two."

"Does he know what's going on?" asked Macintyre, suspiciously.

He'll have seen the papers by now, Antony thought; his answer was perhaps less than candid. "He agreed to take the brief."

"Did he, though? And what if Hammond's charged with murder? Tell me that."

"A brief is a brief is a brief," said Antony, suddenly abandoning his cautious approach. Surprisingly, the doctor chuckled.

"That's true," he acknowledged. "But do you really think amnesia makes a good defense?"

"Of course not. But unless he recovers his memory before the trial, we've got to explain his silence somehow. The trouble is—"

"Well?"

"It's like this—" He described, as briefly as he could, the situation which had arisen following Elaine's arrival on the scene. "Don't you think that might tend to weaken the effect of your evidence?" he asked.

There was a pause. "No," said the doctor, at last.

"The police think it accounts for Hammond's story. Heads they win, tails we lose," he added, in gloomy parenthesis.

"I don't understand you."

"Well, he's in an awkward situation, which they think a fair enough reason for pretending to have lost his memory . . . in addition, of course, to the fact that it saves him having to explain himself about the heroin. But my trouble is that it might equally be held to explain genuine amnesia . . . that 'retreat from reality' you talked about."

"A man who got himself into a dilemma like that would have enough gumption to talk his way out of it, wouldn't he? But why does it matter?"

"Because . . . well, because I don't think it's true."

"You're harking back to this lunatic idea about a drug," said the doctor accusingly.

"I know you said you didn't know of such a thing. But there could be, couldn't there?"

"You've been looking it up. A little learning," said Dr. Macintyre, bitterly, "is bloody dangerous."

"That's why I'm asking you about it," Antony pointed out.

"Well, if you're thinking Hammond may be an addict, forget it. Have you any idea of the effects—"

"Loss of memory can be one of them."

"Not by itself . . . completely isolated . . . there's nothing wrong with Hammond," said Macintyre, in the tone of one goaded beyond endurance.

"You thought he might have had some scopolamine, but would he be taking pills for seasickness at the end of a voyage? And it's one of the main things used in 'twilight sleep,' isn't it, and that makes people forget."

"It makes them forget a few hours out of their lives . . . not everything that ever happened to them. I'll grant there are combinations of scopolamine and morphine used—for

98

instance—before an operation. But the effects are nothing like Hammond's symptoms . . . or lack of them."

"I know that, doctor. But perhaps some other combination . . . one nobody has tried yet—"

"I can't help you, Maitland," said Macintyre positively. "Go away and read *The Boy's Own Paper*—you'll find plenty of 'drugs unknown to science' there." Antony reflected sadly, as the phone clicked in his ear and then went dead, that this wasn't really his day. He sent Willett out for sandwiches and coffee, and worked steadily through the lunch hour toward producing an opinion for that good-natured and long-suffering solicitor, Mr. Bellerby.

"And for once," he said later to Geoffrey Horton, "I was probably able to tell him what his clients want to hear. However . . . here's what the captain of the *Atlantis* has to say."

Geoffrey eyed the stout envelope with alarm. "All that?" he said.

"To be accurate, the information he collected for me. But it doesn't boil down to much. He says there have been rumors for some time that the drug traffic was pretty heavy now, and occasionally the police have been asking questions about this person, or that. But none of his officers had observed anything suspicious on this trip, no unauthorized goings and comings, nothing. He gives the names of the people who sat at table with Peter, and such information about them as he could glean . . . not very much. According to the steward who came to see me, these same people were the ones Peter saw most of . . . and a pretty innocuous bunch they sound," he added, mournfully.

"You're working on the theory that someone planted the stuff in Hammond's luggage," said Geoffrey. "But why pick on him?"

Antony balanced the "out" basket, which was empty, precariously on top of the "in" basket, which was overfull, and seated himself on the corner of the desk. "Because he wasn't a regular traveler," he said. "And because he was going straight to the Chiltern Hotel the night they docked."

Horton thought about this for a while. "That's why you're interested in the people he associated with," he said at length.

"Because they'd be most likely to know where he was going. Exactly."

"I don't see it. To begin with, how do the Customs officers separate the sheep from the goats?"

"Check the passenger lists, I expect."

"Yes, I suppose . . . well, what use was the stuff to 'them' if Hammond had it?"

"You haven't been talking to Sergeant Watkins. He told me: one, Peter arrived at the Chiltern at eight o'clock on Friday evening, and went straight down to get a meal; two, Wilson (you know, the chap who was killed) ought to have been on duty that night, but wasn't. That would explain why the package was still in Peter's suitcase on Saturday afternoon. If he'd woken up normal that morning, he'd probably have unpacked and found it. Or perhaps not . . . he'd not have been needing those rather heavy walking shoes in town."

"You're saying Wilson would have taken it, if he'd been there, without Hammond's knowledge?"

"I think so. Of course, there'll be other hotels involved. And in each case the person concerned would have to be in a position of some authority—like Wilson—who could find out which room the passenger was allocated, send the regular valet on an errand somewhere, and take his place for half an hour. Not too difficult, really."

"It's insanely complicated," said Geoffrey, flatly.

"It has its attractions. Think about it," Antony advised him.

"I should probably end up as mad as you are," said Horton rudely.

"Well, don't think about it, then. But can you give me one good reason for Wilson being murdered in Peter's bathroom, other than that he was mixed up in the racket somehow?"

"No, I can't. But you haven't explained—"

"Why Peter lost his memory . . . why the police were told the heroin was in his possession . . . why Wilson wanted to go on duty on the third floor on Monday evening . . . why he was murdered, even allowing him to be a member of the gang . . . and why the police were told about *that*," said Antony. "Of course I haven't explained to you . . . I don't know yet."

"You're not even doing a good whitewashing job," Geoffrey told him disagreeably. "All this can be just as easily accounted for by assuming Hammond's guilt. I'll grant Wilson was probably mixed up with whatever was going on; but isn't the most likely thing that Hammond killed him, because he let him down in some way? Or perhaps he blamed him for phoning the police."

Antony slid off the desk corner. "Definitely not my day," he said. The gleam in his eye might have been amusement. But Geoffrey was following his own train of thought.

"I never liked this business," he grumbled, "and I like it still less since the murder. If you'd only keep clear."

Maitland had walked to the window, and was looking down with apparent interest at the narrow street, but now he turned and grinned. "The situation is rather more complicated than you know," he said. "I gather that Inspector Conway has cast me for a leading role in this melodrama."

"What do you mean?"

Antony told him. "And I must say," he added, "I rather fancy the part."

Geoffrey was not at all deceived by the flippancy of his tone, but nonetheless found it annoying. He said the first thing he could think of to bring his friend down to earth. "Have you told Sir Nicholas?"

"Have a bit of sense, Geoffrey. I'm not daft," said Antony. But by the time Horton had spent five minutes seriously trying to convince him of the error—or, at least, the folly—of his ways, he was beginning to wonder. He listened without any visible sign of repentance, however, and when the diatribe had worn itself out said only: "You won't forget I want Dooley's address."

Horton looked at him without speaking for a moment. He seemed undecided whether he should regard this as the last straw, or relax his indignation a little. Finally he smiled, though rather sourly. "I'm ahead of you there," he remarked. "He's in the phone book—lives at Notting Hill."

"The same chap?"

"I got Cobbolds' to check that—and they were so quick I expect they'll charge you with a taxi fare," said Geoffrey, not without satisfaction. "It seems to be the man you were talking about."

"Then may heaven bless you," said Antony, devoutly; and went away to find—in the interests of economy—the nearest tube station.

By contrast, his meeting with Patrick Dooley took on almost the flavor of a reunion, after the first misunderstandings had been cleared away. "Not that I'm not glad to see you, Mr. Maitland," his former client assured him, "but if it was you set the police on to asking me questions . . . well, was that a friendly thing to do?"

"I didn't do anything of the sort," said Antony. "In fact . . . far otherwise. I was lucky," he added, "to find you home."

The address Geoffrey had supplied was in a street of terraced houses, most of them with an air of gentility despite their shabbiness, and the one where Dooley had his lodging was no exception to this rule. They were talking now in his own room, the first-floor front, where the bed was demurely hidden under a folk-weave cover, the window shrouded in lace, and there was even—or so Antony told Jenny later—an aspidistra on a plant stand in the corner. (It is sad to record that she thought he was making it up.)

Dooley seemed to feel this casual remark called for explanation. "I don't go on duty until six o'clock," he said. "Me being in the restaurant business now, in a manner of speaking." He was a small man, with a shock of black hair, a warm voice with just a tinge of brogue, and a manner which—as it had always done—bordered on the sanctimonious. His neat serge suit was rather shiny, but as genteel as his surroundings. He was watching his visitor rather anxiously as he spoke, so that Antony thought if he hadn't known his ways he'd have taken it for granted he was lying. Even as it was:

"I suppose you mean, you're a waiter," he said. "Where are you working?"

This rather free translation of his own version of his activities was apparently accurate enough, though it was noticeable that—as Maitland had expected—Dooley himself was not altogether pleased with it. "At the Night Light in Charing Street," he said. "And I can tell you, Mr. Maitland, it isn't altogether nice for a respectable man to be mixed up with someone that's murdered. I'd not have thought it of Jim Wilson, that I wouldn't."

"Not at all nice," agreed Antony solemnly, "for a respectable man." Dooley seemed rather pleased than otherwise by the remark.

"It's a long time," he said, reminiscently, "but I wouldn't say you'd changed, Mr. Maitland. Not at all, you haven't. Not that I'm blaming you," he added, "for what happened when we met before. You were younger then, and the jury . . . a dull lot, wouldn't you say? But when you infer that the word I used is not the right one, you're making a mistake." From this oracular style he descended suddenly to plain speaking. "I've been going straight for years now, Mr. Maitland. Years and years."

"Then you won't mind helping me, I expect. It is about Wilson, as you guessed."

"Well, what with the police coming," said Dooley—and again he spoke defensively—"and, of course, I'd seen your name in the papers, Mr. Maitland." He eyed his visitor in a speculative way. "For that matter, there've been bits about you every now and then, sir. All this time."

Antony did not altogether relish this reminder, but he had no intention of showing it. He said, casually: "You were a friend of Wilson—" and Dooley responded, as he had known he would.

"The merest acquaintance, Mr. Maitland. You'll know the Night Light is not too far from the Chiltern, and sometimes we'd meet in the Red Lion in Bedford Court; going off duty, or on duty, as the case might be."

"How did you meet him?"

"At the Red Lion . . . casually."

"But you've known him for some years now."

"About three years. We had a mutual interest in the Pools."

Antony grinned at that. "Any luck?"

"Not," said Dooley sadly, "so's you'd notice."

"Well, apart from that, you must have learned something of him. His family . . . his friends—"

"He talked of his kids, rather too much, I'd say. And sometimes he'd mention it if he'd had a tiff with the wife." He paused, and seemed to be contemplating sadly this instance of human frailty; and Antony was suddenly convinced that there was more behind this "acquaintanceship" than met the eye. Dooley was too casual, too incurious, too determined to keep the matter of his discourse on a superficial plane.

"Wilson was murdered," he said, bluntly. "Do you know why?"

The little man's eyes were reproachful. "How would I know a thing like that, and me knowing no more than I read in the papers," he protested.

"Well then . . . his other friends?"

"I'll not say he didn't know a few chaps at the Red Lion, to pass the time of day when he met them. And once he brought a girl in; one of the chambermaids from the Chiltern, at least that's what he said. The police thought I might be able to help them, Mr. Maitland, but I think I was able to convince them—"

"That you were the 'merest acquaintances.' *I* know."

Dooley lifted his chin, and said with dignity: "I told them the truth."

"I'm sure you did," said Antony. As much as was expedient, and not a word more. Dooley might not have been altogether successful as a confidence trickster, but his wits were quick enough to keep him from incautious speech, or so it seemed. "Did Wilson ever come to the Night Light?" he asked.

"I don't think . . . I don't really remember." And this time Dooley was definitely stalling. "It wouldn't have been surprising, would it, if he had sought me there sometimes?"

"I imagine it would have been more surprising if he hadn't. And what about last weekend? Were you looking for him?"

"Last weekend?" His eyes were wide and innocent, his tone couldn't have been more surprised if he'd been accused of going big game hunting in St. James's Park.

"You phoned him, didn't you?"

"Now if I had, sir . . . how could you know that?"

"If you didn't want to get in touch with him, why were you hanging round the hotel?"

"Well, I may have wanted to speak to him," said Dooley in a grudging tone. "I wanted to tell him I'd had a win on the Pools." To judge from his suddenly cheerful demeanor, this answer ought to settle the matter, but he didn't ask where Maitland had got his information. They parted a few minutes later on almost affectionate terms, and Antony went away hoping that he had at least shaken his former client's composure.

A phone call to chambers disposed of any hopes old Mr. Mallory might have had of seeing him again that day; and Antony was still feeling guilty when he dialed Shenstone's number and asked Peter to meet him in Kempenfeldt Square.

It took longer than he expected, getting home. Jenny was still out, but Peter had arrived and been immured by Gibbs in the study, with all the butler's usual disapproval. Antony rescued him, and took him upstairs. "Go in and sit down," he said. "I'm going to make some tea."

Peter followed him into the kitchen. He had sounded embarrassed on the phone, and seemed no less so now. One hand was pushed into his pocket, as if the feel of the coins there gave him confidence. "Tell me," he said, raising his voice a little to be heard above the running tap, "what am I going to do?"

Antony did not pretend to misunderstand him. "How happy could I be with either," he murmured, "were t'other dear charmer away." He put a tray on the table, and went to the cupboard for cups, ignoring Peter's glare.

"It isn't funny," Hammond snapped. At least, the new twist in his affairs seemed to have shaken him out of his lethargy.

"No, it isn't, is it?" Peter looked suspicious, but Antony seemed serious enough now. "The police have decided your rather tangled love life provides a reason for your convenient loss of memory. And that, my lad, is not a good thing."

Hammond seemed to be struggling with this pronouncement, but when he spoke again he had returned to his grievance. "I suppose I must be a—a sort of Lothario," he said gloomily. "I wouldn't mind that so much if I felt like one."

"How would that be?"

"Well . . . gay and dashing, I suppose. Not caring very much who got hurt—"

Antony, his preparations complete, sat down at the table and waved to Peter to take the other chair. "Elaine Burdon is very beautiful," he said, unkindly.

"Yes, isn't she?" Peter didn't sound very enthusiastic. "But the other girl . . . Nan . . . was she very upset?"

"Well—"

"My brother-in-law . . . Bernard . . . tells me I was engaged to her before I went away," said Peter, dismally. "And I suppose it's good of him to put me up, but I must say it's pretty damned uncomfortable. I mean, I can tell he thinks I'm shamming, and—"

"Uncomfortable or not, a hotel would be just as bad," said Maitland firmly. "You're better where you are."

"So you keep saying." He paused, and added despondently, "If I could only remember."

"It will come." He pulled himself up on the edge of saying, "Don't worry." So easy to give reassurance, and probably so unjustified.

"Well, so far," said Peter, "I haven't remembered a thing. And God knows, I've tried. I did get Bernard to tell me something about the job I was doing in Ceylon," he added, warming to the theme, "and it's absolutely tantalizing; I mean, it's all quite familiar and natural, but still I can't remember that it's anything to do with me."

Just then the kettle boiled over, and Antony got up to make the tea. When everything was ready, Peter got up without comment and carried the tray into the living room. Antony, following, was again shaken by a moment of doubt. Was Peter observant enough to have noticed that there was something wrong with his shoulder? Or did he really remember—? But a moment later he was noting Peter's haggard look, and thinking only of the difficulties that faced them.

Funnily enough, Peter's mood seemed to have changed. He sipped his tea, and said out of the silence, "That girl, Elaine—"

"What about her?"

"She's . . . well . . . rather overpowering. Of course," he added, endeavoring to be fair, "I don't expect I'd think so in—in other circumstances. But I do think I've been rather clever in taking advantage of the fact."

"How?"

"Well, first of all I asked her to have dinner with me to-night." For a moment he sounded ridiculously, to his friend's ears, like a boy boasting of his first date. "Then I said how much I'd like to meet some of the people we knew on the ship; I said I thought it might help me to remember. And she said, yes it might, and there had been a group of us who got to know each other quite well."

"The five people," said Antony, "who shared your table."

"That's right. So then it was decided we'd have dinner at her place, and she'd ask some of them to come in afterwards; those who are still in town." He paused, and eyed the other man with sudden doubt. "You said you wanted to meet them."

"I certainly do. But—"

"It's all fixed. I mentioned you . . . pretended I'd have to call off an arrangement we'd made, as a matter of fact; and she said to bring you to dinner. She said it might make things less awkward, which is true enough. Of course, she doesn't know who you are . . . nothing beyond your name."

"She knows if she's opened a paper within the last two days," said Antony. "Still, it's a good idea, and will save a lot of bother."

"That's what I thought," said Peter, and added inconsequently, "She lives in Chelsea," as though this might somehow prove an added inducement. "The only thing is . . . Nan Robbins. I ought to see her, I think."

"Tomorrow is also a good day."

"Well, actually, I can't say I'm looking forward to it. But at least I owe her an apology. I can't understand . . . but I suppose it might be true, that sometimes it's easier to forget." A moment ago, Peter had sounded almost complacent, but now Antony thought there was no less uncertainty in his manner, no real adjustment to the strange world in which he found himself. He said, on an impulse:

"Peter, how do you feel . . . really?" The abrupt question brought a startled look and a simple answer.

"I keep remembering how I felt when I woke up on Saturday," said Peter Hammond. "That ought to be explained by what has happened; if I'm mixed up with smuggling dope, I suppose I can reasonably be afraid of the consequences. But somehow I think there's more to it than that . . . something I ought to know."

"You won't improve matters by imagining things," said Maitland. He spoke roughly, because, just for a moment, he had seen the fear in his friend's eyes, and he didn't want to remember . . . He was almost relieved when, before he could say anything more, the telephone rang.

He thought it would be Jenny, who should surely be back from Midhurst by now. He was so certain he would hear her voice when he lifted the receiver that he hardly had a thought, for a moment, for the identity of the man who addressed him.

"Mister Maitland?" inquired the caller, with a queer emphasis on the words which made them sound almost like an insult. Afterward Antony realized it was probably an educated voice, though overlaid with a deliberate roughness. He acknowledged his identity. "Then," said the caller, "I've got something to tell you."

"Who is that—?"

"A friend," said the caller, and chuckled, so that Antony moved the receiver a little away from his ear. "I'm giving you a warning, mister, and you'll be wise to listen." There was a pause, and Antony thought he could hear a clock ticking in the unknown room at the other end of the wire. "It isn't always healthy," said the voice, "to ask too many questions." And there was a click in his ear as the connection was broken.

He put down the telephone slowly, and looked up to find Peter's eyes fixed on him. "Someone with an odd sense of humor," he said thoughtfully. But he was thinking, it's funny . . . that's almost exactly what Sergeant Watkins said.

CHAPTER VIII

Jenny was still out when it was time to leave. Antony propped up a note for her on the mantelpiece, and thought a little sadly how all their plans had gone awry these last few days.

Elaine Burdon had a flat in Chelsea that was probably expensive, though the house it was in had seen better days. She went in for a severely modern décor . . . rich, plain colors, against which her beauty showed, perhaps, to the best advantage. They had been admitted by a maid in uniform ("from one of those places that look after your entertaining for you," their hostess told them later). Now, as they entered the big living room, Elaine came forward to greet them, took Peter's hands, and raised her face in the obvious expectation of a kiss. Peter hesitated, and after a moment she raised a hand and patted his cheek, and said lightly: "Never mind, darling. I shall just have to make you fall in love with me all over again." (Watching them, Antony could well believe that this would present no particular difficulty.)

She turned to him then, and held out her hand with a movement he thought just a little too studiedly graceful. "I'm so glad you could come. Yesterday . . . it was *too* awkward. All this is such an ordeal for Peter, isn't it?" she added, smiling. "And I'm afraid I haven't made it any easier for him.

But really, I don't see what else I could have done, do you?"

Antony bowed over her hand. He never could resist playing up to a good line, and here his cue was unmistakable. "Peter will realize later," he said, "what a lucky man he is." Her eyes were deeply blue, he noticed, and sparkled as though in appreciation of the compliment. He released her hand, and she dropped her own slowly to her side, and turned away from them to take a low chair by the fireplace. The room faced east, and was already dim, and the lamp behind her spangled her ash-blond hair with threads of gold. She watched the two men seat themselves, gave Peter a warm, affectionate smile, and then turned again to his friend.

"Do you really think it will help," she asked, "seeing these people tonight?"

"I don't know, Miss Burdon. I think we have to try everything."

"To bring his memory back?"

"What else?"

She tightened her lips at that, but there was no real pretense that she was angry; her eyes were still laughing. "You're not being honest with me, Mr. Maitland. All these dreadful things that have been happening . . . you're trying to help Peter, aren't you?"

"Anything I can do, of course—" said Antony, noncommittally. But her high spirits were infectious, he found himself laughing back at her. "You see," he confided, "he can't tell me what happened on the voyage."

"No, but . . . why is that important?" He did not answer immediately, and after a while she went on, thinking it out as she spoke, "I suppose you think someone else put the drugs in his suitcase. I suppose that must have happened. But . . . one of us?"

He was relieved when the maid came in just then, to ask if she could serve the meal. There was no further opportunity for serious talk while they were at table, and though Peter was silent the conversation went merrily enough between the other two. Elaine's interests, it seemed, lay in the world of fashion, and she mentioned her trustee ("my dear Sir Charles") who had at last agreed to her buying a share in the establishment of a well-known modiste. "One must have an occupation, after all."

"If it isn't too discouraging for your clients, Miss Burdon, to know they can never equal—"

"You're a flatterer," she rallied him. "And not even subtle about it. And they don't think that, you know; if they did, no one would ever employ a model again."

"I suppose not. Anyway, I gather you find it amusing. Do you go to all the dress shows?" She had accused him of lack of subtlety, and he thought he was proving the truth of the assertion; but the next cue she gave him might not even be as good. Elaine seemed quite happy to field the balls he threw to her, and answered without hesitation.

"I go to Paris all the time, and often I'm in New York. This trip—when we met, darling—I'd been out east because we wanted ideas for some perfectly gorgeous materials . . . silks, and shantungs . . . people get awfully tired of all these synthetics, you know, and there are still a few who don't mind about the price, if only you can give them something different." She turned again to Peter. "I had a dreadful time with the Customs, though all I had were some samples, and of course I declared everything."

For the moment, the three of them were alone. "Did you see Peter go through Customs?" Antony asked her.

"Yes, of course, he was just behind me, and so patient. But then the man just asked him a couple of questions, and didn't even open his cases. I thought it was very unfair," said Elaine.

"Did you see any of the rest of your party go through . . . the people, I mean, whom you'd seen a lot of on board?"

"Only Miss Winthrop. She was ahead of me, and they looked in all her cases and even her handbag; it was one of those big ones that would almost hold an elephant. I teased you afterwards, Peter, because they seemed to be discriminating against the women."

"I dare say it would have been better," said Peter, "if they'd found the stuff on me then. At least, I suppose I was still normal—"

"Oh, yes, my dear, perfectly normal," Elaine told him. "We'd just got engaged the evening before." Again she smiled confidingly at Antony, sure of his sympathy. "It will have been a surprise for the others," she said. "At least, not for Greg—it was only fair to tell him—but the others could only have guessed—"

"You haven't told me yet," said Antony, "who 'the others' are."

"The people we sat at table with. Peter was the last to join the ship, you know, the rest of us were good friends already."

"You mentioned Miss Winthrop," Antony prompted.

"Yes. She was older, but . . . very pleasant. And there were Julia and Tom Brayshaw, and Gregory Miller. Miss Winthrop is the only one who doesn't live in town, and she's still at a hotel here . . . still on holiday."

It was a good enough meal, though lacking in inspiration. Peter was eating little, and talking less. Apparently he had shot his bolt in arranging the gathering, now he seemed detached, as if what was going on was no real concern of his; even Elaine's frequent, intimate asides didn't succeed in rousing him.

The first of the after-dinner guests to arrive was Gregory Miller. Antony, who for no reason at all had been expecting Superman, took a moment to adjust his perspective. Miller was tall, it was true; not angularly thin, but slender; beautifully turned out, down to the last detail, so that Antony— who had previously been feeling in fine form—was conscious, suddenly, of his own imperfections. He watched critically as the newcomer took his hostess's hand and looked deeply into her eyes. Miller's eyes were brown, and rather mournful; his hair was chestnut, too, and inclined to be curly, and certainly too long; his features were delicate, and yet somehow there was about him no real hint of weakness. An interesting chap, thought Antony; and settled himself to listen.

"My dear," Gregory was saying, "you have broken my heart."

"No, really, Greg?" It was said with every appearance of enjoyment. "But you knew, I told you; and you've had two whole days to get over it."

"What are two days," said Miller, "when one's whole life is blighted?" He had a soft voice, and somehow managed to speak quickly, even at his most dramatic. He looked now at Peter and said amiably: "I shan't wish you happy. I hope you lead each other the hell of a life."

Elaine looked from one of them to the other. To Peter she said: "It's Greg Miller, darling." And, turning back to the newcomer she went on reproachfully: "He doesn't know you, Greg. I told you he wouldn't."

"I heard what you said, my dear, but I'm afraid I thought . . . a convenient tale, no more." He's like a wasp, thought Antony, and as though Miller divined the thought the sad brown eyes moved around to meet his own. "A new face," said Gregory with something like enthusiasm. "You didn't tell me, darling, you had such a treat in store for us."

"It's Antony Maitland, Greg . . . a friend of Peter's. He's a barrister." A smile touched her lips as she turned to look at Antony. "I'm afraid Greg's manners are awful," she apologized. "I hope you'll forgive him, he means well."

"Now that," said Gregory, with more energy than he had previously displayed, "is too bad of you, darling. A frightful thing to say about anybody. I've heard your name, Maitland," he added, "so I take it you're either famous or notorious . . . which would it be? And Peter's gone to you for advice; perhaps not altogether wise of him, do you think?"

"As to that," said Antony equably, "who lives may learn."

"A philosopher," cried Gregory, joyfully. "As I live and

breathe, a philosopher." He looked at each of his three companions in turn, and added in a tone which seemed to deprecate his own enthusiasm, "I can't think of anything I've done to deserve such good fortune, unless, of course, it's bearing my troubles in a *manly* way."

"You're talking a lot of nonsense," said Elaine. "Peter, darling, will you see what everybody will have to drink. You were going to bring Emma Winthrop, Greg; don't say you forgot her."

"How could I forget?" asked Miller fervently. "Apart from the fact that your wish is my command—and that's a stupidly-worded phrase, if ever I heard one—how could I forget so forceful a personality as Miss Winthrop?"

"Well, I'm sure you couldn't, darling. But did you?" said Elaine; betraying, in spite of the rather complicated nature of this utterance, an excellent grasp of the situation. Miller looked reproachful, and shook his head at her.

"She declined," he said. "She told me she appreciated the invitation, but we should enjoy ourselves better without her." He looked at Antony, taking him into his confidence. "So refreshing to be classed as 'a young person,'" he said. As he spoke the two mellow notes of the doorbell sounded from the passage, Elaine turned her head to listen, and a moment later Tom and Julia Brayshaw were coming into the room.

This time the greetings, introductions and explanations were more involved, and Antony had time to study the two latest arrivals for a moment before he was called upon to take part in the conversation. Tom was a big man, not quite so tall as Miller, perhaps, but strongly built and aggressive-looking; as for Julia, the steward's description was quite uncannily accurate: "another looker," he had said, "but not so much class." Her hair was dark, with a shade of red where the light touched it, and her make-up was just—but only just—too heavy. Her black dress suited her, but her pearls were of a size and color that couldn't possibly be genuine. She inclined her head in response to Elaine's introduction, but her eyes were alert and, he thought, wary. By contrast, Tom Brayshaw gave him his hand; surprisingly, for so virile-seeming a man, his grip was limp, so that Antony felt as though he had been given a jellyfish to hold. But when he met Tom's eyes a moment later the thought came to him that perhaps it was one of the stinging kind . . .

Elaine indicated chairs, got them all seated in a rough semicircle. Peter completed his duties by pouring himself a brandy. He was very quiet; but then, he couldn't possibly have been unaware of the appraising glances that were being thrown in his direction. As he seated himself in the low chair that had been left for him next to Elaine, the girl looked round at her guests and said warmly:

"You know I'm pleased to see you all. But this isn't just an ordinary social gathering." She did not look at Peter, but she laid a hand on his arm in the intimate gesture that was becoming familiar. "I'd better explain. Peter *said* he wanted to see you because he thought it might—might stimulate his memory—"

"Well, it was true," Hammond protested. "The doctor said he didn't know what might do the trick." Elaine gave him a sweet, patient smile, and he relapsed again into an uncomfortable silence.

"That's what he told me," she repeated. "But you see— you've all read the papers, haven't you?—Mr. Maitland wants to find out what happened on the voyage. And, of course, Peter can't tell him."

Tom Brayshaw said, "Why?" in his deep voice, and Miller answered him quickly, almost slurring the words in his haste.

"But it's too obvious, my dear. He thinks one of us planted the stuff the police found in Peter's suitcase." He looked at Antony, who returned his gaze calmly. "Don't you?" he challenged.

Maitland took his time to look round the circle: at Peter, whose face was expressionless; at Elaine, a little flushed, but with a brightness of eye that might reflect some inward

116

amusement; at Gregory, lightly malicious, hoping his dart had gone home; at Julia, whose face had fallen into sullen lines; at her husband, coldly incredulous, and just working up to a slow anger.

"Is that true?" demanded Tom Brayshaw.

"From what I've been told," said Antony, "you people saw most of Peter Hammond on the *Atlantis*, would have had most chance of knowing if anybody tampered with his luggage or was seen making unexplained visits to his cabin." Julia raised her eyes at that, and darted a look at her hostess that was queerly triumphant. "It is also true that this fact might make you suspect, if the question of suspicion arose. But all I'm trying to do is dig up some sort of defense to the charge that has been preferred against Hammond under the Dangerous Drugs Act. So let's stick to that, shall we?"

"It isn't only that," said Tom. "What about the murder?"

"I can't see that that touches . . . any of you . . . at all."

"Perhaps not. But I don't like it," Tom grumbled. Antony gave him his sudden smile.

"I can't say I like it much myself," he remarked. "But I hope you'll help me."

Brayshaw relaxed a little. "I can't think of anything that would interest you," he said.

"The phrase is, 'any detail, however slight,' " said Miller, with one of his darting looks at Antony.

"That's right." His tone was still friendly. "If we could just chat for a while, informally." Anyone who knew him would have been suspicious of this artless approach, but in that company only Peter looked slightly puzzled. "Did any of you know Hammond before you met him on board the *Atlantis*?" Both the Brayshaws shook their heads; Gregory, back in his tragic mood, looked at Elaine and said, "Oh, no," in a falling voice.

"Do you get abroad much, Mrs. Brayshaw?" He was leaning back in his chair, with a studiedly casual air; but, surprisingly, he had hit on the right question to ask. Julia started to answer in a complaining tone, Tom was concerned to put what she said in a more amiable light; and suddenly there was no further need of prompting, they were all talking at once, tossing reminiscences back and forth, and incidentally telling him . . .

Tom Brayshaw and Julia had been on the ship from Singapore. He was "always away" on business, but this was the first time his wife had accompanied him. Miller had been in Hong Kong, getting material for an article which was to appear in a popular magazine. (Good lord, thought Antony, *that* Gregory Miller. Now, who would have connected this wasplike creature with the saccharine quality of his literary style?) They had shared a table from the beginning, with Elaine and two other people who were only traveling as far as Calcutta. There Miss Winthrop had joined the party, and at Colombo Peter had been added to their number. They had all, of course, had numerous other acquaintances on the ship; but they couldn't think—and they gave at least the appearance of trying—of anyone who had seemed to hang round them, or ask them too many questions. "And I don't mind telling you," said Tom Brayshaw ruefully, "I'd be only too glad if I could."

Were any of their cabins near Peter's? Only the Brayshaws were on the same deck, and they weren't really near. And, anyway, there had been too much coming and going, too many people you knew vaguely by sight, for you ever to think twice as to whether your fellow-passengers had a right to be in any given place. "Couldn't the cabin steward help you?" asked Julia, and when Antony said, "Yes, I shall be seeing him," there was a little silence while they thought that out and he wondered if it was his imagination that one of them was afraid.

The talk went on endlessly, of course, but that was really all about the voyage. Every one of them had a grievance to air when it came to the Customs (which meant, Antony supposed, that Sergeant Watkins's "screen" was still working well). "I'm afraid," said Elaine, when at last they had all left

118

but Antony and Peter, "you didn't get too much out of that."

"I wanted to meet them," said Maitland, "and I'm grateful for the opportunity. Though I didn't expect," he added, smiling at her, "quite the introduction you gave me."

"You may not know it," said Elaine, "but I did you a favor. It was stimulating, wasn't it . . . something to make them talk?"

"I'll take your word for it." He got up as he spoke, and looked inquiringly at Peter, who showed no disposition to linger but came to his feet with unflattering alacrity. Elaine made no comment, but went with them to the door.

"Good night, Mr. Maitland. Good night, Peter darling." She gave each of them a hand, but her eyes were on Peter. "It won't always be like this, will it?" she said sadly. Peter made no direct answer, but grabbed her shoulders, pulled her toward him, and kissed her clumsily over the left eye. He then pounded down the stairs, leaving Antony to follow at his leisure; when his friend joined him he said: "God, what an evening!" and started to walk briskly toward the King's Road.

Antony fell into step beside him. "If that's how you feel, I'm glad you can't blame me for arranging it," he remarked.

"Oh, I'm not blaming you," said Peter, unnecessarily. "But can you imagine . . . all those people . . . I suppose they *really* know me? It made me feel like something in the zoo."

"At least," said Antony lightly, "we now know pretty well everything about conditions in Hong Kong." The street they were in was quiet, but a car was coming slowly up behind them. He added, "I wonder if that's a cab," and turned his head to look.

"Not a taxi," said Peter. "Something much—" But he had no time for more; Antony grabbed his arm and jerked him back so violently that he lost his balance and they fell together down the steps of an area they had passed only a moment before. Dimly he heard the roar of the car's engine as the driver accelerated, and was aware that this had started even before they fell. The beam of the headlights, full on now, danced against the wall of the house as the car bumped up onto the pavement, and then swerved away as it took to the road again. After a while the sound died, to mingle with the hum of traffic in King's Road.

It was a moment before either of them moved, and then Peter—whose fall had been to some extent cushioned by his friend—scrambled to his feet and put out a hand to help the other man rise. "Steady," said Antony, ignoring the gesture. He got onto his knees, and pulled himself up with his left hand on the railings. In the dim light that fell into the area from the street lamps his face was ghastly.

"You've wrenched your shoulder." In his anxiety, Peter's voice was sharp, almost accusing.

"Not too bad . . . soon be all right." He sounded breathless. "Did you remember that, Peter? Or—"

"I noticed," said Peter, shortly, "that there was something wrong. The first time I saw you . . . the first time I remember seeing you, I mean."

"Well, be that as it may, we'd better be moving. Someone doesn't like us. I wonder which of us they were after."

"You think it was deliberate?" Ridiculously, in the circumstances, he sounded shocked. Maitland, who had gone painfully up two of the steps from the area, stopped and looked down at him.

"A drunk?" he pondered. "Somehow I don't think so." He reached the pavement, and looked across the street to his right, where he thought he heard someone approaching. A shadow, dimly seen, slipped back into the deeper shadows beyond the range of the street lights. Above them the house loomed dark and seemingly deserted. "There doesn't seem to be anybody in," he said. "We'll try next door."

: :   : :

"But the police weren't really interested," he told Jenny a couple of hours later. They had turned on the electric fire in the bedroom, and the room was comfortably warm. "Of course, if we'd told them to get on to Conway, or the Narcotics people, it would have been different. But I didn't feel like facing an inquisition, and Peter's shadow will put in his report soon enough. There isn't anything they could do about it, after all. Peter says the car was an Aston Martin, but even that's too vague. As it was, the local police decided the driver was drunk."

Jenny was curled up on the hearth rug. She shivered and said, not looking at him, "If someone was trying to kill you—"

"Or Peter. Most likely Peter. It's absolutely infuriating, you know. He must have found out something on the ship, and if only he could remember."

"He wasn't hurt?"

"A few bruises, I expect. He says he'll take care, but I don't know if I really convinced him—"

"What did Doctor Prescott say about your shoulder?"

"There's nothing he can do, you know that, love. He's tied it up so tightly it's damned uncomfortable, and he told me I should use a sling, but that's just to remind me not to use my arm. It'll be all right in a day or two."

"Yes, of course," said Jenny. She reached up and took the tumbler from the table at his left hand, and took a sip, and grimaced, and gave it back to him. In that little silence, a hundred things were left unsaid.

"You didn't tell me how you got on today."

"Oh, we got Nan's things, and made sure everything was all right at the cottage, and stopped the milk and the newspaper, and talked to the postman, and went to see the vicar. Then we came back to town, and found her somewhere else to live . . . a sort of hostel in Earl's Court. At least, it calls itself a club; the bedroom's tiny, but it's cheaper—and nicer —than that stupid hotel."

"You found my note?"

"Yes, I brought Nan back with me, so she got your message about going to work right away for Mr. Kendal. I was so glad, because it must be awful to be really hard up like that, and somehow I don't think she wanted to borrow."

"I don't suppose she did." But when the phone rang he was thinking of Elaine.

Jenny was already in the hall when Antony caught up with her. "I'll take it, love," he said, and put her aside firmly. He hadn't told her about the mysterious caller, which seemed silly when he had had to admit to the car episode.

When she reached the living-room door he had the receiver to his ear, was saying "yes" at intervals, and scribbling awkwardly on the message pad. "It's a cable from Uncle Nick," he said, as he hung up at last. "He's still in Paris. And he must be really annoyed," he added, gloomily. "He's quoting Johnson." He held out the pad for Jenny to see, and she read the message aloud.

" 'Sir, that man is a fool who intrudes himself rashly upon the affairs of his neighbour.' It's . . . it's awfully apt, isn't it?" said Jenny. "But I don't believe Johnson really said that. I think he made it up."

"That only makes matters worse," said Antony, declining to be comforted. He reclaimed the pad and scowled down at it, but after a moment he looked up and saw Jenny's smile, and an amused look crept into his eyes. "Two can play at that game," he remarked, with an air of satisfaction, and went over to the bookcase.

CHAPTER IX

HE SLEPT LATE the next morning, after a night disturbed by
the pain in his shoulder, found on rising that he was stiffer
than ever and that the left side of his face was a sight, and
went to breakfast in his dressing gown. Jenny had set the table
by the open window, where at this hour the sun only slanted
in, and the breeze was fresh and pleasant. She poured coffee
and handed him the paper. "There's a paragraph in the 'Stop
Press,' " she said. "But no names."

"I forgot to ask you," said Antony. "Have you heard from
Aunt Carry?" Jenny pulled a face at him.

"She phoned yesterday evening," she said. "She'd been
trying to get me *all* day. But I rather think she's disowned
us altogether now, so she may not ring again for a day or
two." She didn't sound particularly worried, and Antony reflected, not for the first time, how much better women were
fitted for dealing with the slings and arrows of outraged relatives than were their menfolk. He hesitated on the edge of
telling her about the anonymous phone call, and again decided against it. But it wasn't any use trying to keep her from
answering the telephone, as he had done instinctively the evening before, because obviously he couldn't stop it ringing
while he was out.

Peter phoned while Jenny was helping him into his jacket;

she had a brown silk scarf round her neck, which was obviously destined for use as a sling. Peter, too, seemed inclined to solicitude, and Antony cut short his anxious queries. "I'll meet you for lunch," he said. "Astroff's at twelve-thirty." He turned back to the room to find Jenny's eyes on him. "You'd better come too," he told her. "But I'm going to try to see Miss Winthrop first. So will you phone Roddy for me?"

"What do you want me to tell him?"

"I want a statement from the cabin steward about whether he saw anybody unauthorized in, or near, Peter's cabin during the voyage. So will he ask the captain of the *Atlantis* to find out for me? And tell him—if he doesn't want my undying curse to haunt him—to stick to his brief this time."

Elaine had given him the name of Miss Winthrop's hotel, and fortune favored him when he presented himself at the desk. Miss Winthrop was in, and would see him. She would join him in the lounge in just a moment. He walked up and down waiting for her, not daring to take one of the deep armchairs; he was pretty sure that when he did one arm wouldn't be enough to get him out of it quickly.

His expectations had ranged a good deal, because he couldn't quite reconcile the steward's description with the fact that Miss Winthrop had sought—and so presumably enjoyed—the company of the five people with whom he had spent the previous evening. The woman who came toward him a few moments later was sixtyish, he thought; thin, with clothes unfashionable but not outrageously so, a firm chin, and a mouth like a rat trap. But her iron gray hair was thick and curly, and only tidy—he was sure—because it was cut severely short; and her blue eyes were warm and friendly. The apologies he had started for the trouble he was causing were never completed. She waved him to a chair and took one herself, managing somehow not to sprawl in spite of its invitation to inelegance.

"I've as much curiosity as the next woman, Mr. Maitland, and of course I've read the papers. You needn't apologize for troubling me." She smiled, tight-lipped; Antony thought that, if it weren't for the friendliness of her eyes, he'd be frightened out of his wits by that smile. Even when she said, "You've had an accident?" her mouth belied the sympathetic tone.

"Yes," said Antony. He did not mean to elaborate, but found himself adding, "Someone tried to kill Peter Hammond." And then he wondered if that were true, or if he himself had been the target.

"Good gracious! I hope—"

"No damage. Well, only bruises. We fell down some steps." He told her briefly what had happened, and she shook her head over it, though not—it seemed—in disbelief.

"I suppose it's nothing to be surprised at, after all I've been reading about him in the papers," she said. "Do you think . . . but you're his friend, I shouldn't ask you—"

"If you mean, do I think he's really lost his memory— yes, I do. And I don't believe he's been smuggling drugs either, but it's rather hard to prove when he can't tell me anything." And suddenly her smile had real humor, mouth and eyes alike.

"So you're wanting me to supply some answers for you, Mr. Maitland. I wonder what you think I can do."

"Well, you see," said Antony carefully, "if we assume his innocence we're left with two possibilities. The package of heroin was put in his luggage on board the *Atlantis*; or later, while he was at the Chiltern Hotel. The first seems more likely."

"And what led you to me?"

"You dined at the same table. I'm told you were part of a fairly close-knit group—"

"And you're wondering, no doubt, what I was doing in their company."

"Well . . . yes, I was." His tone was cautious still, and this time she laughed aloud.

"Not looking for someone on whom to—er—to plant a parcel of drugs," she assured him. "As a matter of fact, I was fascinated by those two young women—Elaine Burdon and Julia Brayshaw." She saw him frowning over this, and added with a touch of impatience, "The rivalry between them."

"I . . . see," said Antony, doubtfully. "Who were they after?" he added; and saw her compress her lips at the vulgarity.

"You're asking me to gossip, Mr. Maitland. It's one thing to be an observer—"

"It could be important," he said; and left it at that. After a moment she smiled at him.

"Then I'll be indiscreet, and hope I'm not misjudging you. They weren't after anyone in particular, as you put it, but they both wanted attention."

"You mean . . . any of the male members of the party—?"

"That's right. Elaine had an advantage in a way, because Julia could hardly be expected to compete for the favors of her own husband. And if Julia persuaded—say—Mr. Miller into paying her any extraordinary attention, Elaine could always revenge herself by walking off with Tom Brayshaw under her nose."

"Well, what I want to know," said Antony, "is where Peter stood in all this."

"I should have said he felt there was safety in numbers. Modern young people allow themselves a good deal more license than was customary in my day, Mr. Maitland."

"You *would* have said—?"

"Until Elaine told me she was engaged to him."

"Did that surprise you?"

"Not when I thought about it; not that he should have asked her to marry him. But I was under the impression—she flirted so lightly, so attractively—that I thought her affections already engaged."

"You mean, someone not on the ship?"

"That's exactly what I mean. Besides, she was carrying a photograph . . . but I suppose I'm old-fashioned, to think that would mean anything at all."

126

"Did you see it? The photograph, I mean."

"Only a glimpse, and by accident. She dropped her handbag one day. And Mr. Hammond helped her to pick up the contents, but I've no idea whether he saw the photograph too."

"But she didn't talk of anybody else?"

Miss Winthrop shook her head. "Obviously, I was wrong in my assumption. I also thought that if she showed a distinct partiality for anyone on the *Atlantis*, it was Mr. Miller. But that, I suppose, is what is known as 'leading them on,'" she added, austerely.

"Do you remember Peter coming on board?"

"Yes, very well. I didn't go ashore at Colombo, but I was on deck and watched the few passengers who came on board there."

"Do you happen to remember his luggage?"

"Certainly. He had a brief case and a largish suitcase, which he asked to be taken to his cabin; and there was a trunk, too, labeled 'not wanted on voyage.'" She saw his puzzled look, and added briskly, "And the reason I remember is simple. I was the first through Customs at Southampton, and waited to say good-bye to the rest of the party. So I saw his luggage again then."

"It wasn't examined?"

"No. He was the only one of us to go straight through; I can't think why."

"Had you been long abroad, Miss Winthrop?"

"Oh, yes, quite some time. I had been to Singapore, and thought I should see something of India before I came home. An overrated country," she added, "but I feel one should take an interest—"

He waited for her to finish the sentence, but she seemed to have nothing to add. "Was it your first trip?" he asked.

"My first trip to the East. I have been several times to see my sister in America," she told him.

"Do you happen to know Mr. Brayshaw's occupation?"

"Something to do with cotton goods, I gathered. And if

you are chary of asking a direct question, Mr. Maitland, *I* am a retired schoolteacher, with a little money of my own which enables me to gratify my reasonable desires." She saw his look of dismay, and smiled her grim smile. "I am not accusing you of anything worse than a pleasant delicacy of feeling," she assured him.

He didn't get away without to some extent satisfying the curiosity to which she had admitted; and when he asked her if anybody on board the *Atlantis* had seemed to be asking too many questions—about the destination of their fellow passengers, for instance—she thought about it for a moment and then professed herself unable to help him. "Though I was making inquiries about a hotel, myself, Mr. Maitland. I have never made a prolonged stay in London before," she added.

He got away at last, and stood on the pavement outside the hotel; the sun was hotter now, and the breeze had died, and he wished suddenly, with a quite alarming intensity, that he could phone Jenny and tell her to pack and meet him at the station, and they would take off as they had meant to do for Bill Cleveland's farm in Yorkshire. And it might be no cooler there, but at least the air would be fresh and you wouldn't be condemned to wear "suitable" clothes.

Putting this thought regretfully behind him, he waved at a passing taxi, and watched it swing round to his side of the road. He'd be early at Astroff's, but he could phone Mallory, and then try to get in touch with Greg Miller and Brayshaw. It might be helpful to see those two alone, if they didn't take fright at the very suggestion.

Mr. Mallory was querulous, but Antony had no intention of going near chambers that day. Miller was reported to be putting in a day "at the office," which turned out to be in the editorial room of the *Woman's Review*. He professed himself delighted at the prospect of another meeting ("though it's a pity, dear boy, that this thing you're working on isn't in my line—journalistically, you know"). He was also able to give Antony the name of Tom Brayshaw's firm. They arranged to meet for dinner the next evening at the Night Light; Maitland was feeling a certain curiosity about the place, which might or might not be illogical. He didn't trust his good friend, Patrick Dooley. The next call he made was not so successful, however: Mr. Brayshaw was in conference.

Jenny arrived a few moments after he left the phone booth, and he took her into the bar, where he had told Peter to meet them. It was cool in there, they were able to appropriate their favorite corner, and Jenny didn't ask him how he was feeling. After about five minutes, Antony was beginning to relax, if not to feel actually comfortable. But that was before Peter Hammond arrived.

Maitland had realized for some time that the strain on his friend was increasing, rather than easing, as the days went on. Today he watched him crossing the room to join them, and noted his haggard look, and thought with sympathy that the situation must be almost unbearable. But it wasn't until the waiter brought the Scotch that Hammond had ordered and he emptied the glass at a gulp and ordered another, that Antony became aware of a radical change in his mood.

"Something's happened," he said; and then, as a possible solution occurred to him, "have the police been at you again?"

Peter avoided his eye. "It isn't that," he muttered.

"What, then?" The waiter returned before Peter could answer, and Antony reached across and moved the tumbler to his own side of the table. "You'd better tell us," he said, "while you're still sober." Hammond looked up at him briefly, and then fixed his eyes on the table again. Antony thought, he doesn't want to tell me, whatever it is. But I bet he will. "Somebody phoned you, perhaps?" he asked, thinking of his anonymous caller the previous day.

"Well, yes, but—"

"What did he say?" said Antony, at the end of his patience.

"It was one of my—my associates," said Peter, carefully. And then, in a rush, "It seems it's all true . . . the construction the police put on things. I think I knew all the time really, only I didn't want to admit it, even to myself."

"I see. What did this chap say that convinced you?"

"Quite a lot." He did not seem inclined to elaborate, but after a while he added: "I didn't mean to tell you. I don't quite know why—"

"George Washington complex," said Antony succinctly. "You always had it." And, surprisingly, Peter laughed and looked up to meet his eyes without apparent embarrassment.

"Then can you tell me, Antony, what the hell I was thinking of, to get mixed up in something like this?"

"Are you so sure—?"

"I suppose I may as well tell you. But I can't ask for your help any more," said Hammond, with a return to gloom.

Antony pushed the glass back across the table to him. "You'd better drink it after all," he said. "And if you're guilty, you'll still need defending, you know. I take it you're only admitting the charge of smuggling . . . not to the murder, too?"

"Not the murder. I told you the truth about that. I know what I did that night." He shot a look at Jenny, who was sitting very quietly listening. "I'm sorry," he said, "to have let you in for all this."

"Would you like me to go? Then you can tell Antony—"

"I'd rather you stayed. If—if you don't find it too sordid." His tone was bitter, and Jenny smiled at him encouragingly.

"You'll feel better when you've told us," she said.

"Shall I?"

"The phone call," Antony prompted him. "It was made to you at Shenstone's house, I suppose?"

"Yes."

"How did he know you were there?"

"I . . . he said he tried the firm, and they gave him the number. He must have known where I used to work."

"It was mentioned at least once in the newspapers," Antony pointed out.

"Well . . . he knew," Hammond repeated. "For that matter, how did you guess—?"

"I had a call yesterday myself, probably the same chap." Jenny turned her head to look at him. "Rather a rough voice —sounded like an educated man who'd seen too many gangster films."

"Yes, that's it exactly. So he phoned you?" said Peter. And now his eyes were fixed thoughtfully on his friend's face.

"I didn't tell him your number," said Antony, giving the truth a Jesuitical twist. "I didn't like the sound of him," he added; and that was also true. But he was cursing his own carelessness. He had made an informed guess at the cause of Peter's uneasiness, but it could have sounded like knowledge; and remembering how suspicious the other man had been— of him, as of everybody else—when first he lost his memory, Antony thought now he should have known how it would sound. But better bring it into the open. "What's worrying you?" he asked.

"Something the police said. Well, something they suggested," said Hammond, slowly. "They kept hammering away at it . . . why did I go to you? And it didn't make any difference whether or not they believed me about having lost my memory . . . the inference was the same."

"That somehow I was mixed up in the drug traffic myself . . . I know," said Antony, mildly. "They hinted as much to me." Beside him, he heard Jenny catch her breath on a gasp of pure surprise.

Peter said violently, "I didn't believe it . . . I don't believe it! But it's true I don't know why I came to you that day." He met Antony's meditative look squarely, but it was suddenly intolerable to him that the other man showed no sign of anger.

"I can't tell you that," said Maitland, still very gently.

"I thought . . . I don't know what I thought. I'm sorry. I shouldn't have said—"

"I'm sorry, too. The trouble is, you know, I don't see who you can turn to, if you don't trust me."

"I realize that. I've said I didn't mean—" He looked up and saw with compunction how white Maitland had gone, and the lines of pain about his mouth. "You saved my life last night," he said.

"Forget it!" Antony smiled, but his eyes were still serious. "It doesn't matter . . . any of it. Are you going to tell me about the phone call? You may as well, you know." As he spoke Peter, again abnormally observant, saw his left hand, which had been tightly clenched, relax slowly. He hurried into speech.

"Of course I'm going to tell you. He asked first 'Is that you, Hammond?' and said his name was Godley; and when I said I was sorry I didn't remember him he gave a nasty sort of laugh and said 'You needn't try to pull that one with me, old man.' I protested a bit, and he said 'All right! If you want to keep up the pretense. But you're not very popular round here, you know, since the police got their hands on the doings.' I told him I wasn't popular with the police either, and he laughed again and said that's what he wanted to talk to me about. Who did I think had tipped them off? And, of course, I didn't know." He paused, and looked from Jenny, who was twirling her glass by the stem, to Antony, who might have seemed equally casual if his eyes hadn't betrayed his interest. "He said again it was no use pretending, and I asked him what the—what it had to do with him."

"And I take it you didn't like the answer." Antony spoke to bridge the gap of silence, but when he went on again Peter ignored the query as though he hadn't heard it.

"He said if I wanted it spelled out, I should have it. I'd taken the package over, by arrangement, from one of their agents on the boat, and was to hand it on as soon as I got to London. He said this could be proved, so I'd better co-operate. Well, what he said was, they'd 'shop' me if I didn't. I suppose he meant there was some further proof they could provide. He wanted to know what had gone wrong, and wouldn't believe me when I said I didn't know. All this time I was trying to—to digest what he'd told me, and I expect I sounded pretty stupid, because at last he said, very sharply, 'I want to see you.' And he told me where. I said I wasn't at all sure I wanted to see him, and he said quietly, 'Don't try any tricks with me; you're in this up to your neck, and you'll be there if you know what's good for you.' And then he rang off."

"A gentleman," said Antony, "with a highly developed sense of melodrama." In spite of the apologetic tone in which Hammond had started his recital, it was obvious that this light comment offended him. "The question is, what are you going to do?"

"I thought you'd tell me," said Peter.

"You could go to the police . . . the Narcotics chaps . . . I expect you feel you can trust them." Antony spoke slowly, thinking it out, and was surprised by the vehemence of Hammond's reaction.

"I've apologized, haven't I? Can't you forget what I said?" But there was no regret in his tone, only a furious and irrational anger; and he was unreasonably glad to see an answering spark of resentment in Maitland's eyes. "If that's what you advise, I'll go to the police," he added; but it sounded more like a challenge than a promise. "But it won't be because I don't trust you."

"D-do what you d-damn' well l-like," said Antony explosively. "Only I'd have thought the w-weather was rather h-hot to ask to be put in prison."

"It might be as well to get it cleared up. I mean it's obvious—isn't it?—that I've had some part in what's been going on."

"Is it?" said Antony, coldly. He turned and looked at Jenny, and said as though she had spoken: "You'll have to forgive me, love. The names I should like to call this—idiot—aren't at all fit for your ears."

"But don't you think—?"

"I think that your friend Godley was concerned to scare you. I think he succeeded," said Antony.

"Well, why?"

"He wanted you to meet him, didn't he? This way he thinks he'll make sure no one else knows of the appointment; and that you'll obey him. And if you ask me 'why?' again, Peter," he added, apparently discarding his grievance and speaking naturally again, "I'll probably hit you. And our good friend, Astroff, wouldn't like it."

Peter eyed him uneasily, and smiled in a tentative way. "I dare say I shouldn't like it much myself." He glanced at the sling, and added unaccountably, "You always used your left for preference, didn't you?" And then, before Antony could speak, his head jerked up. "Did I remember that?" he asked. "Is it true?"

"It's true enough." He waited, but after a while Peter shook his head despondently. "Nothing else?" he asked.

"No, I . . . I don't even know why I said it."

"Never mind, then. You were asking me what I thought about Godley's story. As it affects you, I think it's full of holes . . . it isn't even circumstantial . . . it doesn't prove anything."

"I thought—" said Peter. He gripped his hands together on the table in front of him. "I hope to God you're right," he said.

"Of course I am."

"Then why . . . I'm sorry . . . why did he spin me such a yarn?"

"To persuade you to meet him. And that, I think," said Antony, without any expression in his voice, "is because he wants to kill you."

Hammond took a moment to think that out. "But you still don't think I should tell the police?"

"What do you think it would sound like to them? They'd be as suspicious as hell," said Antony flatly. "And that's not contradictory, my love," he added, without turning his head. "I'm working on the theory that Peter's innocent; they presume his guilt."

"Then what—?"

"It may be a lead . . . our first contact with the smugglers. Where does Godley want you to meet him?"

"In Putney Park Lane, Saint Margaret's Church. He said it would be a nice, quiet place for our discussion."

"It would be that, all right. All the same, our best hope of proving you aren't involved is to demonstrate who is."

"Then you think I should keep the appointment," said Peter. He picked up his glass and drained it, and there was now an odd note of satisfaction in his voice.

"Not exactly." Antony spoke with unusual diffidence. "I think we should both go to the rendezvous, but you should keep out of sight," he said; and got up to shepherd his party lunchward before either of them could protest.

CHAPTER X

ON HIS WAY TO Putney that night, Antony was recalling the arguments which had followed his announcement. "No, I say," Peter had protested, as they seated themselves in the dining room, "after last night it doesn't seem they mind who they kill."

"I don't mean to show myself, either, if I can help it; but you *must* keep out of sight. I'm pretty sure you're the object of the exercise."

"Then, I don't see—"

"If the light's right, I may get a look at Godley," Antony explained, with more patience than he felt. "At the very least, I hope we shall be able to follow him." The very fact that he knew his proposal was foolhardy lent a certain speciousness to his remarks, but Peter didn't seem to find them convincing.

"Apart from anything else," he said, "he won't appear until he sees me."

"He'll be there," Antony reminded him. "And if we wait long enough, he's bound to go away again. But you're the target, you'll have to keep well out of sight." The plan of campaign which was forming in his mind would give Peter's policeman, he thought, plenty of chance to keep tabs on him; but he didn't want the chap clumping on to the scene in regulation boots and scaring off the quarry. He wondered for a moment whether it would be wise to tell Peter to ditch his shadow before they left—it was odd that he never seemed to realize the police would be keeping an eye on his movements; but he decided against this on the score of prudence, which later he found ironic.

All the time they were talking Jenny had said nothing at all, which he found so unnerving that his resolution was almost undermined. He knew that she was upset by his proposal, and the fact that she did not protest made him so angry that by the time they got back to Kempenfeldt Square he could willingly have shaken her; and would probably have done so if the pain in his shoulder hadn't been a constant reminder that his arm was very little use at the moment. "Don't you see, love, it could be important?" he said, breaking a silence that was becoming oppressive.

"Of course you think so, or you wouldn't be going," said Jenny, indifferently. She threw handbag and gloves on a chair, and went across to push the window a little wider. This was the point at which his mood might easily have exploded into violence; instead he said—as he had said earlier to Peter: "I'd like to get a look at this chap myself. And I can't let Peter go alone, because I'm pretty sure it's a trap." Jenny had been straightening the curtains—an unnecessary task—but now she turned slowly, and her eyes met his with an intent look.

"Do you think, if it is, it's better if you walk into it?" she asked. "They weren't very particular who they killed last night."

He knew this must have occurred to her—Peter had mentioned it, hadn't he?—but he had nourished a faint hope she wouldn't bring it up for discussion. "That would have been put down as an accident," he said slowly. "Two for the price of one . . . all well and good. But if they've arranged an 'accident' for Peter tonight, they won't waste it on me."

Jenny left her place by the window, and crossed the room slowly to stand near him. "You're an awful liar, Antony," she remarked, dispassionately. He tried to catch her eye, but she had found something else to fiddle with now, and was arranging the folds of the scarf.

"It's true," he insisted.

"Well . . . perhaps it is." She looked up at him and smiled apologetically. "I'm being difficult, darling. I'm sorry." He knew then that she had capitulated; Jenny, whatever her inward fears, had never, in all the years of their marriage, tried to hold him back. And he wondered—not for the first time in his life—why this should be so, and whether she understood the compulsion which drove him at a time like this. He thought perhaps she did; he had, after all, given himself away pretty thoroughly once or twice.

But there had been another point, mentioned at luncheon, which still required explanation; and, in its way, it was even more difficult to deal with. "I was wondering if it's true . . . what you said to Peter . . . about the police?" She wasn't withdrawn any longer, and her gray eyes were troubled. This time it was he who looked away.

"It's a queer story, love, from their point of view."

"You mean, they really think you're . . . involved?"

"Conway does . . . or Sergeant Watkins says he does."

"Oh, I see." What had been said couldn't possibly have satisfied her, but she didn't ask any more questions.

Now Antony sat beside Peter in the Jaguar, while they drove across Putney Bridge and up the High Street. "Straight across at the lights," he said, "and then you can take the next turn right into Hazlewell Road." One thing he'd been sure of, that he wasn't going to accept Jenny's offer of her services as chauffeur; so it was a good thing that driving a car was obviously one of the things on which Hammond's instinct retained a firm grip.

The arrangement was that Antony would approach the meeting place by the footpath from Luttrell Avenue, while Peter drove round into Dover House Road. They had explored earlier, to let him see the lie of the land and decide where he should park the car, and his job was to have it ready for a quick getaway. He might have to reconnoiter a little, but he had promised to take care. He was, however, so obviously cheered by the prospect of action that Antony reminded him again of the need for caution when he got out of the car; and the grin he got in response cost him some misgivings. Peter, in fact, seemed so much more like himself than he had done at any time since he turned up the previous week, that his friend placed no reliance on his discretion at all. But he wished he could feel a little of Peter's simple enjoyment in a dangerous situation.

They had synchronized their watches—"twenty-one fifty-seven"—and Antony watched the Jaguar's tail light disappear round the corner into Howard's Lane before he turned into the footpath. A moment later another car took the same route; a police car, most likely. Unless they knew the district well he thought it unlikely they would realize that Peter had dropped his passenger.

It was dark under the trees . . . a good place for a secret meeting . . . a good place for a murder? He reminded himself that it suited his own purpose too. He went along the narrow path soft-footed, with the church on his right, and paused in the shadow where it merged into Putney Park Lane, straining his eyes. Opposite, a belt of trees separated the lane from Dover House Road, where Peter would be parking; but here it was quiet and lonely enough. He moved forward cautiously, keeping near the wall, and presently could distinguish a bulky figure, silhouetted against the light of a street lamp some distance away. He realized later that this should have warned him, but at the moment he was only puzzled that the man wasn't keeping out of sight.

He did not hear footsteps, or anything at all until a voice spoke in his ear. "Don't look round," said the man who had spoken to him on the telephone, "at least, not unless you want a knife between your ribs." A pause, then, "I'm glad you could make it, Mr. Hammond."

It wouldn't be wise to risk a look at the chap now. But he

wouldn't have thought he could pass as Peter, even in the dark. He stopped in his tracks and said querulously: "What is this? What do you want?" pitching his voice high to avoid recognition.

There was a moment's silence. "Maitland?" said the man with the knife incredulously. "Now who'd have supposed he'd have been fool enough to tell you?"

Antony thought, he's got a good ear for voices. No use trying to bluff, then, not on the point of identity. "If your name is Godley, I brought you Hammond's apologies," he said, in his normal tone. "He was sorry he couldn't come himself."

"I wouldn't try to be smart, if I were you," Godley advised him. He was very close now, and Antony was wondering how best to take advantage of the fact, when he added, softly, "I know you know all the tricks, Mr. Maitland, but so do I. Forewarned is forearmed, as they say. So I really don't think I'd chance it." Antony could feel the knife at his back now— at least, he supposed it was a knife. There was one very simple way of finding out, but he'd no intention of trying it. The big man ahead had moved a little, and seemed to be looking thoughtfully in their direction; of habit, Maitland tried to keep his presence in mind, as well as in sight, but it was hard not to give all his attention to the man behind him. He said, mildly:

"I didn't expect quite so hostile a welcome. And aren't you going to introduce your friend?"

"Cut it out," said Godley, roughly. Antony still thought the roughness was assumed, though not as a disguise; he was positive he didn't know the voice. A man with a feeling for drama living up to his part, perhaps? And not too well . . . it was noticeable that the words he used did not always match his tone. But he wasn't allowed much time for contemplation. "Where is Hammond?" Godley demanded.

"He went to the pictures." Antony allowed himself to become gently garrulous. "I didn't mean to tell you, because it seems rather rude in view of your invitation, but there was a film at the Empire he didn't want to miss." There was no doubt about it now, it was a knife; he stood very still, forcing himself to disregard it, but he hoped Godley knew what he was doing, because a thrust just there . . .

"You'd better tell me." The voice was softer now. "I don't want to hurt you, but my friend—as you call him—might get impatient." Again Antony felt the prick of the knife.

"I'm doing my best," he said, plaintively. "I say, you do know what'll happen if you lean on that thing, I suppose?"

"I know exactly what will happen."

"Well, I just thought . . . I mean, if you want me to tell you—"

"*Don't turn round!*"

"We could converse so much more easily," said Antony, freezing again.

"Talk, talk, talk," the other man grumbled. "Comes of being a lawyer, I suppose."

"I'm a trial to all my acquaintances," said Antony, sympathetically. But he couldn't keep it up indefinitely, and he couldn't think of any way to end the conversation. Godley, of course, could bring it to a close in any one of a number of ways; he had a shrewd suspicion that none of them would be pleasant.

"I'll say you are," said Godley, unappeased. (Definitely rehearsing for a part in a gangster film.) "Just shut up for a minute, and tell me where Hammond is."

"I expect he's at home."

"Then how did you get here?"

"By bus."

"Your car was seen coming along Old Brompton Road about nine-thirty. Who was driving?"

"I was."

"I said I know a thing or two about you, Mr. Maitland. And one of the things is, you don't drive yourself. War wound, or something."

"Or something," agreed Antony, equably.

141

"And your arm was in a sling earlier today; did you hurt it last night?"

"I've been meaning to ask you about that. Are you the chap who arranged the 'accident'; or do you prefer murder?" There was a silence. "I'm asking you if you killed Wilson," he explained. Godley swore at him, and Antony clicked his tongue reproachfully. "I don't believe one person organized both," he said, slipping back into his talkative role. "And when I decided to come here this evening, I was hoping you weren't the impetuous sort. So easy to—er—eliminate anyone who gets in your way. But then there's the body to dispose of—" He broke off with a gasp as Godley, who must have shifted the knife to his left hand, grabbed his right arm just below the elbow and twisted it behind him, wrenching his shoulder even more badly than the previous night's fall had done. For the moment he shut his eyes against the pain, and his only conscious thought was that he mustn't cry out a second time. When he opened his eyes the big man, whom he had still seen only in silhouette, had come much closer.

"That's enough," said Godley, unnecessarily. And then, addressing his colleague, "Take a look round, Danny-boy. If you find Hammond, bring him here."

The big man turned away without speaking. "We'll continue our talk elsewhere, Mr. Maitland," Godley said. There was a note of cold savagery in his voice now which was much more intimidating than the pseudo-American accent had been. "That is," he went on, "if you still feel like talking." But before he could finish, the world exploded in the sound of a shot and the big man pitched forward onto his face.

Godley swore again. Antony felt the grip on his arm tighten, and then mercifully relax; a hand took him between the shoulder blades, so that he went forward a few stumbling steps before he fell on his knees. For a moment he could do nothing but struggle against a feeling of nausea; then he raised his head to listen, though it still did not occur to him to move. Godley's footsteps were retreating down the passage to Luttrell Avenue . . . quietly, but not quite quietly enough. From the direction in which the shot must have come there was no sound at all. Then somebody came crashing through the belt of trees which divided the lane from the housing estate beyond . . . Peter, taking no precautions. Farther away, somebody shouted. A car started up, he heard it reversing, so that the headlights swung round and presently he was caught in their glare and put up his left hand to shield his eyes. So for a moment he did not see that the big man lay less than a foot away from him . . . and that he was very still.

: :   : :

"And a fine fool I must have looked," he complained later to Jenny (much later, when time had done something to discount the evening's humiliation), "kneeling there by the corpse in an attitude of prayer, right in the glare of the headlights, with a couple of cautious bobbies stalking me through the trees." But at the time there was nothing at all funny in the situation, and still less to laugh at when the police arrived, almost as quickly as Peter did. The big man was dead, but he had guessed that already. He had never seen him before.

He supposed the two men to be Peter's shadow and a squad car driver; one of them was in uniform, and the other wasn't, so he was probably right. They were courteous, and firm . . . particularly firm; and it was uncomfortably obvious that they saw no reason to look any further for the author of the shooting.

This attitude, of course, made a certain awkwardness in dealing with the situation . . . they had to send for assistance, they couldn't leave the body, they had to keep an eye on their suspects, and they wanted to look for the weapon. So it was some time before they got back to the local police station. Later still, "Inspector Conway would find it convenient if you could see him at the Yard, instead of here," one of the local men told them. Adding, "if you don't mind," with blatant insincerity. There followed a certain amount of argument about the Jaguar, the police position (that they had no intention of letting either of these dangerous characters out of their sight) being complicated by their unwillingness to admit it. But at last they were back at New Scotland Yard, in one of the peculiarly cheerless waiting rooms which seemed specially designed to break the spirit of the most stouthearted wrongdoer. By midnight, a doctor had been and Antony's arm was back in an improvised sling again. But they were still waiting for Conway.

He arrived at last, stiff as a ramrod, and frowning with tiredness. He was accompanied by a shorthand writer, and the veneer of courtesy had worn very thin indeed, so that his greeting was of the briefest and he added immediately: "In the circumstances, I must warn you, Mr. Hammond—" Antony, who had been half-asleep a moment before, straightened up and prepared for trouble. As Conway finished speaking the door opened, and Sergeant Watkins sidled into the room.

"And does that also apply to me, Inspector?"

"Certainly it does, Mr. Maitland," snapped Conway. And Watkins said to the room at large:

"We shouldn't wish to omit any legal formality." The mild brown eyes met Antony's and undoubtedly there was amusement in them. "You might throw the book at us," he added, reproachfully.

Antony achieved an answering smile. "I certainly should, if you gave me half a chance." He turned back to Conway again. "Well, Inspector?"

"You've no objection to this being recorded?"

"None at all. And to save time I'll add: we neither of us want to consult a solicitor, because we know what happened and he doesn't, and it would be a shame to drag him out of bed. But we *do* want to make a statement."

"Is Mr. Maitland speaking for you in this, Mr. Hammond?" Peter, who seemed to have been holding himself aloof

144

from the conversation, though his eyes were alert enough, nodded and began to feel for his cigarette case.

"I'm quite willing to be guided by him, Inspector." Antony met Conway's eyes and grinned, and this time he was really amused.

"You see!" he said. And noted with satisfaction that the detective's expression became even more bleak and forbidding.

"Then perhaps you'd make a start by telling us what took you to Putney this evening." He was looking at Peter as he spoke, but Antony interposed swiftly.

"I said a statement, Inspector. I'll tell you as much as I can, and Mr. Hammond can say what he did after we separated. Which will, no doubt, confirm what your own officer has already told you."

"Very well, then." He flashed an angry look at Watkins before he went on, as though the man from the Narcotics Branch was somehow to blame for the situation. "But first, Mr. Maitland, I should like an answer to my question."

Antony (who was working on the simple theory that if he talked enough there was a good chance the two policemen would forget what they wanted to ask him) was slightly put out by this pertinacity. "I suppose if I told you we were going for a walk, you wouldn't believe me?"

Conway shook his head decisively. Watkins said, "Well, I might, because I have a very trusting nature. It's a great handicap to a police officer." He seemed to be enjoying the situation.

"Then I'd better tell you," said Antony, with an air of candor. His description of the telephone call was brevity itself, but he gave a fairly complete account of what had happened later, at the end of which Conway's frowning gaze turned to Peter again.

"You stayed in the car, Mr. Hammond?"

"Yes. I parked in Dover House Road, as we'd arranged, and stayed in the car until I thought I heard someone call out.

Then I thought I'd better see what was happening, but before I'd gone very far through the trees I heard the shot. So I started to run, because I wondered—"

"You didn't see who fired the shot?"

"It came from my left, I think. It sounded as if the person who fired was standing a little farther down the lane, nearer the Upper Richmond Road."

Antony said, again with a casual air, "Your own chap can confirm that, Inspector," and Conway turned on him, suddenly furiously angry.

"I'm afraid I must disappoint you, Mr. Maitland. The officer who was following Mr. Hammond lost sight of him as soon as he entered the belt of trees. He could easily—" He broke off, perhaps seeing too late that the information was just what the other man was angling for. "Well, you have given an account of your movements," he said repressively, "but you haven't explained why you accepted this invitation."

"We were willing to do anything we could," said Antony, with a maddening assumption of virtue, "to get this business cleared up."

"Yes, but why should you think—?"

"He didn't, I suppose," said Watkins, making one of his unpredictable incursions into the conversation, "phone up and say, 'good evening, I'm a smuggler'?"

"We suspected him because he'd phoned me before, and warned me to keep out of Hammond's affairs," said Antony. "I thought we could see without being seen, but this other chap was standing where I expected Godley to be . . . what was his name, by the way, I'd never seen him before?"

Perhaps because he wanted the information himself, Inspector Conway glanced inquiringly at Watkins, who seemed quite willing to accept the unspoken invitation. "Racketeer . . . strong-arm stuff . . . several convictions for 'disturbing the peace' and carrying concealed weapons. A flashy dresser, and outstandingly vain. Almost certainly involved in some

146

really nasty incidents, but no proof of that. We've suspected him lately of being tied in with this drug business; again, without anything we could act on." He had been speaking directly to Conway, but now he turned a little and added: "Not at all the sort of person to make an assignation with on a dark night, Mr. Maitland." Antony shuddered elaborately.

"No, indeed. But his name, Sergeant; you haven't told us his name."

"Daniel Brown. At least, that's the name he used," said the sergeant doubtfully. And at the same time Antony exclaimed with an air of enlightenment:

"Danny-boy!" He looked at Conway, who was positively bristling with suspicion, and added hastily: "I told you . . . Godley spoke to him."

"Ah, yes. Godley," said the inspector. His voice was heavy with disbelief.

"Don't you know him?" Antony sounded discouraged. Conway merely shook his head, but Watkins said:

"Not by that name. If you could describe him, now—"

"I told you," said Antony again. "I never saw him." He found Conway's eye fixed on him, skeptically, and added from sheer perversity, "But I can do his voice for you, if you like . . . you lousy, flat-footed son of a bitch." The last words were spoken in a tone so unlike his own that Watkins looked round instinctively to see who had come in, before giving a loud guffaw and disappearing behind his handkerchief in a fit of coughing. Conway, quite stiff with disapproval, said incredulously:

"I beg your pardon!"

"Don't you ever go to the pictures, Inspector? Godley does. Hollywood gangster . . . I told you." And Conway, upon whom this repeated statement seemed to be having an unfortunate effect, flared again into anger.

"I'm not interested in fairy tales, Mr. Maitland. I don't for a moment believe this man Godley exists."

"Oh, yes, he does," said Peter. "I talked to him." He slipped a hand in his pocket, and seemed to be playing with the loose change he carried there.

"I'm not saying, you know, that's what he said to me," Antony explained, with an earnest, painstaking air that made Watkins resort to his handkerchief again. "For one thing, he'd lost his script; and for another, I'm not a policeman. But if he were here—"

"If he were here, I shouldn't have found it necessary to caution you," said Conway, still furious. Antony abandoned his theme, and took time to think that out.

"It's obvious," said Watkins, helpfully, "that you couldn't have shot Danny-boy yourself."

"No . . . I see." Antony was too absorbed even to notice how this interruption was taken by Inspector Conway. "He wasn't shot at close quarters, and he was facing down the lane, and I was behind him. Your men saw enough to confirm that, though they didn't see Godley."

"They did not," said Conway, grimly.

"So the idea is, I went there to meet Danny. We were talking, and he attacked me—"

"Which very likely he would, Mr. Maitland," said Watkins, "if you started playing any of your games with him." Antony smiled at him absently.

"Then I suppose you think Peter shot him to defend me . . . it's a pretty thought, it just doesn't happen to be true. For one thing, he'd have been shot in the back."

"Not," said Watkins, "if he'd heard Mr. Hammond coming, flung you to the ground—as somebody did—and turned to face him." He paused, and added innocently: "If Mr. Hammond's counsel made a good tale of your war injuries, and you admitted to calling for help, he might even get the charge reduced to one of manslaughter." He watched without surprise as Antony came to his feet, his chair scraping back on the wooden floor with the violence of the movement.

"I t-told you," he said. "It isn't true!"

148

"Then there's no need to get so excited . . . is there?"

"I d-don't l-like the s-suggestion."

Peter said suddenly, "Let it go. I don't believe they can prove anything, Antony. How can they?"

"How, indeed?" said Antony, wearily. "For one thing . . . has the gun been found, Inspector?"

"Not yet."

"Well, Hammond didn't have it on him, and your men were with us almost at once," Antony pointed out. "So I'd say it was pretty important to find it, from your point of view."

"Almost as important," said Watkins, staring at the ceiling, "as it is for you to prove you didn't know Danny-boy."

"We didn't," said Antony, shortly.

"What about you, Mr. Hammond?" Peter shook his head, and the sergeant went on in his casual way, as though the whole matter was really of no importance, "Well, if you didn't know him it's odd he was trying to get in touch with you. He phoned the Chiltern Hotel five times on Wednesday, asking for you."

"Damn that receptionist!" Peter was suddenly angry.

"He said he gave you the message."

"Well, he did. I just thought it was someone I knew before I lost my memory. So I didn't bother much about the name; it could have been Brown."

"It was."

"But still, I don't know him. Anyway, not during this last week," added Peter conscientiously, and to Antony's exasperation.

"We've told you about Godley," he put in. "Why should we trouble to hide a connection with this other chap?"

"Because Danny-boy is dead," said Watkins, as one stating the obvious.

"Well, was there a car abandoned anywhere near?"

"Not so far as we've been able to ascertain," said Conway. "And if you're going to tell me that means 'Godley' drove it away, Mr. Maitland, it certainly doesn't follow."

"There's an excellent bus service," Antony agreed. "But I thought, perhaps—"

"No car," said Watkins. "Not even an Aston Martin, if that's what you're getting at."

"So you've heard what happened at Chelsea?"

"I've read a report." That was Conway taking over again, and stiff with annoyance. "You didn't see fit to ask if I should be informed, or to mention it to me yourself."

"What would you have said?" asked Antony, gently. "More imagination!" He looked at Conway. "Anything else, Inspector?"

"I think not, Mr. Maitland." Conway was once more coldly master of himself. "Unless you wish to explain—"

"You have all the facts, Inspector. My opinions are my own . . . and probably bloody silly ones," he added, with the glimmer of a smile. Conway didn't actually agree with him, but he felt it was touch and go.

Instead, the detective got up and said formally, "I shall be glad if you will both come here tomorrow morning to sign your statements. That will give us an opportunity to go into things at greater length."

He took Peter home with him for what remained of the night. Considering the matter, as they went, he thought despondently that the provocation Sergeant Watkins had given him was probably not undeserved; he had, after all, done all he could to annoy Inspector Conway. But losing his temper completely, as he had done for a moment, always left him self-reproachful. In a happier mood he might well have considered his exchanges with Conway the one bright spot of the evening.

CHAPTER XI

BREAKFAST TIME on Friday was enlivened by another cable-gram from Sir Nicholas. "Questioning," it stated flatly, "is not the mode of conversation among gentlemen." "Obviously a soul mate of our elusive friend, Godley," said Antony; and left the table to telephone Geoffrey Horton.

Peter was looking much more alive and energetic this morning. He indicated with a gesture the paper on which the message was written. "That's worried him, hasn't it?" he asked. "I don't quite see why."

"Well, you see," said Jenny, "if you knew Uncle Nick—well, of course, you do, but if you remembered him—you'd know he's always creating about something, and often it doesn't mean much. But he never sends telegrams unless it's terribly important, and when he starts quoting it means he's really annoyed. Once he was at Liverpool Assizes, and Antony was trying to disentangle a stockbroker—I never really understood what the poor man had done—and Uncle Nick kept sending those night letter things, full of quotations from Gilbert and Sullivan. And when he came home there was a frightful row."

"He likes sending cryptic messages," said Antony, who must have been listening with half an ear even while he got his connection. "And it doesn't do to look too closely for the meaning, because it's mostly unpalatable." He came back to the table, and poured himself another cup of coffee. "He'll meet us there," he added, to Peter. "I said ten-thirty."

The session at Scotland Yard was no more enjoyable than he had expected, and nothing new emerged from it. For form's sake, they took Geoffrey Horton with them, and Antony—less garrulous this morning—had opportunity to reflect on the paradox of his friend's character; the most cheerful of companions off-duty, but a very pillar of orthodox propriety when occasion demanded. Sergeant Watkins was not present, which was perhaps a good thing. But Conway's immediate superior, Superintendent Forrester, was there; a man whom Antony found much more congenial than the inspector . . . and thought far more dangerous.

He attempted only one small diversion, when Conway—who was nobody's fool—referred back to his colleague's inflammatory suggestion concerning the possible reduction of the charge to manslaughter. Antony was still in an unusually chastened frame of mind and quite determined not to lose his temper again; and it was to answer this sort of thing that he had brought Geoffrey with him. But before the solicitor could speak, he had taken up the point himself.

"If I thought that suggestion was disingenuous," he said, "I suppose I should be grateful. As it is, I don't much fancy having Hammond plead 'Guilty' to manslaughter, only to have you hit him with everything you've got over the Wilson business. Besides—" he took time to look challengingly at Forrester, before his eyes went back to Conway's face again—"if we wanted an alternative to a straight 'not guilty' plea, I know a trick worth two of that."

"Do you, Mr. Maitland?" said Forrester, in his quiet way.

"Coke's definition of murder," said Antony, "calls for a person of sound memory and discretion. Well, we don't have to go back to Coke, really, but we might as well for all the use any of the later decisions are. And think what fun we'd all have," he added, enthusiastically, "setting up expert witnesses like ninepins for the other side to knock down."

Forrester said only, placidly, "We don't have to worry about that, Mr. Maitland. We can safely leave it all to the Director of Public Prosecutions." He paused, and eyed Antony reflectively. "If the point was valid, it would be interesting to see how it affected a possible charge as accessory," he mused. "It would give me great pleasure to allow you the opportunity to argue *that* point in court."

Geoffrey embarked on a scandalized protest; Inspector Conway could be heard muttering something in the nature of a fervent agreement; Peter looked worried; and Antony burst out laughing.

"The Homicide Act's quite clear there," he said, "I wouldn't have a leg to stand on."

But it was a long meeting, and tiring. When at last they got away, Peter pleaded a previous engagement for lunch, and Horton took Antony back to his office and went away to raid the senior partner's supply of sherry. "And I don't mind telling you," he said severely when he returned, "I came near to throwing the whole thing up, once or twice."

Antony picked up the glass left-handed, and raised it a little as if in an ironic toast. "You're so kind to me," he murmured. "The ship may be sinking, Geoffrey, but don't give Jenny the chance to call you a rat."

Horton smiled for the first time that morning. "I'm not very likely to, but I wish I knew what was happening," he said.

"The police are pursuing their investigations, and after last night I think it's a wonder they haven't got us both in prison," said Antony soberly. "And I'm following my own line, and getting nowhere fast."

"I didn't know you had one," said Geoffrey, with the devastating candor of long friendship.

"Perhaps you're right. I'm working on the assumption of

Peter's innocence of the smuggling charge, and it doesn't seem to lead anywhere."

"There could be an obvious reason for that," said Horton, brutally. He expected a flare of anger at the suggestion, but Antony only said wearily:

"You're right, of course. It's one of the considerations," he added, "that I find most helpful." Geoffrey found this meek acceptance of his strictures so unnerving that he immediately started to argue on the other side.

"At least, you've worked out a possible *modus operandi* for the drug traffic," he said.

"Possible," said Antony. "I wonder if it's even probable."

"In view of Wilson's death," said Geoffrey, "I think it's more than probable that an organization exists very much as you outlined it. Anyone can get the stuff onto the ship—or plane, I suppose—"

"Ship . . . for this particular idea," Maitland interrupted him. "No chance of transferring the stuff on a plane, and still less chance of finding out where your fellow-passengers were going to stay on arrival."

"All right, then . . . anyone can get the stuff aboard, and then look round for someone whose luggage is unlikely to be checked in Customs because he's just making the odd journey, and who proposes to stay at—say—the Chiltern Hotel."

"Their list of hotels must be quite a long one." Antony seemed to be regaining interest.

"Yes . . . well . . . at the hotel the package is removed by—let's stick to the one place—by Wilson, and he passes it on to—"

"I imagine his contact was Dooley. You see, nobody expected Wilson to be off duty when Peter arrived, and that's why Dooley was hanging round the hotel during the weekend looking for him."

"Because Wilson hadn't shown up at whatever meeting place they had arranged? But take a case where there were no snags—"

154

"Dooley passes the package on to the chap who distributes the stuff, I expect; who could be Godley." Horton was looking doubtful, and he added impatiently, "I'm only guessing, Geoffrey, I didn't say this was gospel."

"And you think Godley may be the head of the whole operation?"

"No, I don't. I think—and for the record, this is another guess—that there is one chap at the top, who is quite divorced from the day-to-day running of the business. And I say that because if I were peddling dope, that's the way I'd want it."

"In the circumstances," said Geoffrey, "the fewer remarks of that kind you make, the better."

"You're probably right. But how do you like my theory?"

"It sounds . . . reasonable," said Horton, grudgingly. "But it doesn't cut out the likelihood that the people who actually bring the stuff through Customs know what they're doing and receive some sort of consideration."

"I agree that would obviate one risk—that they'd find the stuff themselves. But think how much more likely they'd be to be searched if they had a guilty conscience and went through looking furtive. Besides, this way the gang can't lose; if the 'carrier' himself finds it, or if the Customs find it on him, they're in the clear."

"They'd have lost the consignment," Geoffrey pointed out.

"An ordinary business risk."

"I still think—"

"Yes, I know you do. But, look here, Geoffrey, why do you think Peter Hammond lost his memory?"

"It happens."

"For heaven's sake, stop being reasonable for a minute," said Antony irritably. Horton grinned at him. "It's such a coincidence . . . just now."

"The police don't believe he has amnesia; or, if he has, they think it's because he's been up to something he doesn't want to remember," said Geoffrey.

"Let's forget the police for a moment. Supposing he saw

something on the ship that made him dangerous . . . it would give them a motive for making sure he couldn't remember, don't you think?"

"*If* they had the means. But why not kill him?"

"I'm not quite sure. They've tried to since, so it may just have been they wanted time to stage an accident. Which is odd, because they obviously don't mind killing." He broke off there, as an idea struck him; but Geoffrey didn't notice the suddenly intent look.

"I'm glad you admit there are some things this theory of yours doesn't explain," he said, a little sourly.

"Oh, a hundred," said Antony, growing more cheerful as the other man became depressed. "Is there any more of that sherry, and can I use your phone?" Horton pushed the bottle across the desk toward him, and waved invitingly toward the telephone. "I want to call Tom Brayshaw, I couldn't get hold of him yesterday."

"You really think one of those five people planted the stuff on Hammond?"

"Well, if they didn't, I haven't a lead at all. Anyway, they're the most likely."

"Why not one of the stewards?"

"How would he find out which hotel Peter was going to?"

"Only by accident," Horton agreed.

"Besides, there's another possibility. What could Peter have seen on the *Atlantis* that was suspicious?"

"Don't ask me. It isn't my theory."

"What I've been wondering is, if one of those boon companions of his might not have been someone important in the racket." He paused there for so long that Horton got up, placed the telephone at his elbow, and poured the sherry himself.

"Seen a flaw in the argument?" he inquired unkindly.

"No-o. Not exactly. Anyway, that's why I want to see the two men again. Miss Winthrop is also a possibility, theoretically, but somehow I don't know—" He was feeling in his pockets as he spoke, and finally produced a ragged envelope with some figures on it which he regarded with something very like despair. "One of these numbers is Brayshaw's," he said, "but I can't remember which."

Geoffrey had been considering a protest . . . a warning . . . but he knew it wasn't any good. "If you'll tell me the name of his firm," he offered, "I'll find it for you. It's obvious you're not in a fit state to take on the London Telephone Directory singlehanded."

Antony thanked him and complied. "And then we can have lunch," he said, picking up his glass again. "I can't understand why a crisis always makes me so hungry."

         : :   : :

Peter had seen Nan briefly when she left the office the evening before, and had made the arrangement for lunchtime today. He was a little surprised when she told him to meet her at the Tower of London, even when she added that it was near the place where she was working; but when he saw her coming toward him with a brown paper bag in one hand and a Thermos flask under her arm, he felt he should have known all along that she meant to make a picnic of it. They found an unoccupied bench on the side overlooking the river, and he watched her as she unwrapped two packets of sandwiches.

It was really hot, without the breeze that had made the last few days so pleasant, but after a year in Ceylon Peter found it nothing out of the way; and Nan—brown as a berry already —seemed unconscious of the heat. She was looking very neat today, in the green linen suit which she had meant to "go away" in; but what Peter noticed was the deftness of her hands, her vitality . . . and her nervousness. He was as aware of her as, at their earlier meetings, he had been apathetic, and when she looked up she found his eyes fixed on her.

"I hope you don't mind," she said. "The office boy told me this is a good place to come, and I felt I couldn't bear to be indoors all day." She wasn't exactly apologetic, but he sensed her need for reassurance.

"I think it's a splendid idea," he told her. "I take it you don't care for London."

"Well—" said Nan, and flushed; so that he remembered for the first time that he was asking her questions to which he should have known the answers. "I've always lived in the country, you see. I used to go into Midhurst every day, to work for one of the doctors; but that's not quite the same."

"It was good of you to stay, then." How could he be reassuring, when he was so uncertain of himself?

The formal words seemed to embarrass her. She pushed the sandwiches toward him and said: "The buns looked awful, so I thought we'd make do with these. And there's coffee, but we'll both have to drink out of the thing from the top of the flask. Do you mind?"

"Of course not. Nan—"

"Yes, Peter."

"When were we going to be married?"

She raised her eyes to his for a moment. "It doesn't matter, Peter, really it doesn't. I do understand."

"When?" he insisted.

"Well . . . tomorrow. But there's nothing for you to worry about," she added hurriedly. "Jenny took me home, I told you that. And I unarranged everything."

"I see." This was a side of Peter that she had never seen before. He looked remote . . . angry . . . she wasn't quite sure. "Nan—this is important—when did you last hear from me?"

"You phoned me from Southampton."

"Antony told me. I meant . . . before that."

"A postcard," she said, "from Gibraltar. It's very wasteful," she added irrelevantly, "to send postcards by airmail."

"I suppose it is," he agreed absently. "Well, I don't understand it, but it doesn't really matter. Because it's just as well for you, Nan, that we aren't going to be married tomorrow."

She took that in silence, but after a moment picked up the flask and poured some coffee and pushed the cup toward him. "A loving cup?" said Peter. "The last time it was champagne, the night before I went away, and we drank to my safe return." He stopped short, and stared at her, but his eyes had a blank look. "Nan . . . did we do that?"

"Of course we did! Oh, Peter, you're remembering."

"Yes, I—" He shook his head, as if he were trying to clear it. "It's happened before; once yesterday, and again this morning. It's as if there was a gap in the fog, but then it closes in again. Does that sound stupid?"

"Not at all. The other times—?"

"Things I remembered about Antony Maitland. This morning, for instance, he imitated somebody's voice; and it seemed quite natural to me, something I knew he could do. It's difficult to explain."

"But it must mean . . . you ought to see the doctor again . . . it must mean you're getting better."

"The trouble is, Nan," he said somberly, "I don't know if I want to remember."

"You must. There are so many things—"

"I've been thinking about it," he said, as if she hadn't spoken. "I don't think I've done anything worse than agree to take a package through Customs; but if I did, I must have known what was in it, and that makes a difference, doesn't it?"

"Is that why you said it was a good thing we weren't going to be married?"

"That . . . and other things."

"I know I've no right, but . . . Peter, please tell me. That man who was killed—"

"I didn't kill him."

"Of course not, but—"

"I shall probably be arrested. Not for that, but for what happened last night. I'd better tell you, because it will be in the evening papers." He drank some of the coffee, and passed the cup back to her again. The sandwiches lay on the bench between them, disregarded, and presently the ravens would have a feast. "And don't talk about 'rights' to me, Nan. Do you hear?"

She was very quiet while he told her about the events of the past few days. "You'll see why I think I've got myself mixed up in something," he said when he had finished. "They're going to so much trouble to get me out of the way."

"I don't agree at all, there could be lots of reasons. What does Mr. Maitland think?"

"He hasn't told me. He says he still thinks I'm innocent."

"Then couldn't you believe him?"

"I do . . . I suppose. But that doesn't make me believe myself."

"If the police arrest you—"

"I don't know. I always thought . . . but everything's such a muddle, Nan. I just don't know what will happen."

They sat in silence for a while after that, until she looked at her watch. "I'll have to go, Peter. Will you walk back with me?"

"Yes, of course. Shall I see you tonight, Nan? Jenny Maitland asked me to bring you to dinner at Kempenfeldt Square . . . if you'll come."

"You don't want to see Elaine?" There was neither reproach nor coquetry in the question, and he accepted it at face value. Yesterday the true answer would have been, "I don't want to see either of you"—though, of course, he wouldn't have given it. Now, things were different.

"She's very beautiful," he said slowly. "I suppose a man might be flattered if she seemed to like him . . . perhaps that's what happened to me. But I know one thing now, I must have been mad if ever I thought I preferred her to you."

Nan was screwing the top on the Thermos; it seemed to be taking a remarkably long time. She looked up at last and smiled at him. "I'd like to see Jenny again," she said.

: :   : :

Antony had insisted on a quiet corner in a quiet restaurant.

"Have you never given any thought," he asked, " to the difficulty of eating soup left-handed?"

"You could always do without," said Geoffrey reasonably, which earned him a reproachful look.

Antony talked most of the time he wasn't eating, because he was still suffering a reaction from too much Inspector Conway. Geoffrey—who knew him very well—bore with him patiently, and resisted the temptation to resume his lecture. He was, in fact, so silent that, if Maitland had been less nervously on edge, he must have noticed the fact.

He found Tom Brayshaw in his office, in a hot and grimy section of north London. He didn't look particularly busy—in fact, he took his feet off the desk and put down the evening paper as Antony went in; but perhaps yesterday's conference had settled all his problems. He had taken off his jacket and loosened his tie, and he greeted his visitor with an odd sort of grin—almost a leer—which Antony didn't understand until he saw the headline running across the page of newsprint. "PUTNEY DEATH GANG KILLING?" it asked, with comparative lucidity.

"Things have been happening since I saw you," said Brayshaw. But he seemed more amused than shocked by what he read, and waved a hand hospitably enough to offer a choice of chairs. The office was comfortably, almost luxuriously furnished, in spite of its rather dingy surroundings. Antony chose a chair as near as possible to the open window, and then wished he hadn't because such air as did come in had practically a hundred per cent soot content.

"May I look at the paper?" he asked.

"Of course. Of course." Brayshaw pushed it toward him. He was definitely on top of the world today, and Antony wondered how much this had to do with his own predicament. Last time they met, the other man had been on the defensive; now he saw no cause for alarm. Properly played, that might be a good thing, even though he was irritated by Tom's rather boisterous air of condescension.

The newspaper report was cautious . . . so cautious as to

be amusing . . . well, nearly. But the writer, or his editor, had a fine mastery of the art of innuendo; nothing was said openly, a great deal was hinted. "As a lawyer, I have to admire it," said Antony, putting the paper down on the corner of the desk.

"Funny thing, I always put Peter Hammond down as rather an ineffectual sort of chap." Brayshaw's tone was almost admiring.

"You wouldn't think that if you knew him well."

"You may be right. But what I don't see, Maitland, is what you're doing in all this."

"I told you . . . remember?"

"I remember what you said." Again Brayshaw's smile was knowing. "But all this . . . gang warfare," he said, with a gesture obviously intended to indicate a reference to the visitor's bruised face and damaged shoulder. "It all seems so damned unlikely."

"I just went along for the ride." To anyone who knew him, Antony's tone would have seemed suspiciously mild. Brayshaw chose to take what he said as a witticism, and began to laugh.

"But I wish you'd tell me—"

"No." Antony's tone was decided, but oddly enough Brayshaw did not take offense. He said only:

"It seems a pity," and leaned forward and clasped his hands together on the desk. "Well?" he asked.

"There are one or two questions I should like to put to you." For a moment, as he spoke, he saw himself as he must appear to the other man. In view of the reports in the paper, the dryness of the formal approach must seem ridiculous. "I think I should explain that I am putting them in the interests of my client,"—no need to go into the exact position there—"but there is very little likelihood of your evidence being required. It is merely that I thought your remarks might be more illuminating if I spoke to you alone."

For a moment he thought Brayshaw was going to take fright at that. He reached out and straightened the newspaper

which was lying across the 'corner of the desk . . . an unnecessary gesture, but perhaps the reminder of its contents
stiffened his resolution. "I'll be glad to help," he said. "Not
that I think I can." And then the grin was back again. "In
the absence of the ladies—" he said.

"Precisely," Antony agreed. "Your cabin was on the same
deck as Peter Hammond's, wasn't it?"

"Not really near."

"But if you saw one of your group on that deck, who wasn't
visiting you—?"

"I'd have thought they'd looked in on Peter. That's fair
enough."

"But nothing like that happened?"

"Nothing that I remember."

"Mrs. Brayshaw, then?"

"Not really. Look here, Maitland, what are you after?"

"The person who planted heroin in Peter's suitcase."

"If anyone did. All right. But Julia knows nothing about
that." Antony sat looking at him in silence, and after a while
Brayshaw went on in a grumbling tone: "You know what
women are to gossip. She told me she saw Elaine coming out
of his cabin one night. Not terribly late, but she'd gone to
bed early with a headache. And I don't know where Peter
was that evening . . . not with us. But you're not interested
in that."

"Am I not?"

"Women's talk!" said Brayshaw. "I dare say it was true,
but what does it matter?"

"That would depend," said Antony.

"Well, I'll tell you what Julia says, if you like. If it happened once, it wasn't the only time. And when we heard
about the engagement—"

"When was that?"

"Elaine told Julia when she phoned to ask us to go to
Chelsea on Wednesday."

"There was no hint of it the last morning of the trip?"

163

"They didn't say anything. I'm not very good," said Brayshaw, with obvious sincerity, "at the finer shades."

"Well, were you surprised when you heard they were to be married?"

"I was at first, but Julia had it all worked out. She says it was Elaine's idea, not Peter's. That Elaine knew she saw her that night, and told Peter he'd compromised her. I suppose it's possible," he added doubtfully. "It sounds a lot of rot to me."

Antony smiled at him. "Obviously, Mrs. Brayshaw has a romantic mind," he said. Any of his friends would have recognized, at that moment, the likeness to Sir Nicholas.

"Well, it's just talk, you know. You said yourself you weren't looking for evidence," said Tom defensively.

"For guidance only. So do you mind telling me what you did when you left Miss Burdon's flat on Wednesday?" He changed the subject abruptly, and the question was deliberately clumsy.

"What on earth—? Well, I drove Julia home, of course. We live at Golders Green."

"And last night—"

"Now, see here, Maitland, I don't have to take this kind of thing. You've chosen to involve yourself in Hammond's affairs, but you're not dragging me in . . . not if I know it."

"I couldn't anyway, unless you're already involved. So why not answer my question?"

"Why should I?"

"Because I have a very inquisitive disposition. Because I might try to find out by more devious means."

"There's nothing to stop me throwing you out," said Brayshaw. But he sounded more sulky than threatening.

Antony got up. "Only considerations of humanity," he agreed, amused. "Your corridors are so very dusty." He began to move toward the door. "I seem to have worn out my welcome," he murmured. "Are you sure you won't tell me—?"

"If you must know, I was at home . . . alone. So you can make what you like of that." Antony gestured apologetically. "And if you try to see Julia again," Brayshaw added, "I'll break your neck!"

"My dear sir, there isn't the slightest need." Antony paused in the doorway, and looked back smiling. "After all . . . you've given me all the gossip."

He had a feeling that Brayshaw threw something at the door as it closed behind him. Or he might merely have been breaking up the furniture. Antony was smiling to himself as he went through the outer office, and down to the street.

: :   : :

But his lighter mood didn't last long. It was swelteringly hot outside, and the short walk to the bus stop was anything but pleasant. He was tired after two bad nights, and his whole arm, from the shoulder down, was aching. And he hadn't liked what he read in the paper.

So he sat at the front of the bus, on the top deck, and watched the pageant of London unfolding slowly, and tried to think things out. He wasn't very successful. By the time he got back to Kempenfeldt Square all he could think of was a cool bath and a drink; but he hadn't sufficient strength of mind left to decide which should come first.

Luckily, Gibbs wasn't about; he might even be treating himself to a day off, in Sir Nicholas's absence. Or perhaps his worst fears had been realized when he read the evening papers, and he had left in a huff. But he had been expecting the worst for so long now, that his most likely reaction would be to take a perverse pleasure in finding how right he had been.

When he opened his own door he thought at first Jenny must be out. Then, as he crossed the hall, he heard her voice from the living room. The idea of visitors nearly made him change course, but then he realized it was a one-sided conversation, and pushed the door open in time to hear her saying, "I think he just came in, Doctor. I'll go and see." She put down the receiver and moved away from the desk to make room for him. "It's Doctor Prescott, darling. He wants to speak to you."

He achieved a smile as he passed her, but he wasn't feeling very cheerful, and the genial rumble of the doctor's voice did nothing to reassure him. "How's the arm, Antony?"

He wanted to say, "It hurts like hell, and there's nothing you can do about it. So what?" But, of course, he didn't. "Not too bad," he lied.

"In spite of last night . . . eh?"

Even from here the folded newspaper thrown on the sofa showed a startling headline, not very much different from the one he had seen in Brayshaw's office. There'd be one on Dr. Prescott's desk too. As he hesitated, he heard Jenny go out of the room, closing the door so that it clicked firmly. He said carefully: "The police doctor looked at it, so I didn't bother you. There's no real harm done, you know."

"Good . . . good. You needn't sound so cautious, Antony; I'm not going to ask any awkward questions. I just thought . . . something to make you sleep?"

"Thank you, Doctor." He was suddenly, out of all proportion, grateful—not for the offer, but for the one person in London, it seemed, who didn't want to lecture him; or to ask him questions, and then refuse to believe the answers he gave.

"Now, there's something else. What's all this Macintyre tells me . . . says you've been bothering him . . . eh?"

There were a good many things Antony could have replied to this, on his dignity as a barrister of the Inner Temple and a member of Sir Nicholas Harding's chambers. Instead, he sounded almost guilty. "I only asked—"

"I know all about that, and you ought to know better. Macintyre's a cautious old . . . Scot," said Dr. Prescott, leaving Antony to wonder hazily what his original thought had been, "and he's not likely to give you anything in the nature of a theory. Nothing less than rock-hard, copper-bottomed facts," said the doctor, "and probably not even those unless he'd actually done the experiments himself."

One thing emerged from this rather complicated statement. "You've got something to tell me," said Maitland hopefully.

"Mind you, it won't prove anything. But if you think it will help to be able to show that amnesia could be produced by a drug—"

"Your worth is above rubies, Doctor. Tell me everything," said Antony fervently.

Dr. Prescott chuckled. "Now you sound more like yourself," he remarked. "All I've got for you is a nice little story, contained in a letter to the Editor of *The Scalpel* about three years ago, about a chap who was experimenting for better results in preoperative sedation. He wanted something that could be taken orally—not everybody cares for an injection; and what he came up with was a mixture of scopolamine and morphine (he didn't give the amounts), and he quite literally 'tried it on the dog.' But that was an accident, he says."

"The dog ate—or drank—or whatever—some of this sedative?"

"That's what I'm telling you. Then it went to sleep. The chap wasn't worried, of course, thought it would wake up naturally in a few hours' time . . . which it did. I said it was a family pet, didn't I? Well, they didn't realize at first there was anything wrong, but after a while it became obvious the animal was definitely not normal. It seemed to be thirsty, but didn't know where its water bowl was. It didn't react at all to people it knew, though it was usually very demonstrative. No reaction to the words it knew either—it wasn't a pup, you know, it had been with these people for years. No reaction to its food being prepared, though it ate hungrily when the plate was put in front of it. And it snarled when its master tried to pat it; as I've said, it was affectionate with people it knew, but didn't like strangers to take liberties. In other words," Dr.

Prescott concluded, with an air of triumph, "It seemed to have lost its memory."

Antony breathed a long sigh. "Can I have someone look up this letter?"

"No need. That's what I've been doing in my spare time these last few days. I'll send the magazine round this evening, with a prescription for you. But Antony—"

"Yes, Doctor?"

"You're not counting too much on this? I mean, it only shows what could have happened." He sounded really worried. "I hope I did right to tell you. Are you sure you feel quite yourself?"

Antony laughed at the anxious tone. "All the better for hearing from you, Doctor. By the way, what happened to the dog?"

"It was quite fit, as far as I know."

"I mean, did it recover its memory?"

"I don't think that was recorded."

He put down the phone a few minutes later, and sat for a while, thinking. It was surprising how much the information had cheered him, though he knew its only value was as an unconvincing confirmation of something he already believed.

While he was at the desk, he thought he might as well phone Roddy Gaskell, but the cabin steward's statement was an anticlimax after what Brayshaw had told him. Mr. Hammond hadn't been in the habit of entertaining in his cabin, and had only had one visitor there, so far as the steward had noticed: a woman passenger, a Miss Burdon. She had dropped in once or twice, he didn't remember when. Day or late evening, it would be . . . he wouldn't know what went on at night. The captain might have been exercising his reputed flair for discretion, but read with the gusto Roddy imparted to all his utterances the whole thing sounded like a chapter out of Decameron. Antony listened, suppressed a desire to laugh, thanked Roddy, parried his questions, and at last rang off.

Jenny came back into the living room as he replaced the receiver. He hadn't had time to notice her before, but now he saw she was looking worried. He thought at once that there had been another telephone call from Godley, and when she said, "I went to the bank today," he felt a sense of relief which the cheerless tone of the announcement would not normally have induced.

"We can't be overdrawn," he protested.

"No, we aren't. I asked for the balance because I wanted to be sure we were all right for the long vacation, and it was far more than it should have been. So then the cashier showed me, and someone had paid in three thousand pounds . . . last Wednesday. And I expect I looked astonished, because he went and brought the paying-in slip, and it was quite clear . . . your name . . . and it was paid in notes, not a check . . . and the name of the depositor was 'D. Brown' in a great, sprawling handwriting." She saw Antony's expression, and her own grew tragic. "I don't understand it," she said, "but I knew it wasn't a good thing."

"How right you were." He kept his voice level, but he had a nasty feeling this was the worst thing that had happened, so far. "What did you do, love?"

"I said it must be one of the clerks, and you'd forgotten to tell me," said Jenny. "But—I know it's a common name, Antony—but isn't Brown what the papers said the man who was killed was called?"

"It is. I . . . don't worry about it, Jenny. It doesn't matter . . . until the police find out."

"You won't tell them?"

"Not unless I have to. I don't see how they'll know."

"Then why—?"

"A sort of insurance policy, I imagine. In case I get too close. And if they did but know," he added, gloomily, "there isn't much chance of that."

CHAPTER XII

A FEW INQUIRIES had made it obvious that there was no need
to book a table at the Night Light for the dinner hour; the
restaurant catered largely to the theater crowds, and would
be busiest in the late evening. Antony thought this ominous,
and was pleasantly surprised to find that the place—though
ill-lit and a trifle "arty" in decoration—had a brisk air about
it. Clean linen and bright silver didn't necessarily mean the
food would be eatable, but on the whole the omens seemed
good.

He arrived a few minutes early, and Miller was late. He was
able to select a corner table, from which he could survey the
room in comfort; the headwaiter didn't seem to be in attendance, but his own waiter fussed helpfully before retiring to
await the guest's arrival, and after a while Dooley appeared
through the service door with a tray of drinks for a nearby
table. He made no sign that he had seen Antony until all his
customers were served; then he gave a quick look round, and
sidled up to him.

"Mr. Maitland, sir," he said reproachfully, "is this a friendly
thing to do?"

Antony considered. "Not unfriendly, surely?"

"Checking up on a chap. You lawyers," said Dooley bitterly, "wouldn't believe your own grandmother if she told you where she worked."

"But I did believe you," Antony told him gently; and rather spoiled the effect by adding, "that's why I came. And to have dinner, of course."

"If that means more questions, Mr. Maitland, I've nothing to tell you. Nor I couldn't talk to you here," said Dooley. Antony grinned at him.

"For old times' sake," he said, "I wanted to be able to imagine you in your new surroundings. I find it so much easier," he added unkindly, "to think of you in prison."

"You wouldn't want to get me in any trouble." But there was no confidence in Dooley's tone.

"I'd like to wring your neck," said Antony, truthfully; and watched with amusement as the little man registered hurt surprise. "Who did you telephone after I left you the other day?"

"Why, I . . . nobody, Mr. Maitland. Not unless it was a matter of business; nothing to do with you," said Dooley earnestly. He looked all round the room again. "Well, I can't stay here talking. But . . . was that a nice thing to say, sir? I liked you better when I first knew you, I can tell you that; even if that judge did give me two years." He turned and sped away.

It wasn't long before Gregory Miller arrived apologizing for his tardiness, but exquisite and unhurried as ever. Antony felt the sharp eyes taking in every detail of his own appearance. "Such a ghastly thing to happen," cried Miller; but the effect was one of gaiety. "No, don't tell me! Even the newspaper account . . . I was quite prostrated by the thought of so much violence. And a man killed! Altogether devastating."

Antony resisted the temptation to reply in kind, and broached the subject of food and wine. When that was dealt with, Greg said more normally: "It's a pity, of course, that it isn't in my line. Just think of the material this would give me—"

"Orpheus in the underworld," said Maitland; and let his eyes roam deliberately round the big, low-ceilinged room. The headwaiter had made his appearance now . . . at least, he supposed it was the headwaiter. An elderly man with white hair and an air of authority. And wearing, unexpectedly in this dim light, dark-tinted glasses. As he watched, Dooley sidled up and spoke to him, and after a moment he turned and went back through the service door.

Greg was eyeing Antony uneasily. "Not this place, dear boy," he said. "Very respectable, really."

"Is it?"

"Oh, yes. At least, so I'm told," said Miller. "The dinner hour," he explained, "is for the discriminating. Later, there'll be a crowd; but at any time you'll find the service excellent. Henri—oh, he's gone again—keeps things running smoothly. Remarkable chap, considering."

"Considering what?" asked Antony, idly. He wasn't really interested in Henri (who was probably the headwaiter), except insofar as he was interested in any contacts Dooley made.

"He's an albino," said Greg. "Which means he has shocking bad eyesight. It's surprising, really, he manages so well." He went back then to the point from which he had made this detour. "Nothing wrong with the place," he insisted. "It's on the 'recommended' list in the *Woman's Review*," he added, with a grin. "What I meant—"

"It would be better 'copy' if Hammond were here," said Antony caustically. He found Greg's eye upon him . . . speculative, unapologetic . . . and began to laugh. "It isn't really funny," he said, as the other man joined in.

They finished their martinis, and the hors d'oeuvres arrived. The service was certainly deft and unassuming. The headwaiter had not appeared again, but Dooley was flashing about with a great air of efficiency (he had really learned his job), and carefully ignoring the table in the corner. "I saw Tom

172

Brayshaw this afternoon," said Antony, pursuing an olive across his plate.

"Ah, yes . . . Tom." There was so much venom in the words that Maitland looked up, startled.

"I thought he was a friend of yours."

"There has been a great deal said about this 'close-knit' group of ours on the *Atlantis*," Miller told him. "It was quite simple really. For my part, I attached myself to Elaine . . . can you imagine a more reasonable thing to do? So did Tom, I imagine; bringing Julia along with him, willy-nilly. You know," he added, "every day the evils of the married state become more apparent to me; it's very trying to have a mission to spread sweetness and light, but that's what *Woman's Review* expects of me."

"How very frustrating." The sardines were easier; after all, he didn't really care about olives. "And was Elaine also the magnet where Peter was concerned?"

"I should think so, wouldn't you?"

"So you weren't surprised when the engagement was announced?"

"Nothing surprises me," said Greg, positively. But he contradicted himself a moment later. "Well, I did wonder . . . a little."

"When did you hear?"

"Elaine told me—I think it was Tuesday. You know, Maitland,"—his smile was malicious—"that girl really thought I wanted to marry her. She broke it to me . . . oh, so gently."

"Kind of her," said Antony. As long as his companion was in the mood to talk, he was very willing to listen, whatever the content of his discourse.

"Oh, I appreciated it. Don't think I didn't appreciate it. And that's really why I went to Chelsea on Wednesday night," said Greg. "I thought, Julia will be furious, and there'll be some amusement in that. I take my amusement where I find it; what else can one do?"

"I hope you weren't disappointed."

"No, indeed." Greg put down his fork to gesticulate more vehemently. "I realized at once, of course, that you were an acquisition to my list of acquaintances; but it wasn't until I read the paper this afternoon that I realized . . . now, don't be offended, dear boy," he added, with an air of alarm. "It's nothing to me if you go round hobnobbing with dope fiends, or getting yourself beaten up, or even whom you kill."

"I haven't met any fiends in this business . . . yet," said Antony mildly. "And if you mean the bruises on my face, I fell down a flight of steps." Gregory gave a sort of moan, which might have been intended for sympathy. "As for murder, I gave it up in Lent, and I haven't started again . . . so far."

"Oh, I have offended you," said Miller. "You're quite upset." Just another person who doesn't believe a word I say, Antony thought; and it doesn't matter, except as a reminder . . .

"You left Miss Burdon's party with the Brayshaws on Wednesday night," he said. "Had they come by car?"

"Yes . . . a monster," said Miller. His gesture might have been intended to illustrate a fishing story. "They offered me a lift, but I wanted to be alone."

"With your broken heart?" suggested Antony uncharitably.

"I was quite, quite shattered," Greg assured him.

"So you didn't join them."

"I was not in the mood," said Gregory, suddenly irritable, "for Julia. I walked and walked . . . at least half a mile. And then there was a taxi."

And what good was all this, Antony thought, discouraged, while their plates were changed and sole marchand de vin was produced with a flourish for approval. Even if Miller was telling the truth, there could have been a phone box before the taxi came along. When you were dealing with a gang, alibis became a nonsense. As for last night . . .

"Did you get your job finished in good time yesterday?" he asked; which was reasonable enough, as Greg had pleaded pressure of work as an excuse for not meeting him on Thursday. He picked up his fork and prodded the sole despondently, in a way which would have mortified the chef beyond bearing. And looked up to find his companion's eyes fixed on him with a disconcerting awareness.

"Are you still trying to protect Hammond's interests? But I forgot . . . your own are rather tied in with his now, aren't they?"

"They are," said Antony wearily.

"Well, I'll answer your question," said Miller, with a return to his normal manner, "and it won't help you unless all that in the paper is a fake. I worked at the office until nine-thirty, and then I went home. I live at Richmond, rather a jolly little place—" His voice ran on, but still his eyes were watchful and alert. Finally he broke off and asked abruptly, "Was it true . . . all that stuff in the paper about what happened last night?"

"Rather less than the truth."

"The inference was the police didn't believe anybody else had been present, but you, and Hammond, and the man who was shot."

Antony looked across at him with the glimmer of a smile. "If you saw the same report I did, it was a masterpiece," he admitted.

Gregory allowed a pause to lengthen, while he occupied himself with his dinner. Antony took a mouthful, and then laid down his fork. It wasn't often he felt completely indifferent to food, but tonight he was becoming conscious of a dull conviction that nothing mattered at all. Dr. Prescott's call had cheered him momentarily, but what Jenny had had to tell him had fixed that. And what was he doing, wasting his time here? A movement in the doorway caught his eye, the small stir of a new arrival; Elaine Burdon came into the room, and behind her Bernard Shenstone.

"You know, you puzzle me," Miller was saying. He saw that Antony was looking past his shoulder, and turned his head a little. Henri, the headwaiter, was still absent; another man came forward to escort the newcomers across the room. "Well!" said Gregory. "The fair Elaine; and not in mourning for Peter's lost memory, by the looks of it." He turned back to Antony again, and once more his mood had changed, the animosity of a moment before forgotten. "Who's that she's with?" he asked. "Handsome brute, isn't he?"

"Bernard Shenstone," said Antony. "Peter's brother-in-law."

"Eligible?" said Miller, again wasplike in his interest. "A better catch than Peter?"

At the moment there could hardly be a worse matrimonial prospect in London than Peter Hammond. "A wealthy man," he acknowledged. "A widower."

"So-o-o." Greg drew out the word, obviously delighted by his discovery. "Will you introduce me?" he asked.

"Presently," said Antony, and picked up his fork again. The sole was delicious, after all, a pity to waste it. "If you can stand so disreputable a sponsor," he added. "Shenstone hasn't much time for me, so far as I can tell."

"I don't care about that. I just want to see her face," said Greg, frankly, "when she sees us."

"Will it be such a surprise to her?"

"I took her out on Monday evening," said Gregory, "and she suggested this place. I shall say I am hurt she didn't keep it . . . our secret," he decided.

And yet I'd have thought, said Antony to himself, that Shenstone was the sort of man to decide for himself where he would dine. Elaine was enough to turn any man's head, of course; and he suddenly thought of the overbeautiful house, the air of untouchable elegance. The setting would be perfect for her beauty; not shadowing, but complementing it. Perhaps Bernard had realized that, too. He wondered what Peter would think of the idea, and put the thought from him, and looked across at Miller again.

"There's one other question I'd like to ask you," he said.

"Do you remember any conversation on board—not necessarily just among your own party—about hotels in London . . . where people were going to stay?"

Miller frowned at him. "That's an odd one," he said.

"Odd or not, will you answer it?"

"Well . . . yes. I seem to remember Miss Winthrop saying where she meant to go, and someone else telling her, 'that's an awful dump, my dear.' It must have been Elaine. So then Miss Winthrop was asking everybody for their recommendations; and I suppose at the same time she could easily have learned where the people who advised her were staying."

"I see." The two newcomers had not seen him, he thought; they were talking earnestly together, making the most of the opportunity to get better acquainted. If he was right about Elaine, she had no need for any gold-digging operations; perhaps she was genuinely attracted by Shenstone . . . perhaps . . .

At the next table, a jovial soul was loudly demanding "Henri." A waiter disappeared, and presently the white-haired man came back into the room. He stopped to speak to the couple at the table nearest the service door; it was too far away to hear any words, but his gesture seemed to indicate that he mustn't keep the importunate customer waiting. Not an elderly man at all, when you saw him closer; and how much could he see behind those dark glasses? It was odd how expressionless a face could seem, when the eyes were hidden. Antony, conscious he had been staring, looked down at his plate again, found to his surprise that the sole had been taken away and he had been supplied with cheese and biscuits; he stretched out his hand to move the coffee cup to stand more conveniently at the left of his plate.

There was a babble of talk from the next table. They couldn't order at all, it seemed, unless Henri would advise them. He murmured something to the jovial man, who seemed to be the host, but the whole party overruled him. No . . . no . . . no . . . they would have only what he chose. And were unexpectedly silent while he told them.

"Then I think, the *Caneton à la rouennaise*. Madame would like that." (There was a bow for madame.) "Or if m'sieur would prefer, the *entrecôte Mirabeau*? I will myself tell the chef—" A smooth way of speaking, a French accent you could cut with a knife . . . Antony, listening, sat suddenly very still. He was as sure as he had ever been of anything that he had heard the voice before . . . last night . . . in Putney Park Lane . . . Godley! He didn't bother to analyze what quality it was that Henri's voice shared with that of the man who had held him up at knifepoint. He only knew they were the same.

He put down his coffee cup as the realization hit him, and looked up, startled, to meet the blank stare of the albino's dark glasses. His curiosity about Dooley's associates had paid off . . . or had it? If he told the police . . .

Shocking bad sight, Miller had said. And Godley had mistaken him for Peter. How much could he see? Far enough to discern the recognition which he knew he had betrayed? He did his best to avoid me, when Dooley told him I was here, but that chap was so insistent . . .

Either Godley had seen he was recognized, or he was confident his voice would not betray him. He finished his proposal calmly, listened smiling to a chorus of approval, and summoned a waiter. Apparently he had forgotten his promise to speak to the chef, for he came next to the table where Maitland and his guest were sitting. Seen more closely, the lack of color was almost shocking, though he might have been regarded as handsome if he had had more animation.

"Is everything to your pleasure, *messieurs*?" He turned his head in Greg's direction. "I believe we have had the pleasure of seeing you before, have we not? That is a compliment, I think, that you return so soon?"

"The place is too adorable," said Miller, with a bad relapse into his normal affectation.

"But m'*sieur* is here for the first time?" The dark glasses were turned toward Antony now. "You are pleased, I hope."

"*Je suis content*," said Antony briefly. He thought the man was studying him; it was maddening not to be able to tell. "*Mais le bouillon était aveugle.*"

"How great a pleasure to hear my own language," said Henri, nodding in a pleased way. "But I must not indulge myself, or your friend will think us ill-mannered. No?"

"*Je m'en moque comme de quatre sous*," said Antony. And he doesn't know, he thought, as he watched the headwaiter threading his way back toward the service door, whether I recognized him as Godley, or just his phoney accent. I wonder how long he's kept that one up, and how he manages when he doesn't know a word of the language . . . except the menu, I suppose. But I was right when I put him down as a chap with a flair for dramatics. Meanwhile, there was the problem of getting away from this place, which might prove difficult.

"You are quite, quite mad!" Gregory was saying. His voice was tragic. "Now if I come here again, the meal will be ruined. They will make soup out of a packet, and they will burn the fish, and the steak will be of a rarity which I do not desire—"

"—and the dessert will make you sick, and the cheese will get up and walk away before you can eat it," said Antony unsympathetically. "Have you finished your coffee? You want to meet Shenstone, don't you?" He got up as he spoke.

"Such energy!" Greg moaned. But he too rose without delay. "I wish you'd tell me, though. What was all that about?"

Antony grinned at him. "I rather gathered you understood what I said."

"Yes, but—"

"*Je me presse de rire de tout, de peur d'être obligé d'en pleurer.*" And there might be cause enough for tears before the night was over, he reminded himself. He was moving across the room, and after a moment Greg shrugged angrily and followed him. But he seemed to have recovered his spirits by the time they reached Shenstone's table.

Elaine looked up, smiling, when she heard his voice, but the smile became a little fixed when she saw Antony beside him. "Why, Greg . . . Mr. Maitland . . . what a surprise!"

"Isn't it?" said Antony cordially. "The last two people I expected to see."

Shenstone had come to his feet. He seemed larger than ever in the dimly-lit room. "Peter told me he was dining with you," he said, and the words only just missed being an accusation. But then he glanced at the girl and smiled. "Miss Burdon and I are improving our acquaintance."

"He must have misunderstood me," said Antony, lightly. "I don't think you know Gregory Miller; he was traveling on the *Atlantis*." He completed the introductions; Shenstone wasn't pleased at being interrupted, but then, why should he be? His voice had less than its usual silkiness when he said:

"You'd better sit down, both of you."

It was Greg who made the correct, polite protests. Shenstone seated himself again, and signed to a hovering waiter to bring up extra chairs. "We can finish our meal while we talk. I've a good deal to say to you, Mr. Maitland."

That sounded ominous, but he was getting used to being out of favor. "Then, perhaps . . . I'll have the waiter bring our liqueurs over here." Shenstone nodded, and he gave the order and turned to Elaine. "I hope you'll forgive us, Miss Burdon—" The apology broke off as he looked at her.

"Peter's affairs are important to both of us," said Bernard Shenstone. His eyes, too, were fixed on the girl.

"I've been so upset," she said. But she sounded vague, unsure of herself. Could she be embarrassed? But now, looking at her more closely, he thought perhaps she was telling the exact truth. There was no flaw in her grooming, the blue gown she was wearing was every bit as becoming as the gray had been; but her eyes were clouded, and there were lines around her mouth, almost as though she had been hurt physically.

Shenstone's eyes were fixed on Antony's face; a questioning look, as he found when he turned his head. "It is something of a coincidence," he said, at his smoothest, "that we should all meet here tonight." Like hell it is, thought Antony. Aloud he said, evasive in his turn, "I gather it's a favorite place of Miss Burdon's." And was immediately aware that he had said the wrong thing; she wasn't just upset, she was frightened. He turned, and saw Henri only a few steps behind him. Now, why does she bring people here if it's an unpopular thing to do? From the corner of his eye he saw the headwaiter move away from them across the room, and at the same time the girl said in rather a high-pitched voice:

"Greg brought me here . . . once."

Miller was obviously just as confused as Shenstone was by the change in Elaine Burdon; equally obviously, he felt he had been silent long enough. "Well, I must say, my sweet, you were a more amusing companion than Maitland." He fortified himself with a sip of Drambuie. "Has he asked you yet where you were last night?"

"Where I . . . I don't understand?"

"He's interested in Wednesday, too, for some reason," Greg amplified his query. "But, of course, we know where you were that evening."

"Well, I was at home yesterday evening, too," said Elaine with more spirit. "Were you really going to ask me that, Mr. Maitland?"

Not in this company, thought Antony, a little grimly. Shenstone is beginning to simmer, I wonder if he really is *épris*? "Let's just say, I'm glad to know the answer, Miss Burdon," he said.

"But can it be confirmed?" Greg sounded inordinately pleased with himself; his voice was gay, but his eyes were sharp and watchful. "If your maid could tell us—"

"This has gone far enough!" Shenstone banged his hand down on the table. Not simmering now, boiling, thought Antony. And what is Miller up to? A mischievous type, in the fullest sense of the word; but can a simple desire to annoy go quite so far as this?

"Oh, do you think so?" Gregory seemed unabashed, but prepared to take the statement seriously. He drank the last of his liqueur and got to his feet. "I can't help feeling you'd do better without me," he remarked plaintively. "So I'll say good night, dear boy, and thank you. I can't promise to return your hospitality, because I have a feeling you may not be around."

"You might visit me in prison," Antony suggested. Miller took his time to consider the point.

"No, I don't think so," he decided. "My sensibilities . . . too sordid. Elaine, my pet, I hope you sleep better tonight. You mustn't get haggard, you know . . . not your type. Mr. Shenstone . . . perhaps you will forgive my intrusion, now I am about to take myself off." He had started to move away when another idea struck him, and he turned back to say earnestly to Antony, "Will they try you at the Old Bailey, do you think? Now I might come there."

"I'll look out for you," Antony promised. He watched Greg cross the room and wondered for a moment if he were wise to let him go. He turned to meet Shenstone's frowning look. "Your friend seems to have an uncommonly acute grasp of the situation," the big man said. His anger seemed to have vanished, he sounded only amused; and, paradoxically, this irritated Antony as none of Miller's shafts had done.

"The police are indeed persistent," he said mildly.

"And you are still trying . . . I warned you, Mr. Maitland, when first you came to me, that I knew Peter . . . rather well."

"I still don't think—"

"Well, I can understand you don't wish to admit you

182

were wrong, now you have got yourself so thoroughly entangled. Innocently entangled, I hope. But I really think you would be more sensible—"

"I'm grateful for your good opinion, of course," said Antony, too politely. (Was it better to be called a fool than a knave?) "But as things stand I have no choice but to go on asking questions. So far I haven't found the answers particularly illuminating."

"I haven't got a maid," said Elaine surprisingly, "if that's what you're thinking about."

"No, I—"

"Mr. Maitland cannot possibly be interested in your movements," said Shenstone positively. "But as I was with you myself for an hour during the evening, the point is in any event immaterial."

"That," said Antony, "would depend on the time." He caught Shenstone's eye, and added hastily, "If the question arose. It hasn't been raised by me."

"I imagine the query can only refer to your—er—adventure at Putney. I called on Miss Burdon to find out whether she would honor me with her company tonight, and left her at about ten-thirty. But, as you say, you aren't interested in that."

Antony thought, I didn't say so, it could have been Elaine who shot Danny-boy. I hadn't thought of it, but I'm thinking about it now. She's plenty of wiles to persuade a tougher nut than Shenstone into covering for her . . . a sob story, perhaps, with me as the villain of the piece. But that doesn't explain her nervousness this evening; if she's so frightened of Godley, why did she come here? He said aloud, with less than honesty: "No. Not really."

"So perhaps," said Shenstone, "we may leave the subject." Antony waited, saying nothing, until the silence became oppressive. Then,

"You said you wanted to talk to me," he remembered.

"More accurately, I want to ask you . . . I think I have

a right to know the position . . . exactly how Peter stands."

"You mean, with the police?"

"Yes, of course. I don't understand that report in the paper—what your purpose was in going to Putney last night; but if the account of what happened there is accurate—"

"The facts are pretty well as stated."

"You saw two men; the man who was shot, and another who threatened you."

"I didn't see the second one. I thought he was an American," said Antony; and resisted the temptation to see how Elaine reacted to the lie.

"So you couldn't identify him, but you'd know his voice again?"

"Well . . . I might."

"And still another person—whom neither you nor Peter saw—fired the shot from farther down the lane? You must forgive me, Mr. Maitland, but really—"

"Not at all a likely story," Antony agreed. He sounded depressed. "But you're wanting to know, I imagine, what the police think about it."

"Yes."

"They don't think anybody else was there . . . not the man who threatened me, nor the person who fired the shot. Just Peter, and me, and the man one of us killed."

"But they have taken no action."

"There's a snag from their point of view," said Antony, deliberately—and still he did not look at Elaine—"they haven't found the gun." And must I spell it out any more clearly, he thought, with sudden weariness? When they find it, Peter will be arrested, and they'll probably take me, too, as an accessory. I don't think they can formulate any further charges against me, whatever Conway suspects; but isn't that quite damnably enough?

Shenstone was taking his time to digest the information. "I can't say I like what you've told me," he said at last, "but—as you can guess—it isn't altogether a surprise. I'm in your debt, Mr. Maitland, for being so frank with me." Antony—irritated, as always, when the other man's tone became honeyed—closed his lips on a retort which wouldn't have been at all polite.

He looked down at his glass and found it empty. Now, how did you dispose of a glass of Chartreuse without knowing it? The waiter had reappeared, removed the used plates, and was inclining his ear for further instructions. Antony took the opportunity to ask for his bill, and while he was settling it Shenstone's attention was diverted to his guest again. "My dear Miss Burdon, I'm neglecting you. I hope you understand—"

No excuse for prolonging their talk. Antony got up and began to make his farewells, and a small amused thought warred in his mind with cold fear; to stay longer would be boorish, but why bother to mind your manners when you didn't know—but had a pretty good idea—what was waiting for you outside. He was under no illusions; unless Godley was insanely sure of himself he couldn't risk letting him go.

Surprisingly and disconcertingly Elaine gave him her hand, a clumsy business, as he had only his left to offer her. It lay in his for a moment . . . smooth, and delicately brown, and very, very cold. He thought she was going to speak, but then she didn't. The courtesies were over, and as he turned away he heard Shenstone's voice, again satin-smooth. "A tiresome business. I'm sure you'll realize now you have been foolish—" So he was trying to persuade her out of her fancy for Peter, was he? Much good that would do him.

A few minutes ago he had seen Henri come through the service door and cross the restaurant. The man was standing now, talking to someone, near the table he had previously shared with Miller. Antony started to thread his way, not directly to the door, but toward the wall where a broader path would make the going easier. And there he turned, not left toward the entrance, but sharply right through the door that led to the kitchens. Once there, he moved quickly.

185

A waiter said: "M'sieur is mistaken—" Dooley looked round from a consultation with the chef. Two women in overalls who were washing up, blinked at him through a cloud of steam and then went on with their work. A young boy darted forward eagerly, leaving the pan he had been stirring: "Let me show you, sir—" But none of them, except Dooley, seemed in any way surprised.

There were three doors out of the big room. Antony made for the nearest, and found he was in luck. A long, bare corridor, and a door with glass panels that must surely lead to the street. He dodged round a pile of crates of empty bottles, and went toward it at a run. Though even if Godley had seen him, he could hardly risk starting a hue and cry.

He came out into a narrow passageway, and turned right without hesitation, away from Charing Street. That was where the danger would lie, and he spared a thought for the form it would have taken; a taxi, perhaps, to get him well away from the premises. The organization would have some resources, after all.

He slowed to a walk as he neared the end of the passage, turned circumspectly into a street he didn't know. A shop with its blinds down on his right, and a little farther on the lights of a pub. He chose the shop doorway, which was deep enough to conceal him, and could be relied on to do so without comment. It was less than a minute before he heard a clatter of footsteps from the alley; Henri was a fast worker then, and really meant business. He braced himself for action if the man should turn his way.

But he didn't. Not a very intelligent type, after all, and perhaps there'd been no time to give him specific instructions. He ran out into the middle of the street, and stood there in full view, looking round. A broad-shouldered man in a badly fitting suit, and not in training: he was breathing heavily. After a moment's indecision he made off across the road, and disappeared round the corner. Which most likely meant that was the nearest way to a more populous area . . . the way he himself would have taken if he knew the district better. Well, he must content himself with a more circuitous route; but he thought any of the turnings opposite would be bound to land him in Shaftesbury Avenue before long.

Half an hour later he was approaching home from what he hoped would be an unexpected quarter, coming into the square only a few doors away from Sir Nicholas's house. He paused in the shadows to find his latchkey, and to swear at the restrictions which his injured shoulder imposed. There was no sound, no movement. The street lamp on the opposite corner illuminated a bare stretch of pavement; the dusty trees beyond the railing in the center of the square did not even stir in the warm, heavy air. And then he heard footsteps approaching . . . slow . . . steady . . . no attempt at concealment. Not an ambush, surely . . . one of his neighbors . . . ? He came out into the square, knowing he could now be seen with the lamp behind him, and walked along slowly toward his own front door.

Past the Holmes's house . . . the footsteps were still approaching, but he couldn't see anybody yet; past Dr. Nelson's, who insisted on living here, despite all the precedents which should have taken him to Harley Street; past old Miss Webber's . . . he could see the chap now, but he couldn't quite make out . . .

"Good evening, Mr. Maitland," said Sergeant Watkins amiably, "I was hoping I'd bump into you."

CHAPTER XIII

IF THE SERGEANT was surprised at the reaction to his greeting, he didn't show it. Antony gave a shout of laughter, hastily stifled, grabbed his arm, and pulled him up the steps. "We'll talk inside, if you don't mind," he said, and only relaxed when the door was shut behind them.

"More trouble, Mr. Maitland?" Watkins asked, as he followed him across the hall. "Or . . . you wouldn't be pulling my leg, by any chance?"

"I wouldn't dare," said Antony. He opened the door to Sir Nicholas's study, and fumbled for the light switch. "Come in, Sergeant, and tell me what's on your mind."

Watkins followed him, looking round with an appreciative eye at the comfortable room. Antony waved him to one of the chairs near the fireplace, glanced at the clock and noted that it was nearly eleven, and said, "Could you regard yourself as off-duty? Then I could offer you a drink." It was much too late to ring for Gibbs, but he could always scrounge for himself.

"I suppose you could call this visit unofficial," said Watkins. "But as for being off duty . . . not with such a desperate character as yourself, Mr. Maitland." He was smiling as he spoke, but there was just sufficient bite in his tone to disturb Antony's already ruffled feelings.

"What do you want?" he asked.

"Well, mainly, Mr. Maitland, to inquire after your health." He was looking up at the other man as he spoke, noting the signs of strain and tiredness and—oddly—of excitement. "And, having reassured myself on that score, I'd like to know where you've been tonight, and what's been happening. But I'll admit—before you point it out to me—that I've no shadow of right to ask you that question."

"I've been dining out—with Mr. Gregory Miller, Sergeant—at the Night Light in Charing Street." He saw the sudden intentness in his visitor's mild blue eyes, and added quickly: "Does that interest you particularly?"

"I was wondering what took you there. And why you arrived home like a cat with its fur rubbed the wrong way," said Watkins. Antony laughed again.

"You practically told me to take an interest in the place when you put me in touch with Dooley," he pointed out. "As for the other—" He hesitated.

"Don't tell me it was Mr. Miller's conversation," Watkins advised him. "I know he's an erratic gentleman, but I've no doubt you could hold your own with him."

"All right, then. What do you know about the Night Light, Sergeant?"

"Patrick Dooley works there."

"Yes, I know that. I mean—"

"Inquiries have been pursued," said Watkins. He paused, and added, "*Stringent* inquiries," as though the word pleased him.

"Well?"

"Come, Mr. Maitland, do you want me to remind you that I'm here to ask questions, not to answer them?"

"Then I've n-nothing more to s-say."

Watkins eyed him reflectively. "There's some who think a tale's more believable if not told too willingly," he remarked.

"There's s-some," Antony retorted, "think it's h-helpful

to make a c-chap lose his t-temper." This time it was the sergeant who laughed.

"Shall we call a truce," he suggested. "Tell me why you want to know about the Night Light—" He allowed the sentence to trail invitingly.

"All right. But you won't believe me," Antony warned him. "The headwaiter is the man who shoved a knife in my back at Putney last night." He paused, studying Watkins's expression, and then added belligerently, "Too much for you to swallow? It happens to be true."

"Now, I've told you, Mr. Maitland, I've a credulous nature," said Watkins. "If you were to tell that to Inspector Conway, now—"

"He'd c-call me a l-liar to my f-face," said Antony. The sergeant waved his hand in a placatory gesture.

"Finish your story," he invited.

"That's all. He isn't a Frenchman. I insulted his soup, and he registered nothing but gratification. But in view of your stringent inquiries, I expect you know that."

"You didn't see him at Putney. How did you recognize him?"

"By his voice. And you needn't ask me if I'm sure. I am."

"Did he know?"

"I haven't the faintest idea. Those dark glasses—"

"I know a good deal about him. Name of Henry Birkett, born in Clapham thirty-seven years ago, father a bank cashier, both parents now dead."

"I was wondering," said Antony, "how he managed to have no French. The restaurant business is usually learned abroad."

"Not Henry. He worked in the bar on one of the big liners until four years ago."

"Well then, who owns the Night Light?"

"You're thinking it's an unusual background for a head-

waiter. The restaurant is owned by a chap called Bailey—
and I think he's all right," added Watkins; the doubt in
his voice seemed directed rather at the general depravity
of the human race than at any particular delinquency of
the unknown Mr. Bailey. "If Henry had good references—"

"From someone who wanted to establish him on shore,"
Antony suggested. "I suppose you couldn't find out—?"

"No, Mr. Maitland," said Watkins, with finality. "You
see, what's going to be asked about this story of yours—
by anyone else, you know, not so trusting as I am—they're
going to ask how, if Henry is Godley, he could possibly risk
letting you get away?"

"He couldn't start anything in the r-restaurant," said Antony, making a fairly good attempt to keep his temper.
"It's a good cover, and apparently he has his character to
keep up. I left through the kitchens, I thought it would
avoid unpleasantness."

"So nothing happened." Watkins was reflective again.
"Well, I'm bound to tell you, Mr. Maitland, that doesn't
exactly make your story more credible."

"Oh, w-what's the use?" Antony had been standing all
this time, with a watchful eye for the sergeant's reactions.
Now he moved away from the hearth and began to stride
angrily up and down between desk and bookcase. "I'll tell
you something you can believe," he said, over his shoulder.
"Elaine Burdon was there tonight with Shenstone—Peter's
brother-in-law."

"I can believe that without any great strain," agreed Watkins placidly.

"But you don't believe—no, of course you don't—that
she's in any way mixed up in what happened to Peter? And
you won't do anything to check on my story about Godley?"

"I shall bear it in mind. I might go so far as to inquire
whether Henry was at the restaurant last night," said Watkins cautiously.

Antony, whose lapses of temper were never of very long duration, laughed and came back to his former position. "Big of you," he said. "And when I'm found with a knife in my back, don't say I didn't warn you."

"I have a good deal of faith in your ingenuity, Mr. Maitland."

"Meaning, you don't believe me. I admit I'm more worried about Hammond; he's a reckless sort of chap."

"And if we're to believe you, there have been two attempts on his life. And—this is something that will interest you—there was a car, an Aston Martin, reported stolen in Chelsea on Wednesday night."

"Was there, indeed?" said Antony. "I'm not surprised."

"Well, it was found only an hour or two later, parked in the next street to the one it was taken from. But you know, even accepting that part of your story, and what you told us about Godley being at Putney last night, that still doesn't explain who killed Danny-boy, and why."

"I realize that, only too well. It's almost as if there were two gangs, working one against the other. But about Peter—"

"I'd have said he was the quiet sort."

"Yes, he is. But he can be reckless too. I've asked him to take care . . . the trouble is, he doesn't realize . . . that's why I'm worried."

"Well," said Watkins, "if that's the truth . . . we're keeping an eye on him, pretty close."

"I don't know that I find that especially comforting. Close enough to scare off an attack?"

"Close enough for that . . . if he doesn't do anything silly," Watkins told him. "But I'll not deny, Mr. Maitland, that isn't our prime purpose. It's just what I said . . . we're keeping an eye on him."

"And the weapon hasn't been found yet?"

"No."

"And when it is?"

192

"Not my department. But I think, don't you, that with the other evidence—"

"Yes, I think so, too." And what then? As if he could read his thoughts, Watkins said:

"Do you still say you didn't know Daniel Brown?" And felt a small glow of satisfaction at his companion's startled look.

"I never saw him or heard of him until he was dead. Why do you ask?"

"We've been over his rooms pretty thoroughly. Naturally," said the sergeant. "And one of the things we found was a notebook, a record of cash transactions. And the very last entry was made on Wednesday, the thirty-first July, on the debit side. Three thousand pounds, which is a tidy sum." He paused, and smiled innocently at Antony. "Now, yours isn't an uncommon name, but not common either. Would you know anything about that three thousand pounds, Mr. Maitland?"

"He made a deposit to my account. My wife found out when she went to the bank today." He kept his voice level, but he felt as if he was suffocating. "I'll send a note to the manager, if you like, asking him to give you particulars." Watkins's eyes were fixed on him, but he couldn't read their expression. "My answer still stands," he added. "I didn't know him."

"In the circumstances," said Watkins, "it's a pity you can't prove it." And he sounded genuinely regretful.

That meant, of course, that they'd press the charge of accessory; and with more chance of success now. Both he and Peter could be connected with Danny-boy, which created a strong presumption that they had gone to meet him. So his own story of what had happened in Putney Park Lane must obviously be a lie designed to protect the murderer.

"You didn't think," Watkins was saying, "that it was your duty to tell us?"

"I shouldn't have dreamed of doing so," said Antony, with more spirit, "if it hadn't seemed obvious you were going to find out."

"You didn't mention your acquaintance with Dooley, either," the sergeant pointed out, giving him another jolt. This time, Antony only laughed, and said easily, "It didn't seem relevant." But he was thinking that Watkins knew altogether too much.

The sergeant went away soon after that, and Antony went upstairs with his mind in a turmoil. Peter and Nan had gone, and Jenny was curled up in her dressing gown on the sofa. She said she had been asleep, but he didn't believe her. "I'm later than I expected," he said. "If you'll give me a drink, love, I'll tell you—"

It didn't take long. He told her the evening's events without detail, but with few evasions either. He didn't stress the new threat from Godley; in fact, it was overlaid in his mind by his talk with Watkins. Jenny was silent for some minutes after he had finished, and when she spoke she ignored altogether the dangers that were foremost in her mind.

"It's funny about Elaine Burdon, isn't it?"

"If you mean, that she was at the Night Light—that's not surprising if she's part of the gang. And I think she is. It would be a good place to pass messages."

"You think she planted the heroin on Peter?"

"Yes. But there are so many questions, love." He sounded tired now, and dispirited. "Nothing seems to follow simply and logically. If two sets of people are working against each other . . . or it might just be that some mistakes have been made."

"Could that be why Elaine was frightened? If she's done something the gang didn't like, I mean."

"It could be that. I haven't explained very well, Jenny. I think someone's been knocking her about." Jenny looked so incredulous that he added irritably, "Knocking her about

. . . beating her . . . *I* don't know. And that sounds more like a lover than the gang. They aren't squeamish, they'd just have killed her, I think."

"It doesn't sound very loverlike either," said Jenny doubtfully. "Though perhaps, if the gang made her say she was engaged to Peter, she might have a boy friend who didn't like it."

"I can't see what advantage it was to anyone for her to say a thing like that, if it isn't true." She had no immediate reply to make, and he took the opportunity to change the subject. "Uncle Nick would have a fit if he heard you say 'boy friend,' Jenny."

"I dare say he's in Lausanne by now," said Jenny, obviously comforted by the thought. "And I dare say," she added, "you're quite wrong about Elaine."

But he was too tired to argue the point, too tired even to put up much resistance against taking one of Dr. Prescott's tablets. He went to bed and slept heavily, for the first time since Wednesday losing all consciousness, even of the pain in his shoulder.

: :   : :

He read the story of the dog who lost his memory over breakfast next morning, and found nothing to add to what Dr. Prescott had told him. He put the paper aside for Geoffrey Horton, and asked Jenny how Peter had seemed the previous evening. He was much more himself, she thought, but there had been no more signs that his memory might be returning. And Nan would make him a very good wife, if only the police, and the gang, and everybody else would leave him alone.

There was a phone call then, and it was Conway wanting to see him. A police car would be in Kempenfeldt Square in a quarter of an hour. He got ready quietly, and concealed well enough his sudden panic that it might be a one-way trip . . . that he might not be coming back.

Sergeant Watkins wasn't present, just Forrester and Conway. But there could be no doubt that his colleagues in Homicide knew all about their talk the night before. Which was only to be expected, though it didn't add anything to the joy of the interview. But the real blow came almost as soon as he was shown into Forrester's office, when Conway informed him, with sharp satisfaction, that the weapon—a Colt single-action Army revolver—had been found in Putney Park Lane.

"May I ask when . . . and where?"

"Early this morning, when the search was resumed. It was under a bush, thrust into the earth as well as could be done with the ground so hard."

So much had been happening, it was hard to realize how short a time had passed since the murder. All the same, "Isn't it surprising you didn't discover it before?" he asked.

"Not really surprising, I think. But there are two other points that will interest you, Mr. Maitland." Conway was being unusually forthcoming; now what was in the wind? "The gun was found farther up the lane than the spot from which the shot was fired; that is, nearer the place where Peter Hammond emerged from the trees."

"If I was planting it," said Antony, "I'd have thought of that, too." And then wished he hadn't spoken, when the serious Inspector Conway grinned at him in triumph.

"I doubt if you'd have been so incautious," he said, "as to plant a revolver with your friend Hammond's fingerprints on it."

"What!"

"Yes, I thought you wouldn't be so confident if you expected that," said Conway with satisfaction. "It was careless of him, I admit."

"But you said it had been pushed into the earth—"

"There had been a certain amount of blurring, and perhaps the experts would not swear too positively to all the prints. But there is one that is very clear, which is quite sufficient, you know, for our purpose."

Antony didn't say anything. He felt as if he had been winded, and could only stare stupidly. After a moment his eyes moved from Conway's face to Forrester's; he might almost have been asking for reassurance, and the superintendent shook his head at him.

"I'm afraid it is true, Mr. Maitland."

"Yes, I know. You don't play tricks . . . like that."

"Hammond was arrested an hour ago," said Forrester, still gently. "His solicitor is with him now." He might have been, thought Antony, with a revival of anger, a doctor with bad news to give, who prided himself on his bedside manner. "So I think," the quiet voice went on, "you must consider your own position."

"Hard as nails," Uncle Nick had said once about this chap, hadn't he? And were they going to arrest him, too? The answer wasn't immediately apparent. They warned him, they questioned him . . . about Wilson and Dooley, and Danny-boy, and Henri the waiter . . . and "do you really expect us to believe, Mr. Maitland" what you told us happened at Putney? And, above all, like a recurrent nightmare, they asked him—in a dozen different ways—to explain the money that had been paid into his bank account. But in the end they let him go.

He left New Scotland Yard by the entrance onto the Embankment, and found a seat, and stared blindly out over the river. His thoughts were churning hopelessly. He thought, I've got to snap out of it; and then he thought, fingerprints . . . incontrovertible evidence . . . no hope of getting round that. He sat there for a long time, until he stopped feeling sick and his mind was fairly clear again.

It was three o'clock by this time, and he went to look for a telephone box. Geoffrey Horton was at home, but it wasn't really a helpful conversation. If there was an explanation, Peter Hammond couldn't remember it. He phoned Jenny then. "Peter's been arrested, love. Could you tell Nan right away, in case she sees it in the paper? Yes, of course I'm all right," he added, "I'm on my way home. They won't let me see him." It was only after he had rung off that he realized that Jenny had been trying to tell him something. Well, it would have to wait.

So he didn't expect anyone to be waiting for him when he reached Kempenfeldt Square, and went up through the quiet house to the upstairs flat. He made for the living room, because if Jenny had left a note it would be on the mantelpiece; and he was halfway across the room before he was brought up short by the sight of his uncle, sitting in his favorite chair. He was the more startled because the question of whether or not he should cable Sir Nicholas had been very much in his mind; he knew he should have done so, but he couldn't think what to say.

"I . . . I didn't know you were back, sir."

Sir Nicholas eyed him with disfavor. He had come home by plane—a mode of travel he detested—after an urgent telephone call from Geoffrey Horton to his Paris hotel; he had given a solemn undertaking not to mention this summons as the reason for his return, which he resented; and he had now been waiting over an hour for his nephew, and worrying himself all that time into an even blacker mood. "As you did not see fit to communicate with me," he said, "I suppose my return may be a matter for some surprise. But there are English newspapers published in Paris, and the French news service, in addition, is quite a good one."

"I knew it!" said Antony.

"I imagined you might," Sir Nicholas went on, deliberately misunderstanding him. "And from my perusal of the available accounts of your activities, I gained the impression that your arrest was both imminent and inevitable."

"You're quite right, sir. They arrested Peter this morning. I've a respite, I gather, only because of some technicality the D.P.P.'s concerned with."

"I see. I admit life might be more peaceful if you were under lock and key, and the experience might even be salu-

198

tary. But, of course, there was no need to tell me; you realized I wouldn't be interested."

"Are we s-still alive after all this satire?" Sir Nicholas heard the angry stammer in his nephew's voice, and his expression grew even more austere. The fact that he recognized the source of the quotation did nothing to placate him.

"Make no mistake about it, I mean every word I say."

"D-do you, sir?" He was still standing in the middle of the room, and Sir Nicholas said sharply:

"Come and sit down, and keep your temper. I want to know—exactly—what has been happening here since I went away."

Antony obeyed only so far as to move to the hearth rug, and stand there in his favorite position with his back to the empty grate. His uncle looked him up and down slowly. He had dispensed with the sling today, and the stiffness with which he moved might have been no more than an ordinary sign of fatigue; but though the bruises had faded to a disagreeable greenish yellow they did not improve his appearance, and he was, besides, unusually pale. Sir Nicholas completed his inspection, taking his time, and raised his eyes again to his nephew's face. "You heard what I said, Antony."

"An exact account, sir?"

"Exact . . . and honest. If that isn't asking too much of you."

"Have I ever l-lied to you, Uncle N-Nick?"

"That's something I'm beginning to wonder," said Sir Nicholas deliberately.

Antony stared down at him blankly, almost as though he did not understand what had been said. Then he turned and flung himself into a chair. After a moment he smiled wryly, but his eyes had an angry glitter. "If we were talking anywhere else, sir, I could storm out and bang the door; on my own ground you have me at a disadvantage."

"Giving further rein to your temper would hardly solve anything," Sir Nicholas pointed out. "And—you may remember—I'm waiting to hear what has happened."

"I suppose I'd better begin at the beginning," said Antony, disconsolately. The events of last night and this morning overshadowed everything else, so that it was a real effort to think back as far as Monday, and the Magistrates' Court hearing, and the murder of Wilson. "And is it any good, if you've made up your mind not to believe me?"

"I'll believe you if you'll give me the facts. But I can't think of any reason for your failure to advise me," said Sir Nicholas, "except that there's something you wish to hide."

"Not one thing, sir. Just the whole, unsavory mess." He seemed to be lost in gloomy contemplation, but then he looked up and essayed a smile. "I didn't want you to say 'I told you so,' Uncle Nick. And I still don't see what else I could have done."

"Given your disposition, probably nothing," said Sir Nicholas crushingly.

For some reason, Antony seemed to take heart from this remark. But, "It's rather complicated, sir," he warned, "and even worse than you think."

"I'm listening," said Sir Nicholas.

An hour later his expression had not softened. "Incredibly complicated," he said. "And almost unbelievable."

Antony, who had leaned back in his chair and closed his eyes, opened them again. "Thank you for the 'almost,' sir." His tone was flat, exhausted. "Do you think I may be right . . . about the organization of the gang?"

"I think so. Whether Hammond is part of it or not," said Sir Nicholas discouragingly, "is, of course, another matter."

"If Elaine put the stuff in his case—"

"Well, we must leave that open. You postulate that some one person heads this organization—"

"But it must be that way, sir. And if there is a—a sort of Lord High Smuggler, I think he'd be known only to a few people, the next rank down."

"Of whom Godley may be one. And the man you're looking for may be one of the people you've met . . . or it may be Mr. X from Anywhere."

"I don't know how I've managed, sir, without your encouragement," said Antony bitterly.

"You've managed very ill," his uncle pointed out. "But if they feel this need for extra consultation—"

"Don't count on that, sir. I think they'll charge me, and perhaps they won't make it stick. But by the time they've cast doubt on everything I say, and dragged in that three thousand quid . . . well, even being acquitted wouldn't be very much fun. And there's still Peter's side of it."

"In the face of the evidence, do you still persist in this very stubborn defense of him? Even at Putney . . . could you swear he didn't fire the shot?"

"No, sir, I couldn't swear that." He got up as he spoke, but this time he didn't turn his back on the grate, but stood with his left hand clenched on the mantel, looking down at the unlit fire.

"Then I think—" Suddenly Sir Nicholas was angry again. "Have you given any thought at all to what this will do to Jenny?" he demanded.

"I know . . . of course I know. To Jenny . . . and to you." He did not meet his uncle's eyes. "I'll admit anything you like, sir. I've made a mess of things from the start. But if you're going to tell me you shouldn't get into a fight unless you think you can win . . . I can't operate like that."

"I have never suggested—"

"No, sir. In fact, I follow your example. The trouble is, you think Peter's guilty." He brought his hand down sharply on the ledge of the manel, and the clock groaned protestingly, as though it was about to strike. And all of a sudden his eyes became fixed, intent.

"I shouldn't wish to persuade you into doing anything against your conscience," Sir Nicholas said in a troubled tone. He became aware that his nephew wasn't listening to him, and added more sharply, "What is it? What's the matter?"

And as he spoke he heard voices in the hall, and Jenny and Nan came in.

Antony took no notice. He had picked up something from the mantelpiece, and now turned, holding out his left hand so that Sir Nicholas could see what lay there . . . a cloudy white stone, about the size of a crown piece, with a hole at its center. There was some carving on it, not very easily discernible, and the surface was polished and smooth.

"Do you know what that is, Uncle Nick?"

"No." He seemed more interested in his nephew's expression than in the object that was being held out for him to identify. "Are you going to tell me?"

"I don't know either. But—"

"It's Peter's," said Jenny, coming forward. "He showed it to us last night. And after he'd gone I found he'd left it."

"Where did he get it?"

"I don't know." She turned and looked rather helplessly at Nan.

"We think he must have got it in Ceylon." She found Antony's eyes fixed on her, but not as though he recognized her at all. "When he got back to the hotel on Monday . . . when the police let him go . . . it was on the dressing table. And he asked the chambermaid, and she said she'd found it on the floor; and it hadn't been there when the last people left, so it must be his. He's been carrying it in his pocket, with his change; it's a nice thing to—to fiddle with."

"So it is." His hand closed round it, and his eyes moved away from Nan, back to his uncle's face. He was in a blaze of excitement. "I know now," he said. "I *know*."

"If that pebble is so communicative," said Sir Nicholas, tartly, "I think you might share the information with us."

"Well, you see, I've suspected . . . but I still can't prove anything," said Antony. "All the same . . . look here, Uncle Nick, I'll have to go out now. And then perhaps you'll help me—"

"But where are you going?" said Jenny.

"To see Elaine Burdon. I've got a feeling . . . I told you, sir . . . perhaps she'll be willing to talk." The phone rang before he finished what he was saying, and he broke off and eyed it wildly, rather as though he didn't know what it was. After a moment, "All right, I'll get it," he said, and went back to the desk instead of to the door. He put down the white stone on the blotting pad, and reached for the receiver. Both Jenny and Sir Nicholas were watching him, and Nan stared too, but with a feeling she had strayed into a madhouse.

It was only a short conversation, and Antony's part in it almost monosyllabic. At last, "I'll come right away," he said, and rang off. He was halfway to the door when his uncle's voice stopped him.

"Where are you going?"

Antony turned. "I'm sorry, I forgot," he told them. "That was Bernard Shenstone. He says he has something to tell me . . . something he should have told me before . . . something that may help. So perhaps I shall get the proof I need, or perhaps I shall still have to go to Elaine Burdon. But I've got to try everything . . . you do see that, don't you?"

CHAPTER XIV

THIS TIME he was obviously expected when he arrived at the house in Lyall Square. It was much the same hour as his previous visit, and again the big drawing room was filled with sunlight; but the air was warmer today, more oppressive, and no breeze stirred the curtains at the long windows.

Bernard Shenstone was alone when he went in, standing in front of a cabinet at the back of the room. He did not turn immediately when he heard Antony's name, but replaced whatever he was holding gently, and closed the door on it with an exaggeration of care. The parlormaid had retired and the door had shut behind her before he turned.

"Good evening, Mr. Maitland. It was kind of you to come so promptly." He crossed the room, indicated a chair by the window and took one near it, and offered cigarettes. "I owe you an apology," he said.

Antony asked, "Do you?" vaguely. He wasn't sure where this was leading. Shenstone was as elegant as ever, unruffled . . . or was he quite unruffled? Whatever he had to say, he seemed to be finding difficulty with the words.

"I have read the evening papers. After what you told me last night I was surprised—"

"That I was not also under arrest? Some technicality . . .

I imagine they'll get round to it." His tone was sharp, and Shenstone raised a hand, as though in apology.

"This is not a pleasant subject for you, but to some extent I feel myself responsible—" He met Antony's frowning glance, and added with less hesitation, "I warned you, Mr. Maitland, that you should not trust Peter's word. Now I wish I had been more explicit."

Antony thought, sympathy, by heaven! This is what Uncle Nick will have to face . . . afterwards . . . when people try to convey to him, oh, so tactfully, that they don't blame him for what I have done. And it will taste as bitter to him as these words of Shenstone's do to me. He said, aloud, "I'm afraid you'll have to be more explicit now. I don't understand you."

"I'd better start from the beginning. I hope you'll bear in mind it isn't easy for me. There are things I'd rather forget."

"If you're trying to help me," said Antony, "I'm grateful."

"You will remember when Peter started work with Kinlocks, five years ago. That was at my wife's insistence—you remember Pamela, don't you?—because she did not like him to be so much abroad. I realize now that I should have resisted her wishes, but perhaps you will understand that it was not easy to do so. But what I did was against my better judgment, and I have never ceased to regret it."

"He went to work in Birmingham." It was a statement, rather than a question; but some sort of prompting seemed to be needed.

"He had charge of our office there, and I was not at all happy about his management of it."

"It would be better, don't you think," said Antony, "if you said what you mean, right out."

"Very well then. I suspected him of dishonesty. Does that satisfy you, Mr. Maitland?"

"At least, it's plain speaking." He turned his head to look out of the window, but presently, as though his host's stare

205

had a mesmerizing effect, his eyes came back to meet Shenstone's again. "Had you any proof?" he asked.

"I took good care not to obtain proof. This was shortly before Pamela's death, and I felt—I knew it was wrong to suppress the matter, but I didn't want her to know."

"That could have been very unfair to Peter."

"I did not see it that way. After my wife's death I taxed him with the question of these—these defalcations. It was a very distressing business, I believe he was genuinely fond of her, and I . . . all I could think of then was what she would have wanted."

"And he said—?" He was trying to keep his voice even, but the question came out with a startling abruptness.

"He admitted everything . . . everything I had suspected. He said a good deal else, besides," said Shenstone, "that I should very much prefer to forget. I told him I would think things over."

"And then?"

"There was this need for someone in Ceylon. I thought . . . professionally, he's very capable . . . it wouldn't be harming the company. Employed purely as an engineer he would have no opportunity—"

"Of cooking the books? No, I see. I hope you don't think," Antony added, bitterly, "that all this is having an uplifting effect on my morale."

"I think if I can make you realize that your sympathies have led you astray, you might be more willing to be frank with the police," said Shenstone, earnestly. "Would that make no difference to your own position?"

"I don't know." Antony spoke slowly, and just for a moment he felt as if he had glimpsed a flicker of light at the end of a long, dark corridor.

"I am sure . . . but we will discuss that when I have finished my story."

"You had just arranged for Peter to go to Ceylon."

"Yes. As you know, it was only a temporary assignment.

And I am afraid there was considerable disagreement between us as to his future. He felt he should be given a position at least equal to the one he had held in Birmingham. I could not agree to that. That is how matters stood when he came home.

"I was expecting him on Monday. Instead, you came to see me. And you may have wondered why I offered Peter hospitality; or, having done so, why I was so ungracious about it. I wanted to talk to him." He paused, and looked at Maitland with speculation in his eye. "I'm afraid what I am now going to say will shock you."

"Get on with it," said Antony. And again his voice was rough.

"Very well. He arrived here soon after noon on Tuesday, and I arranged to come home from the office. After lunch, we talked. He was angry because the police had been tipped off, he said—those were his words, Mr. Maitland. He said if he could get clear of the smuggling charge he'd throw in his lot with the men who were running the dope business . . . easy money, he said, and the miserable job I was offering would be good enough cover. But first he was going to get even with the man who phoned the police. He said, with any luck you'd get him off, because you were quite convinced he was telling the truth, and everyone knew Sir Nicholas Harding's way with a jury."

"He . . . hadn't lost his memory?" Antony's voice was no more than a whisper.

"Haven't I made that clear? He laughed about that, because he'd never denied his guilt to you, but he said you'd convinced yourself—"

Antony got up, took two steps toward the window, and stood looking out. There was a little table there, with a queerly-wrought bowl of clear green, and the stout, white jade god Shenstone had pointed out to him on his previous visit. After a moment he said, with unnatural steadiness: "I wonder how he persuaded you to keep silent."

"He said he still had a letter that showed I was a party to the things he did at Birmingham. It couldn't have shown precisely that, but a mere admission of knowledge would have been damaging, and the fact that we had been in private correspondence about company matters. Even in my position . . . I'm not invulnerable. But that wasn't all."

"What else?" said Antony. He was still looking out of the window, and spoke without turning his head.

"He said when he 'regained' his memory he'd tell the police he'd found evidence on the *Atlantis* that I was behind the dope smuggling. I laughed at that, at first, because of course there could be no such proof, but then he told me he had that girl—Elaine Burdon—just where he wanted her, she'd back up anything he said. I don't know if that's true; I thought if I got to know her I might be able to tell."

"Was that all the threat he used?"

"He used his own gun to kill Brown, but it was *here*, in a trunk he had stored in the attic. He'll say he didn't remember anything about it . . . and who else but myself could have known where it was?"

"Difficult," said Antony. His tone was flippant, and he was rather pleased with it, in a vague way, because he was feeling cold and sick and quite desperately afraid. He wondered for a moment if he couldn't sidestep what was coming; and he knew as he did so that for him there was one way only . . . the truth must be faced, however bitter, however personally disastrous. He turned from the window and looked down at Bernard Shenstone.

"Why have you told me all this?" he asked. "You couldn't think I'd believe it."

There was a long moment's silence, then Shenstone moved leisurely, and took a cigarette from the box on the table at his elbow. He did not speak until he had used his lighter, and was quite sure the cigarette was burning smoothly. Then, "I flattered myself," he said, "that it was a good story. I only hope the police will prove more credulous." His eyes had again that speculative look, and he sounded genuinely regretful when he added, "It's really a pity. Why didn't you pretend?"

Antony didn't try to answer that; the truth was too difficult. "Would you have believed me?" he asked.

"Yes, I think so. You wouldn't be human if you hadn't had doubts about Peter from time to time."

"Oh, I have," Antony agreed. "But the trouble is, you see, I've also had doubts about you."

The cigarette was going well. Shenstone blew three smoke rings, and watched them drift and dissolve before he looked back at his visitor again. "I must have been very careless," he remarked.

"I had a head start over the police . . . I believed what Peter told me," Antony pointed out.

"That hardly gave you a reason for suspecting me."

"No, but . . . nothing made sense. It wasn't really very difficult to work out the organization behind the smuggling, but only because I accepted Peter's story. And the man on top remained a mystery, and it was in his identity that I had to look for the answers to all the questions that were puzzling me. Why Peter lost his memory? Why Elaine told that preposterous story about being engaged to him? What Wilson was doing in Peter's room the night he was killed. Who phoned the police? Why Peter's death had to be an accident? Why Elaine asked us to Chelsea on Wednesday evening? Why Brown was trying to get in touch with Peter at the Chiltern Hotel? And the rest."

"If you can answer all those questions—"

"I couldn't . . . not till today. But I did begin to think, if you were the man I was looking for it would explain some of them."

"And today?"

"Well, to begin with, the revolver was found—Peter's, with his fingerprints on it. Remember, I was working from the fact of his innocence. Besides, I'd told you last night it was the one thing lacking. You took it away because you didn't want Peter arrested too quickly; you still wanted time to stage that accident. And then, with the police watching so closely, it seemed the opportunity would never come. So you changed your tactics and decided to frame him . . . and make sure the charge stuck."

"You seem to know a great deal, Mr. Maitland." Shenstone's eyes had narrowed; his voice remained smooth as ever, but he looked hard now, and dangerous.

"Quite a lot, really," said Antony. "The other thing that happened today was that I found a 'pebble' that Peter had been carrying about with him all week. That's what my uncle called it, and I'd have thought so too if you hadn't given me so much instruction on the subject last time I was here."

"Where is it?"

"Wouldn't you like to know? Not here," Antony added, hastily. "But I was right, wasn't I, in connecting it with you? And that being the case, it answered a lot of my other questions. If you dropped it at the Chiltern the night Peter arrived there—"

"I have carried it for years." Shenstone didn't seem to be attending. "A ritual disk, the ancient symbol of the Lord on High. Where is it?" he repeated.

"I'm being extremely open with you," said Antony. "Don't you think? But that's something I'm not going to tell you."

"Well . . . no matter." But it was an obvious effort to bring his mind back to their discussion. "You know a great deal," he said again.

"If you spun me this yarn today, I suppose it means Peter is due to regain his memory any time now. But I don't quite see why you bothered to tell me."

"It's a pity I couldn't persuade you. If you turned against Peter, too—"

"Yes, I see. It would help, I suppose."

"Even now . . . I have the greatest respect for your ingenuity, Mr. Maitland, and I am not without imagination.

Between us we could certainly concoct a story which would make your position with the police more satisfactory. It wouldn't even harm Peter . . . he's done for in any case."

"I always thought the devil was a smooth character."

"You won't consider—?"

"No!"

"You may not like the alternative any better," Shenstone pointed out.

"I've been wondering about that. I can't help realizing that the situation is . . . embarrassing."

"Do you really think so?"

"Your word against mine," said Antony, thoughtfully. "As things stand, the police will probably believe you. But if Peter recovers and backs me up . . . what then?"

"My story is designed to discredit his memories in advance. And I think they might still feel some doubt of your honesty, after the events of the last week. However, it's a purely hypothetical case, Mr. Maitland. The police will hear my story, and Peter's in a few days' time. You won't enter into the matter at all."

"I see. And how do you propose to ensure—?" But why ask that? The answer was only too obvious. "The accident you had in mind for Peter, perhaps? It seems a shame to waste your arrangements."

"Not exactly." Another swirl of smoke rings drifted toward the open window. "Peter has always been an enthusiast about cars, you know, and it would have been quite reasonable for him to borrow one of mine. But that wouldn't do for you. Besides, your suicide will tend to confirm the police in their suspicions; and therefore, indirectly, to make them more ready to believe what I have to tell them."

"How very satisfactory. But there are difficulties, you know." All this time Antony had been standing with his back to the window, but now he moved slowly back to the chair he had previously occupied. Shenstone maintained his relaxed pose, but his eyes followed the movement warily.

"Not too many. And don't think I shall feel any compunction. All this"—his gesture seemed to embrace a wider field even than the treasures in the too-perfect room—"all this is too precious to risk because of one man's meddling."

Antony let his eyes wander for a moment. So much that was beautiful, but the house had no heart. "I can see I owe you an apology," he said dryly. And then with sudden anger: "The expense doesn't matter, does it? You don't think about the people who buy the drugs. You don't even have to see them."

Shenstone smiled at him. "No one is forced to become an addict, Mr. Maitland," he pointed out. "You're not a businessman, but this is just a business like any other. Except,"—the smile broadened—"except for the profit. If you can show me any other line with a gross profit of fifteen thousand per cent on turnover, I'll gladly give up the dope."

"Fifteen thousand—"

"We don't sell it undiluted. And, of course, our expenses are heavy. All the same, the net result is not unsatisfactory," said Shenstone, with obvious pleasure.

"Which is why you could afford to be so generous in my case, I suppose." The other man gestured, exactly as though he was waving aside the acknowledgment of a favor.

"That was by way of investment," he said. "And, I think I may say, a wise one. When you are found—"

"If it isn't being too curious, how am I to die?"

"An overdose of morphine seems exactly to meet the case."

"If I hold out for a bowl of hemlock—?"

"No, no, there's a ready-made explanation for the morphine, you know. When the weekend is over you will be found in chambers—" The cigarette was ground out almost viciously in the crystal ashtray at Shenstone's elbow, "—and I don't think anybody will be very much surprised that you took an easy way out of your troubles."

"Well, I don't want to damp your enthusiasm, but you're really going to have to be careful about this," said Antony, earnestly. "Do you usually commit your own murders?"

Shenstone laughed, and sounded really amused. "Do I cook my own dinner?" he said. "Or make my bed, or wash the dishes? But I can do all these things if I have to."

"Very commendable." He paused a moment, and then, "But . . . this time?" he insisted.

"I shall leave the arrangements to the admirable Henri . . . who will be relieved, by the way, to know what is going to happen. Since you obviously recognized him last night he has been anxious about you."

"I'll save my comments for Henri, then."

"Comments?" said Shenstone, coldly.

"The difficulties I spoke of. It's only fair to tell him—" He saw Shenstone compress his lips angrily, and broke off the sentence with a gesture whose vagueness, he hoped, would prove a further annoyance.

"What difficulties, Mr. Maitland?"

"I'll tell Henri. Or shall I just wait, and let him walk into them blindfold?" he wondered.

Shenstone got up, and began to walk across the room to where an ivory telephone—the one discordant note in the room—stood on a table near the door. "If he's arrived," he said, "I'll send for him." He picked up the receiver, and turned to keep an eye on his companion. "But meanwhile, don't think you can start anything and get away with it. Believe me, I have taken my precautions."

Antony had taken the opportunity to move his chair an inch or two nearer the window, and hoped the slight movement hadn't been noticed. Now he thought, resentfully, I'll bet you have; and you haven't even troubled to show your teeth, because you think any opposition from me would be negligible. But he was smiling when Shenstone put down the phone and came toward him again. "Overcautious, surely?" he said, and measured the big man with his eyes. "Believe me," he added, "I know my limitations."

"If you're armed," said Shenstone, "the handicap might

not matter." He paused beside Antony's chair, and put a hand on his shoulder in what might have looked the most friendly of gestures. "Will you accept some advice, Mr. Maitland? You'll find me uncommonly hard to trick. In fact, you'd be very unwise to try to do so." His grip tightened momentarily, relaxed again; he went back to the chair he had previously occupied.

And as he seated himself the door opened and the albino came into the room.

: :   : :

At about the time when Antony and Sir Nicholas were airing their differences, Peter Hammond—uncomfortably lodged in one of the cells at Lennox Street Police Station—had fallen into an uneasy sleep. He didn't even rouse when a kind-hearted constable, who had been brewing up, went along to offer him a mug of tea, though he shifted on the hard bunk, and muttered something.

The constable lingered a moment. A murder charge, he'd heard, and you had to be careful. But there didn't seem to be anything unnatural, except perhaps that the prisoner should be asleep at all. And you never knew how it would take them, thought the constable wisely, as he moved away down the long corridor. Emotion, and all that. Good thing, perhaps, that he could take his rest.

So Peter remained undisturbed, and after a while became quieter, and seemed to be sleeping heavily.

He awoke very suddenly, with all his senses alert, but he didn't immediately open his eyes. His first thought was one of a deep contentment, because today he'd be seeing Nan; but behind that thought there was something unpleasant . . . something he had to do . . .

He had to see Bernard, and he wasn't expecting to enjoy the interview. But first he must talk to Antony . . .

He opened his eyes at that point and found himself staring at a bare wall only a few feet away. After a moment's stupefaction he sat up and looked round blankly. And as he did so he remembered . . . he'd seen Bernard the night before.

But that was at the Chiltern. He'd been surprised when Shenstone phoned, but glad enough to get the meeting over with. Not that the most difficult question had needed asking. . . . "I hear you met a friend of mine on the boat, Peter."

This wasn't his room at the Chiltern. He could remember talking to Bernard . . . he could remember the honeyed tones, and the sudden flame of anger at something he said . . . he could remember . . .

Nothing else.

Calm now, no panic. The first thing was to decide . . . where was he, and how had he got here? There was a barred window, high in the wall . . . a square of blue sky, with a fluffy white cloud in one corner. His watch said six-fifteen; it didn't look quite like morning, out there . . . too mellow. In that case, it wasn't only how he'd got here, but what had happened to the day?

He got up, took two strides to the door, and began to hammer on the smooth surface. There must be someone who could tell him . . .

A voice said, in his ear, "Now, sir. We can't have this, can we?" And he saw for the first time the grille in the door, and outside in the whitewashed corridor a uniformed, but helmetless, policeman.

"Then let me out," he said. "For God's sake, let me out!"

The constable was a middle-aged man with a fatherly manner; at the moment, a father who felt some reproof was merited. "It won't do any good, Mr. Hammond, to carry on like this. You know the position well enough."

"But I don't know. How did I get here? Open that door."

"Well, I wouldn't do that, sir," said the constable, frankly, "not if I was to be paid for it. Not with you looking so wild and talking so strange."

"But you can't just keep me here. You've no right—"

The constable seemed hurt by this suggestion. "You've

seen the warrant, Mr. Hammond. Not one to do things hole-in-the-corner, isn't Inspector Conway."

Peter moved away a little, and put up a hand to clutch his hair. "I've never heard of Inspector Conway," he said. "And what do you mean . . . warrant?"

"So that's it, is it?" The constable came nearer the grille now, and peered through censoriously. "Well, if you're going to tell me you've lost your memory, sir, I'll tell you straight . . . that cock won't fight twice."

"Lost my memory?" Peter seized on the only words in this pronouncement that seemed to make any sense at all. "Of course I haven't lost my memory. It's just . . . well . . . today seems a bit hazy," he admitted.

"You've been asleep," said the constable, relieved, "and woke up muddled. Don't worry, sir, just take it easy and—"

"Are you mad, or am I? If you won't let me out, you'll have to phone Antony Maitland for me." He was feeling in his pocket as he spoke, and after a moment he added, blankly: "My diary's gone."

"Well, it's not a bit of use asking to see this Mr. Maitland," said the constable firmly. "You had all that out in the charge room—I heard you—and the inspector wasn't having any. Besides, you've had your solicitor here, all right and proper, and there's nothing to do but wait for the Magistrates' Court on Monday."

"I haven't got a solicitor . . . and I still don't know who this inspector is, or what I'm charged with . . . and I can't wait till Monday," said Peter despairingly.

"That's something neither one of us can help," said the constable, "things being what they are. And if I weren't a patient man I wouldn't be wasting my time, listening to all this."

"All right then," said Peter, wearily. "Let's start at the beginning. How long have I been here, and what am I charged with?"

"You've been here since this morning, Mr. Hammond. As

216

you very well know," said the constable, beginning to move away down the corridor. "And the charge is murder," he added over his shoulder.

"You've got to listen to me." The note of desperation halted the constable, and he came back slowly. "I don't understand what's happened, but I don't remember anything since last night—"

"Then you'll know about the murder," said the constable triumphantly. "Thursday evening, that was."

"Thursday . . . but . . . we were still at sea . . . and nobody was killed on the ship." He clutched his hair again. "Look here, what date is it?"

"The third of August."

"But . . . I can't have lost a week . . . that's the day I'm going to be married."

"I don't know about that, sir, but it's certainly the third." He eyed the prisoner cautiously, in case he showed signs of becoming violent again. Peter turned away slowly, and sat down on the bunk, and stared blankly at the wall. Presently the constable's footsteps could be heard going away down the long corridor, but he took no notice. After a while his chaotic thoughts came to one focus: I've lost a week, and all that time I don't know what's happened. I don't even know who I'm supposed to have killed. And after a long time he thought, they wouldn't let me see Antony . . . but perhaps I could send a message to Nan . . .

He got up again, and went back to the door.

CHAPTER XV

SEEN IN FULL daylight, the lack of coloring was a good deal more startling than it had been in the subdued light of the restaurant. By contrast, the dark glasses struck a sinister note. But in an ordinary lounge suit—navy blue, and probably off the peg—the albino had shed a good deal of Henri's authority. He looked like any city clerk, and not too sure of himself, either.

He had shut the door carefully behind him, giving it a little pull to make sure the latch had caught. Now he crossed the room and halted about six or eight feet from where the two men were sitting. His head moved slightly, as though he were looking from one to the other of them; and Antony thought how difficult it was to judge a man's feelings when you couldn't see his eyes. From his point of view it was almost as bad as playing the scene blindfold.

Shenstone looked both relaxed and amused. "I don't think you two have met formally," he said. "Henry Birkett, Mr. Maitland; a valued colleague of mine."

"My French friend," said Antony, with a show of enthusiasm. "*Bonsoir, m'sieur l'assassin.*"

A quick frown greeted this. "You had your fun last night," said Henry Birkett. "If you call it fun." His voice was almost

Godley's; perhaps the roughness had become a habit, or perhaps he felt it was called for by the occasion.

"You'd rather we spoke English? Then perhaps 'enter first murderer' would have been a more appropriate greeting," said Antony, still speaking cordially.

There was no doubt now that he'd got a reaction. The dark glasses were turned on Shenstone. "You'd better tell him I haven't murdered anyone."

"My dear Henry, you mustn't let Maitland upset you."

"Well, he knows himself," Birkett insisted. "I couldn't have killed Danny."

"He knows," agreed Shenstone, "but I fear he will not be able to pass on the information. I've decided to take your advice, my dear fellow. Something must be done."

"That's more like it." He turned and seemed to be eyeing Antony appraisingly. "What, for instance?"

"He's going to commit suicide." He held up a hand, as though to forestall comment. "Yes, I know it complicates matters; but it's essential, quite essential." The amused glance turned again on Antony. "You understand, I'm sure."

"What I should like to know," said Antony, "since life's so cheap, why did you drug Peter instead of killing him?"

"It seemed the obvious thing to do at the time," said Shenstone reflectively. "He had to be silenced; but I wanted to leave the way clear for Wilson to collect the heroin. I didn't know he was going to let us down, and a dead body might have upset him." His hand went out to the cigarette box. "But I wonder now if it may not have been a mistake."

"And if your attempts to rectify it were rather clumsy, that was because you were hampered by your relationship, I suppose? Nothing must be done to suggest you were anything but an innocent bystander. I see." Something in his tone seemed to infuriate Birkett, who joined in the conversation again, saying roughly:

"I don't get it. What's the use of all this talk? You can tell me what you want, can't you, in a straightforward way?"

219

"I have already told you." Shenstone's eyes were cold now, his tone commanding. "He can die here, but the details of his suicide are your affair. He is to be found in chambers. You know the address?"

"I know a great deal about Mr. Maitland." The dark glasses gave him an air of malignancy, Antony thought, and spoke quickly into the silence that followed the words.

"The thing is, Henry," he said, earnestly, "you're being had for a sucker."

"What's that? What do you mean?" The man was definitely nervous. He ignored Shenstone's hurried, "I told you not to regard—" and took a step in Antony's direction. "I want to know what you mean," he said again.

"It should be obvious," said Antony, "there are snags in this plan. If you want to be left holding the baby for him . . . go ahead. But let me remind you, he was prepared to double-cross you by letting me live, if he'd been able to convince me that the lies he told about Peter Hammond were true." From the corner of his eye he saw Shenstone sit back again with a resigned air, and quietly take from the drawer of the table beside him a heavy automatic. He held it loosely in his lap, but his eyes were wary.

Birkett had taken no notice of the movement: He was saying vehemently, rather as though he had to convince himself, "He told me you'd not tell the police because they'd never believe you."

"I've already told the police. I told Sergeant Watkins."

"You're lying. He's taken no action."

"I didn't say he believed me. But he's an inquisitive sort of chap, he'll go on wondering . . . why did I tell him that particular lie? . . . and after a while he'll get round to the idea that perhaps there was some truth in it after all."

"With Maitland dead," said Shenstone, "there'll be no one to connect you in any way with what's happened. With his suicide taken as an admission of guilt, any statement he made in the past will be automatically discredited." He must have thought Birkett seemed dissatisfied with this, because he added sharply, "Don't be foolish. You've prospered since I took you up, haven't you, Henry? And hasn't my advice been good?"

"In the past it has."

"And it is now."

"Well, I was thinking. If you go to the police with this statement about Hammond, and if they get to wondering—"

"Leave that to me." He sounded utterly confident, and not, perhaps, without reason. "In any case, there's nothing to connect you—"

"I wonder," said Antony, interrupting him with a diffident air, "whose name Henry used as reference when he got the job at the Night Light."

There was for just a moment a complete and deadly silence. Then Shenstone said softly, "Mr. Maitland. My patience is not inexhaustible." The automatic was steady in his hand now. He smiled as he added: "This time, there is a silencer."

"It would destroy the illusion, wouldn't it, to shoot me now?"

"I should prefer not to, certainly. Don't force my hand."

"I know," said Antony, "while there's life— I suppose you couldn't get hold of a silencer in time to fit Peter's Colt," he added casually, and it took a moment for the substance of the remark to get over to Henry Birkett. When it did he spun round to look at his employer and said accusingly:

"You killed Danny? But you told me . . . I thought it was Hammond."

"The more fool you," said Antony. Shenstone's eyes rested on him for a moment, coldly reflective; then he turned back to Birkett again.

"A man who loses control of his emotions is dangerous, and Danny bungled badly in handling Wilson. As you did, Henry; but your error was not so fundamental."

"I did what seemed best," said Birkett, sulkily, "to cover up—"

"You should have stuck to your orders." He spoke sharply, in complete command of himself and the situation. "But if you obey me now, no harm will be done. I warned you about Maitland, didn't I? He has a viper's tongue."

Again there was a silence. "Very well," Birkett said at last. He seemed to have put his mannerisms aside.

"Have you the morphine?"

"I went down to Purley this morning." This was evidently a satisfactory answer, as Shenstone nodded approvingly.

"Between us," he said, "there should be no difficulty." His eyes went back, appraisingly, to Antony. "And once it is dark—"

Like a blasted undertaker, measuring me for my coffin, thought Antony savagely. "You haven't forgotten the police have a tail on me?" he asked. "He'll certainly wonder what's happened if he doesn't see me leave on my own two feet." Disconcertingly, Shenstone laughed.

"Not so clever, Mr. Maitland," he said. "I'm afraid he lost you on the way here. His attention was diverted."

"I . . . see." That was a blow, and no mistake; and—what was worse—it would strengthen Henry's confidence in his principal. "But you telephoned me," he said; and his tone did not reflect his sudden hopelessness. "I'm known to be here."

"That doesn't matter, so long as there is no one to see when, or how, you leave. In fact, it is an advantage . . . what I had to tell you could well have been the cause of your despair."

"And the—ritual disk, did you say? The chambermaid at the Chiltern saw it."

"I gave it to Peter years ago."

"Weren't you known to carry it?"

"There's a similar one in my collection, though not so old; and none of my friends are sufficiently knowledgeable to tell the difference."

"But you won't risk being seen anywhere near the Temple," said Antony. "So who's to help Henry with that part of the plan?"

"That need not concern you."

"But it concerns Henry . . . doesn't it?"

Birkett said slowly, "I could get hold of Patrick, I suppose. Or perhaps—"

"And when you've got me there, and are busy arranging the details—it'll take time to make it look good, remember, they're always suspicious when there isn't a suicide note—while you're there who's to say there won't be another telephone call to the police."

"But . . . I—"

"I don't know who made the previous calls—about Peter Hammond—but I'm pretty sure the first, at least, was *his* idea," said Antony, jerking his head in Shenstone's direction. "And if he thinks you're getting emotional, Henry . . . like Danny-boy . . . who's to say the next call may not be about you."

"I've told you, Henry," said Shenstone angrily, "don't listen to him." His attention was divided, but there was no doubt where the gun was pointing.

"He can't help listening to me," Antony pointed out. "It's his neck he's risking. Conspiracy to murder," he added, savoring the phrase, "is a much more serious charge even than distributing drugs."

"That's right." Birkett sounded nervous still, but no longer undecided. "I'll give you the stuff, and then I'm going. And I'm getting out while I can."

"But there's no reason—"

"He knows too much. And what he knows . . . do you think no one else can guess?"

"He's bluffing. He's got no proof. And if he had," said Shenstone viciously, "let it die with him."

"There's another weak link," said Antony, clearly, into the

silence that followed this remark. "What about Elaine?"

"Elaine," said Shenstone, "will do exactly as I tell her." And, surprisingly, he laughed.

"I wouldn't be too sure af that. You saw her last night," he appealed to Henry. "What did you think?"

The sullen look had settled about Birkett's mouth again; it was only the tinted glasses, Antony thought, that kept his expression enigmatic. He was wavering still, the instinct to obey a man so forceful as Shenstone must be strong, especially as he had once given him allegiance. He said, as though unwillingly, "I thought she looked scared."

"She was," said Shenstone. "Don't worry about Elaine."

"What made her do it?" said Antony. "Did she fall for Peter? Or was she unsure of you?" Just for a moment he thought the gleam in Shenstone's eye was one of respect.

"If by 'it' you mean that ridiculous tale of being engaged to him, she had some idea, I think, of making me jealous." He glanced briefly at Henry, assessing his reaction to the topic. "She won't do it again," he added, positively.

Antony glanced at Birkett, and then back at the other man again, and let a smile show briefly and then vanish. "I do so admire," he said ridiculously, "a man who understands women." And saw, with a stab of exultation, the anger flare in Shenstone's eyes.

"What do you mean?" he demanded, harshly. And he came to his feet as he spoke.

"That she resents you now, as much as she fears you," said Antony steadily. "You think she loves you? Don't count on it, that's all."

"What do you know of her?" The words were almost a snarl.

"I saw her face, last night." The smile had disappeared now, he was completely serious. "I've seen that look before, Shenstone—during the war, in occupied France—on the face of a young girl who'd just had her first taste of Party 'discipline,' before they got really rough. And there was fear there, all right . . . do you like your women afraid?"

"I've never found it harm a relationship."

"You didn't let me finish. There was hatred, too," said Antony. "You played that hand very badly . . . don't you think?"

The albino had been listening to this exchange, pulling at his lower lip with a hand that was not quite steady. Now he made no announcement of his intention, but turned quietly and started toward the door. Antony did not speak until he had almost reached it, then he said helpfully, with a complete change of tone, "If you're going, don't forget to leave the morphine." Much later, it struck him as amusing that neither of his hearers questioned his motives in giving the reminder.

Henry Birkett swung round irresolutely, and his hand went to his jacket pocket. At the same time Shenstone took three or four paces toward him. I could tackle him now, thought Antony, if things were different. He got up silently, and his hand went out to the table by the window and closed around the little jade god . . . Shou-lao, the patron of long life.

Shenstone said curtly: "I've no time to waste. Are you quite determined?"

"Yes, I am." The words came in a gasp. "You can have the morphine, but I'm getting out." Afterward Antony wondered whether Birkett had even seen the automatic at all; certainly now he seemed unconscious of it, and the look on his face when the shot hit him was almost pure astonishment. Shenstone caught him as he fell and held him with one arm while he looked round coolly, grabbed a cushion from a nearby chair, and lowered Henry onto it so that it was under the wound. Antony spared a moment's admiration for the cool foresight that could think of bloodstains at a time like this; or was it perhaps not foresight, but an almost maniacal pride in his possessions? A cushion was expendable, but the rug was probably priceless, and if once the parquet got soaked the stain would be difficult to move.

All this had been done very silently, the sound of the silenced automatic being certainly unremarkable against the murmur of traffic. And except for a moment just before the shot was fired, Antony knew himself to have been continually under observation. He stood very still, with his left hand behind him, and hoped the pose looked natural.

Shenstone went crabwise to the door, felt for the key and turned it. Then he went back to the man he had shot, and knelt beside him. Eyes and gun were steadily on his remaining companion; his left hand fumbled at Birkett's jacket.

"Is he dead?" said Antony; and was glad to hear that his voice betrayed neither excitement nor fear.

"I wasn't feeling for a pulse," said Shenstone dryly. "If he isn't now, I imagine it's only a matter of minutes. And on second thoughts," he added, "let the morphine stay where it is." He came to his feet as he spoke. "I think we won't delay any longer, Mr. Maitland. You've had your fun."

But he will delay a little, thought Antony. He's got me where he wants me, and there's that streak of sadism to make him enjoy playing cat and mouse. If I show my fear now, will he be satisfied and end it; or will it encourage him to prolong the business?

"To set your mind at rest, Mr. Maitland, I have a perfectly good story for the police."

"One which will s-save you d-disposing of the b-bodies," said Antony. He thought it sounded convincing . . . a desperate attempt to keep up his previous tone.

"Oh, yes. I shall call the police," said Shenstone with enjoyment, "after you are dead. In the course of our talk, you see, you told me certain things about Henry which disturbed me; so I sent for him to give him the chance to deny them. Instead, he went berserk, and shot you. In the ensuing struggle, I shot him accidentally. Admirable, don't you think?"

"Except for one thing. The servants know he was already here to see you—"

"But of course. He was my protégé, after all; as you pointed out yourself, I got him his job at the Night Light. What I didn't know, of course," said Shenstone, with relish, "was that he was the head of this dope racket that Peter has got himself mixed up in. And I'm very much afraid he must have met Peter here just before he went to Ceylon, and thought him a likely prospect as a helper. I'm sorry about that, naturally. Terribly sorry."

"I can just hear you," said Antony, with truth. "And as a m-matter of academic interest," he added, "where did you learn your marksmanship?" He tried to make it sound like a question asked in a hopeless attempt to delay matters.

But Shenstone was inclined to be talkative now. "In the Army," he said. "Where else? But it wasn't really a difficult shot the other evening, you know. From where I stood the light was quite adequate, and that revolver of Peter's is surprisingly accurate. Far more so than this automatic; but in case you're worried," he added, "I don't think I could miss, at this range." And—at last—he stepped across the body . . . a little nearer the man who stood with his back to the window . . .

Antony brought his hand from behind him, and took his eyes from Shenstone's face for a moment to look down at what he held. Shou-lao seemed to leer up at him malevolently. "It's ironical," he said, raising his eyes to meet Shenstone's again. "The god of longevity, you told me . . . didn't you? But I'm afraid he may not survive my death, at least, not quite intact. I can't help but drop him." There was no rug where he was standing, only a shining expanse of polished wood.

"Put it down!" There was panic in the tone. He wasn't stopping to think of the hardness of jade, or of anything but the threat to something he loved.

Antony's hand went back. "Catch!" he said, and tossed the idol straight at his enemy's face. And incredibly . . . beyond his wildest expectations . . . Shenstone let go of the automatic and clutched at it with both hands, with clumsy eagerness. And as he did so Antony threw himself forward; his left shoulder caught the big man just below the knees, so that he lost his balance and fell heavily. With his right hand he grabbed for the gun, and hardly noticed the pain that shot through his arm as the movement wrenched his shoulder again.

The jade god rolled away unharmed across the thick carpet.

By the time Bernard Shenstone had scrambled to his feet again, Antony had backed away toward the window and was leaning, a little out of breath, against one of the big armchairs. "I was always expecting our departed friend to say 'Reach,'" he remarked. "Or should it be 'reach for the stars'? In any case—" He gestured slightly with the heavy gun, which he had shifted to his left hand, and added, almost apologetically, "It's only a suggestion. I can shoot if you'd rather. I'm not very sure of my aim, but I expect I can hit you somewhere."

Shenstone hesitated. He, too, was breathing heavily, and his expression was murderous. But after a moment he raised his hands reluctantly. "Silly, isn't it?" said Antony. "But I don't see what else we can do."

"Nor I. Would you say . . . stalemate?" He was recovering his poise rapidly. "You've turned the tables, for the moment. But where do you go from here?"

"Will you call the police, or shall I?"

Shenstone took his time to review the idea. "I shall be glad to," he said at last, "but are you sure—?"

"Quite sure." There was a grim look about Antony's mouth, but it was impossible to tell the effort it cost him to keep his voice steady. At the moment he resented more than anything else Shenstone's easy resumption of calmness. "Don't say anything else," he warned.

"I shall only speak to the maid. If I say there has been an accident—?"

"That'll do." His instructions were obeyed to the letter; Shenstone put down the phone again and turned to survey the room.

"You've no feeling for beauty, Mr. Maitland. But Shou-lao seems to have survived your rough treatment. May I—?"

"Stay where you are!"

"But surely . . . when the police are on their way. I would so much prefer them to find you armed, rather than me."

"I'd rather they found me alive," said Antony bluntly.

"It's too late to reconsider now, but do you think you were wise to let me call them? All this will be a little difficult to explain, don't you think?" There was no doubt about it now, he was amused by the situation. "You'll tell them the truth, I suppose. How far has that got you this last week?"

"Not so far," said Antony. He was coldly conscious already of the difficulties ahead. Shenstone had intended in any case to talk to the police, and his story was easily adaptable to the new circumstances. He would certainly deny shooting Birkett . . .

"Your word against mine, Mr. Maitland. Which of us do you think they'll believe?"

"You're forgetting one thing." A moment ago it had been easier to talk than to be silent; now each word cost him an effort.

"I don't think so," said Shenstone, frowning. "What do you mean?"

"Your treatment of Elaine. She can blow the whole thing wide open, if she wants to. And I'm betting she will."

"Don't count on it," said Bernard Shenstone. "We're agreed, aren't we, that the police's first instinct will be to believe me, and to think you're lying. Once the preliminary inquisition is over, and I am about again . . . I don't think I have anything more to fear from Elaine. You may have been right in your rather dramatic recital of her feelings . . . she may hate me now. But she's certainly afraid of me."

There was no more talk between them until they heard footsteps on the stairs, and Shenstone moved across to unlock the door. And there was one thing he had been right about . . . Henry Birkett was dead.

CHAPTER XVI

THE HOURS which followed were not pleasant ones. They finished up in Inspector Conway's office at New Scotland Yard —more accurately, it was the superintendent's, but he was at home in bed—and Sir Nicholas said later that when he arrived there at about ten o'clock there were twenty-one people in the room, all talking at once. But the whole affair offended him, so perhaps he may be forgiven some small exaggeration.

Antony's own impressions were too confused to be useful. Shenstone was bland again, and affable with the police, and showed just the right amount of angry impatience when it seemed the accusations being levied against him were becoming too wild to be amusing. His solicitor was also in attendance, a dignified man who appeared quite out of his depth. Inspector Conway was tired, and thoroughly confused by the new developments, and his comments became steadily more acid as the hours wore on. Sir Nicholas was on his dignity; Geoffrey Horton scared out of his wits, and silent because of an uncomfortable feeling that if he said anything at all it would be the wrong thing; and matters were further complicated by the arrival of a small, thin, gray-haired man—known to Conway, but otherwise never properly identified—who seemed worried about Peter Hammond and kept talking about the trouble he was causing at the police station and the wildness of his attitude. "If he's got his memory back, he ought to be here," said Antony; and got well snubbed for his pains. Of all this, Sergeant Watkins was a silent and apparently appreciative observer.

The one thing that Antony held on to was that as long as they were all there Shenstone couldn't be getting away with anything . . . faking evidence, or manufacturing it anew, or scaring Elaine Burdon . . . or leaving suddenly for the other side of the world. It was touch and go once or twice, he realized, and heard his arguments becoming angrier and more desperate. And on one such occasion Sir Nicholas got up quietly, spoke to Sergeant Watkins who was sitting near the door, and went away. Antony, hurt and bewildered by this desertion, but with his mind doggedly fixed on the points at issue, did not realize at the time that the sergeant had gone, too.

Half an hour later, Conway was no nearer to believing him, and he didn't think he could stall any longer. Shenstone looked serious, as no doubt befitted the occasion; but he was winning all along the line . . . as he had foretold. Even the cushion under the dead man's chest had been turned to good account. "I have observed on several occasions, Inspector, that Mr. Maitland has rather an exaggerated sense of humor." In marshaling his arguments, Antony had almost forgotten his own predicament, but it came back to him with sickening clarity now. Conway couldn't be in any doubt that one of them had murdered the albino, and if he decided to let Shentone go . . .

And then Sergeant Watkins came back, sidling into the room with an apologetic, "don't-let-me-interrupt-you" air, which he immediately belied by coughing loudly until Inspector Conway broke off what he was saying and looked at him with a cold, inquiring eye.

"If you'll excuse me, sir, there's a young lady in the next room wishes to make a statement." He looked round in a pleased way, rather like a conjurer who hadn't expected his trick to come off, and added: "It's Miss Burdon, sir. Miss Elaine Burdon."

Conway got up and went out without a word. Watkins turned to Antony, and his brown eyes were amused and friendly. "You'd be more comfortable in another room, Mr. Maitland," he suggested. "You and your friend. And if you'll wait here, Mr. Shenstone—" Looking back from the doorway, Antony saw for the first time a shade of uncertainty in Bernard Shenstone's face.

Once in the corridor, with Horton a pace or two behind, he turned eagerly to the detective. "What's been happening? How did you persuade her—?"

"Sir Nicholas asked me to tell you he'd gone straight home. He thought Mrs. Maitland might be worried."

"You've been to Chelsea? And he went with you?"

"Well, perhaps it's better to say, I went with him. A clear-thinking gentleman," said Watkins admiringly. "Knows his own mind. Now if you'll wait in here, Mr. Maitland—" And ignoring Antony's protests, he went back down the corridor.

The wait was a long one, long enough to sap Antony's initial optimism and set him thinking of all the things that could have gone wrong. But at last Watkins came back, and this time Conway was with him.

He knew with the inspector's first words that things were working out. "I'm sorry you've been kept so long, Mr. Maitland. They were typing your statement. Now if you'll sign it, we needn't keep you any longer tonight."

"Is that all?" said Antony, with dismay in his voice. And then, giving up the pretense that he wasn't interested, "Don't keep me in suspense, Inspector. What did Elaine Burdon say?"

Conway bristled. "I'm afraid—" he began indignantly; but Watkins was answering for him.

"I think you might say she 'came clean,' Mr. Maitland.

233

And her story bears out what you've been telling us all this time. Though I won't say there won't be a good deal of clearing up still to be done. And explaining." He looked at the inspector, who set his lips, and said unwillingly:

"We have made an arrest."

"Shenstone? On what charge?"

"The murder of Henry Birkett. Other charges may be formulated, but—"

"That should hold him," Antony agreed. "And what about Peter?"

"The charges against him will be withdrawn. But for to-night . . . a doctor has seen him, and I understand he is asleep."

"Has he got his memory back?"

"There seems no doubt of it."

"But," said Watkins, "now he's forgotten everything that happened during the last week."

"Oh, lord. Well, you'll take care of him tomorrow, Geoffrey." He went over to the table, and sat down with the long sheets of the statement in front of him, and stared at them for a long time.

After a while Inspector Conway, looking anything but patient, took a chair opposite him and settled himself to wait.

:   :   :   :

"So that's that," said Sir Nicholas, two days later. "No more formalities until the trial, but that will be a tiresome business, I'm afraid." He deposited an inch of cigar ash carefully, and looked round at his audience as though inviting questions.

Jenny had her own favorite corner of the sofa, with the coffee table beside her. The other end was shared quite comfortably by Nan and Peter; they were sitting very close together, and his arm was round her shoulders. Across the hearth from his uncle, Antony was reclining very much at ease, but now he pushed himself into a more upright position and said doubtfully, "If Elaine Burdon comes up to proof."

"I gather from Forrester they're not in much doubt of

that," Sir Nicholas told him. "But they'll still need a good deal from you. And the defense—"

Antony grinned at him. "If Shenstone gets a mouthpiece as fluent as himself," he said, "we should see some fun. I'm sorry, sir," he added, as Sir Nicholas scowled at him, "I should have said 'counsel.'"

"You should, indeed."

"It's mixing with all these bad characters," said Antony apologetically. "But the police have at least six weeks to get the background straightened out; that ought to make everything plain sailing."

"I don't understand," said Peter. "They've charged Bernard with murder—"

"With killing Henry Birkett . . . Godley to you," Antony agreed.

"Yes, well, that's quite clear, isn't it? Do they need bring in the dope ring at all?"

"Two men were present when he was killed," said Sir Nicholas. He looked across at his nephew. "It is necessary to show the jury some reason for believing one of them, rather than the other."

"Well, Elaine won't go back on what she's said," Jenny told him. "I mean, she'd be afraid to, in case they let him go."

"They couldn't do that, could they?" said Nan. "I'd hate to think—"

"'They' could do anything," said Sir Nicholas, dampeningly. He seemed to have taken a fancy to Nan, and was showing this by treating her as one of the family. "But in this case," he added, spoiling his own effect, "they're not very likely to acquit."

Nan smiled at him. "I'm not really vindictive, but after what he did to Peter . . . and I keep thinking—" She broke off, looking dismayed.

Peter shook her gently. "What do you keep thinking, Nan?" and after a moment she went on, reluctantly:

"I didn't mean to say it . . . about Pamela."

"I've been thinking about her, too," said Peter. And stopped, because there didn't seem to be anything else to say. Antony was thinking, a collector's item . . . was any woman more than that to him? And if her beauty faded . . .

"What did Dr. Macintyre tell you today, Peter?" he asked.

"He talked about the stress of modern conditions, and my perfectly normal reactions, and told me I should lead a quiet life," said Peter. "I didn't tell him there was no hope of that, I was going to be married. Oh, and he cursed you pretty freely, Antony. Said your imagination would lead you into trouble, if you didn't watch out."

Sir Nicholas laughed at that, and put down his cigar the better to enjoy his amusement. Jenny said indignantly, "But he was right, it wasn't just imagination. Was it?" she appealed to her husband.

"Shenstone admitted it, and Elaine told us a little more about it," said Antony. "The police have seized masses of stuff; it's too early yet to know how the laboratory tests will go."

"From Lyall Square?"

"Good lord, no. Shenstone was too careful for that. There was a house at Purley, and a chap who lived there who was formerly a doctor."

"You mean, he'd been struck off the register?"

"Yes. Something about drugs, and one of his patients . . . a woman. As far as I can make out now his only duty as far as the gang were concerned was to water down the dope before distribution—"

"That's not accurate," said Sir Nicholas.

"No, but it doesn't matter, sir. You know what I mean."

"A credit to our intelligence, then; not to your lucidity."

"Well, he hadn't much to do, anyway, so he was bored," said Antony. "And he saw that letter in *The Scalpel* and thought it would be amusing to do some experiments of his own, and after a bit he came up with something that worked.

Besides experiments he actually tried it out on the woman who came in to do his cleaning, and she lost her memory all right, but no one suspected anything unnatural about it. Why should they?"

"I don't know," said Jenny, catching his eye and—for some reason—sounding guilty.

"The effect lasted ten days, then she was all right again. After that he sent the stuff to some of his 'colleagues' abroad for testing, and the results seem to have been pretty standard. I expect Shenstone accepted a sample as a joke, Elaine said he seemed amused when he told her about it a year or so ago. Then he saw a use for it."

"But . . . anything might have happened," Nan protested. "How could he be sure—?"

"If you accept the fact that he wanted to kill me eventually," said Peter, "some rather indiscriminate drugging is perhaps not so important. Though I wouldn't want to go through the waking-up process again," he added. "Not for anything."

Sir Nicholas was looking at him reflectively, and with carefully concealed sympathy. "This is an incredibly confused conversation. You had better begin at the beginning," he suggested. "I imagine Hammond would be glad to know something more of the events of the last week."

"Yes, I would. It's the queerest thing, not being able to remember. And I've heard so much during the last two days, but nothing like a connected account."

"You're unlikely to get that now," said Sir Nicholas unkindly. "But Antony will do his best."

"My poor best," said Antony. "But first you should tell us, Peter, the part you remember. Start on the *Atlantis*."

"Well . . . I suppose . . . it started with Elaine. She spilled the contents of her bag one day, and when I was helping her pick them up . . . there was a photograph of Bernard. I wasn't particularly surprised, in one way; we're all so used to saying 'it's a small world.' But I was rather hurt, I suppose; after all, it isn't much more than a year since Pamela died. And so I didn't say anything. But I kept on thinking about it."

"Did she know you'd seen the picture?"

"Not then. Later . . . but I'll tell you. The next thing was she seemed to have decided to—to concentrate on me. I wasn't particularly surprised—"

"The vanity of men," said Nan; and exchanged a sympathetic glance with Jenny.

"—because I know there's no accounting for tastes," said Peter, declining to be diverted. "But now I realize, of course, that it must have been after she found out I was going to stay at the Chiltern. And then, two nights out of Southampton, I went to my cabin one night, and there she was. And I thought . . . well—"

"Well!" said Nan. And spoiled the effect by giggling. Sir Nicholas gave her a cold look; almost as cold as he would have given to one of his own family, in similar circumstances.

"I soon saw I was wrong," said Peter, "because I could tell she was startled. And after she'd gone I sat down to think it out."

"Didn't smuggling occur to you?"

"Of course it did. But I got it into my head she was going to ask me to take something through Customs for her, and then thought better of it. She'd talked a bit about her travels, you see, so it seemed possible she made a habit of bringing stuff in; perfume, or jewelry . . . I never thought of drugs. But when I got to that point I began to wonder about her association with Bernard."

"I don't quite see—"

"I wasn't thinking he might be mixed up in anything criminal. Only that if she was, he might be able to stop her. All next day, I couldn't get it out of my head, so after dinner I took her for a stroll, and asked her what the hell?"

"What did she say?"

"She denied everything, and stuck to it. And she tried to make me believe I'd been right . . . in what I first thought, you know. I got a bit fed up at that point, and told her I'd seen Bernard's photograph, and that really upset her. So I said, all right, and I was sorry; and I went back to the cabin to think. Because it was quite obvious something was very wrong; I mean, there was no reason she shouldn't know him. And that's when I wrote your name down, Antony . . . a sort of doodling, really. I thought you might be able to suggest some answers to the questions that were troubling me."

"I'd have told you, I expect, you were making a fuss over nothing."

"Not if I'd been able to convey Elaine's attitude to you. It was quite obvious she was up to something; and equally obvious Bernard was mixed up in it, or why did she get the jitters when I mentioned his name? I made up my mind to ask him, but I meant to talk to you first."

"You got to the Chiltern at eight o'clock?"

"That's right, but it was after dinner he phoned me. Said he was going out of town for the weekend, and would like a word with me first. So I told him my room number, and he came round."

"And then—?"

"He talked about Elaine . . . she'd phoned him from Southampton. He told me how lonely he was, and wasn't it natural he should seek companionship. And all the time he was watching me, weighing me up. And I got more and more certain . . . I don't know why—"

"Let's put it down to your subconscious, and leave it at that," Antony suggested.

"Well, whatever it was, I was sure now there was something really wrong. And like a fool I blurted out everything I'd been thinking since the night Elaine came to my cabin. I can remember seeing a look of anger on his face, and knowing

I was right. And then he was coming toward me, and he was smiling. And the next thing was Saturday, at the police station."

Sir Nicholas looked at his nephew. "That seems to be your cue," he said.

"Yes, I suppose so. You may or may not have gathered, Peter, what was supposed to happen to the drugs after you brought them safely through Customs."

"I think I've got that clear."

"Right, then. But this time Wilson had been on a jag, and just didn't report for duty. No one realized this straight away, least of all Shenstone, who had no direct contact with him. Dooley rang up his home on Saturday morning—I think—but Wilson wouldn't come to the phone; so he hung round the hotel trying to meet him, and was noticed by the police—who, of course, were pursuing their inquiries about Peter. If Shenstone had known about Wilson's defection, he might have acted differently; but, in any case, he would probably have preferred to gain time to stage a convincing accident, which would have left no awkward questions for him to answer."

"He knew Peter's memory would come back," said Nan.

"Yes, I'll tell you about that in a minute. Elaine phoned him from Southampton, in a panic about Peter's questions. And at all costs, if she was going to be suspected of being connected with the smugglers, there must be nothing to show he even knew her. So Peter had to be silenced. I imagine he gave you an injection, and then put you to bed."

"I don't remember at all. But it would account—wouldn't it?—for the way I felt when I woke up."

"It would. And it would also account for his losing that jade disk . . . if there was a bit of a struggle, I mean. And that's important, because it gave me the answer to quite a few questions, where before I was just feeling my way."

"I don't see how you connected it with Shenstone," said Sir Nicholas.

"No, but you hadn't listened to his lecture on the difference between nephrite and jadeite, and so on. Besides, I'd noticed Peter once or twice during the week put his hand in his pocket as if he were playing with his loose coins. And the gesture seemed both familiar and unfamiliar. I'd seen Shenstone do the same thing, you see; only he took his hand out of his pocket straight away, because the disk wasn't there any more. But the gesture was an unfamiliar one for Peter to make."

"That's all very well, but what did it *tell* you?" said Jenny.

Antony felt in his pocket and produced an envelope which had been cut round the edges, and flattened it out and scowled at it. "I made some notes," he said helplessly. "But they're not really legible. I think I can explain it as I go on, though."

"Well, you'd got to where Wilson didn't do his part; but who phoned the police to frame Peter, and why?" asked Jenny.

"This bit's guesswork—"

"*Only* this bit?" inquired Sir Nicholas, skeptically.

"The other's based on Elaine's statement, sir. And what I learned when I talked to Shenstone."

"Well, let us know what you guessed about Shenstone's motives, if that's the best you can do."

"Look at it from his point of view. Peter has no memory, and therefore no suspicions; but it's only a matter of time before he finds the package of heroin, and what is he going to do then? If he's in touch with someone—a doctor, perhaps —who advises him to go to the police, what will their inquiries unearth? You see, there'd be quite a difference from their point of view between a man already under treatment for amnesia, going to them voluntarily; and the same chap caught with the stuff in his possession, with no explanation to offer and an improbable story of having lost his memory."

"You may be right," said Sir Nicholas cautiously.

"I *am* right." Antony was more positive now. "I don't say Shenstone was correct in his thinking, but he did phone the police, and that's the most likely line of reasoning that would have made him do so. After that, Peter, you were arrested, and released on bail after the Magistrates' Court hearing. And that took us to Monday, and in the afternoon I went to see Shenstone at his office. I was a little worried by the hints he dropped that this wasn't the first thing he'd heard of to your discredit; but in the circumstances, that might have been natural enough. And that night you went back to the hotel, after dining with me, and found Wilson's body in your bathroom."

Antony paused, and looked at his uncle. "I'm going back to Elaine's statement, sir. Wilson was asking for a pay-off, in spite of having failed to complete his assignment, and Dannyboy was sent to reason with him. Bear in mind, in all these transactions, Godley was the go-between, the only one—besides Elaine—who knew Shenstone."

"But why should Wilson and Brown meet in Peter's bedroom?" Nan wanted to know.

"I'm sorry, I'm getting out of order. Shenstone had lost his precious jade disk, and naturally wanted it back. He passed the word to Godley, and Godley told Wilson to have a look round at the hotel. You told me, Peter—at least, you told the police—that he'd come to your room that afternoon, after you were released, but you thought he was just curious. So that's why he fixed that as a meeting place, because if he could find the thing he could give it straight away to Brown. What I don't know—and can't even guess at, Uncle Nick—is what they quarreled about; but Brown had a reputation for violence—which seems to have been just too bad for Wilson.

"At this stage, Shenstone knew nothing of what had happened. It was Godley who decided he'd be pleased if they framed Peter again, so this time he phoned the police. Unfortunately, Peter, you didn't find the body straight away, and then you decided to do nothing about it until I got to the hotel."

"I seem to have been a trial to you," said Peter, thoughtfully.

"You were, believe me. The only satisfactory thing about that situation is that it seems to have infuriated Shenstone. You see, once you were arrested for murder there'd be no bail, and no opportunity for the accident he'd been contemplating. Anyway, he stormed at Godley, and Godley—perhaps not unjustly—put the blame on Danny-boy; and I suppose that was when Shenstone decided the latter was expendable. But he still had a use for him—to make a contribution to my bank balance, for instance."

"Why did he do that?" said Nan.

"He said it was 'insurance.' He didn't think the police would find out unless they were tipped off, and it could certainly have been used to embarrass me if I seemed to be finding out too much. Now, there's something else I'm not explaining very clearly . . . Shenstone had two lines in looking for his lost disk: he invited Peter to stay with him, in case it was among his luggage; and he asked Godley to institute inquiries, too. That's why Danny-boy was asking for Peter at the hotel as late as Wednesday . . . he didn't know he'd moved. It also explains why Shenstone allowed Elaine to invite us to Chelsea on Wednesday, so he'd have a chance to search Peter's luggage. And by the time he'd done that he decided he must be carrying it on him, and that's partly why Thursday's episode at Putney was arranged just the way it was."

"You're getting ahead of your story," Sir Nicholas pointed out.

"Yes, we'd got to Tuesday, hadn't we? I went to find Nan, and Peter went to Lyall Square, and—"

"That's the biggest puzzle of all," said Peter. "Nan told me what happened, but all that about being engaged to Elaine . . . it just wasn't true."

"At this point we have to consider the relationship between

her and Shenstone," Antony told him. "I think it's been going on a long time. All that talk about 'her trustee' . . . she'd been getting money from somewhere."

"It's perfectly clear," said Jenny. "When Pamela died she thought he'd marry her. But if he kept putting her off—"

"You really must control your witness, Mr. Maitland," said Sir Nicholas, at his most repressive.

"My guess is just as good as his," said Jenny, with spirit. "Better, in this case."

"It's quite true," said Antony, "that she thought it would make him jealous. It also gave her a good excuse to go round to Lyall Square, pretending it was to see Peter, though Shenstone had told her they'd better not see each other for a while."

"Of course, said Jenny irrepressibly. "I quite understand that bit."

"I'm not quite sure I know what you mean." Antony sounded doubtful. "And if I do, I'm not sure I like it."

"Well, never mind. You were going to tell us about going to Lyall Square with Nan."

"That was the day I really began to wonder about Shenstone. That house . . . was it always like that, Peter?"

"If you mean, was he always a perfectionist . . . yes, he was. He kept on adding to the collection, of course. But you can't suspect a man of trading in drugs just because you don't like the way he lives," Peter pointed out.

"I can," said Antony, "if he spends as much as he must have done on some of those jade figures. But at that stage it was just a vague feeling, because for all I knew he might have had private means. And I was rather inclined to think he'd have been more careful not to arouse suspicion. It was very noticeable that the other people I suspected of being members of the gang took good care not to appear too affluent."

"I think his collection was a genuine passion. I don't think he could help himself," said Peter.

"I expect that's how the whole thing started. That's Tuesday, and nothing else happened until we went to Chelsea on Wednesday evening, and somebody swiped an Aston Martin and tried to run us down. My guess would be Danny-boy, but it might easily have been some member of the gang we never heard of. Then, of course, I imagined the attempt must have been arranged by one of the people we'd seen that evening; I'd already decided that Peter had been drugged and framed because he'd seen something on board the *Atlantis* that he mustn't be allowed to repeat, and I thought that might mean the Lord High Smuggler himself had been on board. I rather favored Miller, because he seemed on more familiar terms with Elaine; and the only thing that was obvious about the whole affair was that she had planted the heroin. Oh, and that Dooley was involved in some way; because he was the first person I went to see, and immediately afterwards I had that phone call from Godley."

"Which you never told me about," Jenny remarked, accusingly.

"No, well, I'd been to see Shenstone before, but that was as Peter's friend, not as an investigator. That brings us to Thursday, doesn't it? Shenstone's idea was to arrange a car accident for Peter, to which end Godley was to kidnap him. And at the same time, Shenstone thought it would be a good opportunity to get rid of Brown."

"I don't believe," said Sir Nicholas, looking at the ceiling, "that Miss Burdon told you that."

"No, sir; this part is based on what Shenstone told me. He never thought, you see, that Peter'd be fool enough to contemplate telling the police what Godley had said to him; or even that he'd tell me. The idea was, he'd be so scared he'd ditch his shadow before he got to the meeting place; whereas, actually, Peter, I don't believe you ever knew the police were keeping tabs on you."

"I don't remember. But it's not the sort of thing that would occur to one."

"Isn't it?" Antony looked at him for a moment, and then

grinned. "Be that as it may, Shenstone came up the lane cautiously, keeping to the trees, and when he heard voices he thought Godley was talking to Peter; he also assumed that after he'd shot Brown, Godley would carry on with his part of the plan and take Peter away with him. Well, he might have done, of course, if it had been Peter he was talking to, but somehow I don't think Shenstone was an awfully good judge of men. Godley had no guts to speak of; which was just as well.

"You won't remember, Peter, but a good deal of time was spent with the police after that. There wasn't much chance to sit down and think things out, but I was beginning to see a sort of pattern. But not clearly enough to be sure."

"I can't imagine," Sir Nicholas told him, "what made you consider Shenstone at all."

"Prejudice," said Antony promptly.

"That seems a little farfetched, even for you."

"Thank you, sir. But I started from the *fact* of Peter's innocence . . . I explained that. And as I happened to be right, quite a lot of other things had to follow. Then there was Elaine's attitude to Peter, which I didn't quite believe in; she wasn't altogether consistent, you know. For one thing, she told Peter he ought to have written to Nan about their engagement. But if it only happened the last night of the voyage—as she said later—what chance would he have had to do so? And if there should be a connection between the two of them, Elaine and Shenstone . . . I know it wasn't proof," he added irritably. "I'm just trying to explain that when I saw them together at the Night Light on Friday evening I wasn't ready to accept the explanation that they were 'improving their acquaintance.'"

"Go on," said Sir Nicholas.

"I mentioned that I'd heard Godley's voice twice, and Shenstone showed no surprise, though it ought to have surprised him. He had already come round to the idea that Peter had nine lives and the safest thing would be to frame him. At

246

least, I suppose he had, because I presented him with the idea that if the gun was found, Peter would be arrested; and the gun *was* found next morning. I'm not quite sure if that was cause and effect. What I didn't know, unfortunately, was that he'd used Peter's revolver to shoot Brown . . . why did you have such a thing, by the way, and where did you keep it?"

"It belonged to an uncle of mine, who brought it back from the States years ago. It was in the bottom of one of my trunks—which were stored at Lyall Square when I left Birmingham—and I didn't keep it, exactly, I just never got round to throwing it away."

"Well, I found that pretty shattering, when I heard it. Almost as shattering as when Watkins told me they knew— or guessed—about that three thousand pounds," said Antony. "There were your fingerprints still on the revolver, so I supposed he used gloves. But one thing added to another—"

"I can't imagine why you went on bothering," said Peter.

Sir Nicholas smiled at him. "He has a very stubborn nature," he explained.

"I didn't have much chance to give up," said Antony. "For one thing, the police were breathing down the back of my neck; for another, there was Shenstone's plan to incriminate you. And the first move in that game was to discredit in advance your returning memories, if possible to make me believe his story and back him up when he went to the police. Failing that, my 'suicide' would—in an indirect way—tend to confirm what he said." He found his uncle's eyes fixed thoughtfully on him, and went on in rather a hurry. "He was extremely plausible. But you've heard all that a hundred times, Peter. You can't want to hear it again."

"No," said Peter, doubtfully. "But I wish I hadn't got you so involved."

Sir Nicholas cleared his throat, and this time Antony could think of nothing to say. If he were going to ask "Why didn't you pretend to believe Bernard Shenstone?" there was only one answer, and he didn't want to give it. "Because if I had done so, I couldn't face the knowledge that it might have been because I was afraid." Which wouldn't make sense to anybody else, but was as near the truth as he could get. He did not know it, but the look he directed at his uncle was a silent appeal.

If the question had been in Sir Nicholas's mind, he did not ask it. He looked around and said to them all impartially, "What are your plans?" That brought a silence, so he looked at Jenny and put the matter directly to her. "Is there anything to keep you in town any longer?"

"Only that we thought we'd better see them married," said Jenny, and turned to smile at Nan and Peter.

"We'll manage it this time," Peter assured her.

"And, of course," said Nan, "we'd like you to be there."

"All right. And then we'll go away. Have you much more to do, Antony?"

"I'll have to see Mallory, but after that there shouldn't be much to keep me. It's more a matter of pacifying him than anything else." He looked at his uncle and added awkwardly, "Do you think, sir, the papers—?"

Sir Nicholas returned his worried look with one that clearly showed an almost fiendish enjoyment of the situation. "I have made a statement to the press," he announced. "On your behalf, and after consultation with Superintendent Forrester. I don't think you'll have any more trouble."

"But—" said Antony helplessly.

"The matter being *sub judice*," said Sir Nicholas, "there was really very little I could tell them. A dissertation almost without substance, but—I assure you, my dear boy—effective." He turned his head and his eyes met Jenny's with a look of complete understanding. "I don't think there's any more to worry about," he added.

"Then what about you, Uncle Nick?"

"I shall resume my holiday; taking good care, this time, to be quite out of reach of the newspapers. And by the way, Antony, that cablegram you sent me . . . I have been wondering ever since whether you knew how the quotation should have ended."

"I'm not an authority on Johnson, sir."

"No? But you have on your bookshelf a Dictionary of Quotations," Sir Nicholas pointed out. "His cable read," he explained to the others, " 'I hope I shall never be deterred from detecting what I think a cheat.' "

"Which was a very good answer to yours, Uncle Nick," said Antony, abandoning caution. "And it could have gone on '—by the menaces of a ruffian'; but I was thinking of Godley, of course. That was the day he phoned me."

For a long moment Sir Nicholas eyed him consideringly. "Of course!" he agreed cordially.

: :   : :

Later that evening, on the edge of sleep, Jenny roused herself to ask, "Do you really think Peter was—was playing fast and loose with Elaine, or not?"

"I don't know," said Antony. He shifted a little, to ease his shoulder; and suddenly was comforted by all the familiar things . . . the bed's slight protest as he turned . . . Jenny's nearness, and the sheer irrelevance of her question . . . the faint glow from the street lamp on the corner, two floors down . . . even the sound of the rain which had begun to fall, softly and steadily, about an hour ago . . . all these things, by some strange alchemy, filled him with an absurdly extravagant sense of well-being.

"You'd better ask him," he said, "but not just yet. About thirty years from now."

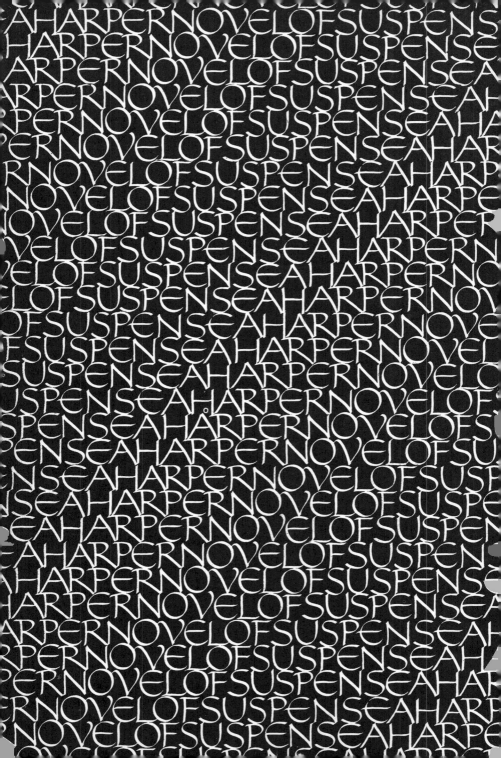